I0588321

The Collected Short Fiction of John R Little

Volume III: A Little Bit More

LVP
PUBLICATIONS

Lycan Valley Press Publications
1002 N Meridian STE 100-153
Puyallup, Washington 98371
United States of America

LVP Publications Illustrated Edition

ISBN-13: 978-1-64562-957-3

For Fatima, my number one fan, my number one inspiration, my only true love.

CONTENTS

INTRODUCTION by John R Little ... 11

SECRETS ... 13

SECOND CHANCE ... 113

THE GOLDILOCKS ZONE ... 131

THE EXCHANGE ... 155

THE FIRST LUNAR HALLOWEEN ... 175

DEMON AIR ... 195

MEMORIES ... 211

THE RULES ... 233

ANNIVERSARY ... 259

BY INSANITY OF REASON (with Lisa Morton) ... 281

ABOUT THE AUTHOR ... 379

Hello again! This volume of *The Collected Short Fiction of John R. Little* contains ten stories that have never appeared in any previous collection.

Does that mean they're brand new? Not quite. They've all previously appeared in a magazine or anthology, but unless you're my wife, it's unlikely you've read them all before. In fact, I'd expect most of these stories will be new to most readers.

That's a good thing!

These stories have all been written in the last few years, and they contain some of my own personal favorites.

As always, I am deeply grateful to the editors who originally published these stories: Christopher Payne, Michael Bailey, Lisa Morton & Ellen Datlow, Brian Freeman, Steve Thompson, John J. Questore, and Roy Robbins. Wonderful people all.

As to this book, I'm thrilled to have it published by Lycan Valley Press Publications. MJae Sydney has ensured the prior two volumes in this series have turned out wonderfully, and I have no doubt this one will be the same.

Once you're done reading these, don't despair. In a year or so, the last volume of the series will be published: *Lost Little Tales*.

See you then!

John R Little
June 2024

Secrets

JournalStone was publishing a new series they called Double Down. In each volume, a well-known author would be paired with a lesser-known author, and each would write a long story to be included together.

Each volume was printed as a flip book, so there were two covers, and depending on which way you held the book, you'd get the cover for one of the stories.

I loved the idea and as soon as I heard about it, I emailed the publisher and asked to be part of the series. Chris Payne agreed immediately, and I selected Mark Allan Gunnells to be paired with.

Mark wrote a terrific novel to go with Secrets.

The fun part was that I wrote a prologue that both of us used to kick off our stories.

I don't think I've enjoyed writing a story more than this one, and I hope you like it just as much.

PROLOGUE

KAREN LOOKED DOWN at the closest tombstone. She'd been walking for almost an hour and still hadn't found what she'd been looking for.

For that matter, she wasn't sure she even knew for herself exactly what she was seeking. The one she was looking at now had a woman's name followed by:

> Born July 4, 1960, Died December 10, 1999
> Beloved Mother and Artist
> She Brought Life to Those Close to Her

A gust of wind blew some loose strands of Karen's long blonde hair, so they covered her view. She pushed them back behind her ears.

"Is that the one?"

The voice behind her was gentle but insistent.

"Are you getting tired of looking?"

Karen smiled as she turned to face Bobby. He stood a respectful two feet behind her, as if he were trying to give her all the privacy she might need while still being there to offer any emotional support.

Not bloody likely, she thought.

Bobby was nineteen years old, just like she was. Somehow, though, he looked older. If she didn't know better, she'd peg him at about twenty-five. He was tall, rugged, and handsome, exactly the kind of guy who would turn girls' heads wherever he went. His deep voice made her wonder if he could have had a future in radio.

Karen, on the other hand, knew she barely looked seventeen, let alone nineteen. She was slim and short and never seemed to fill out like other girls her age.

"Sorry, I didn't intend to sound impatient," he said. "Take all the time you want. Time is the one thing both of us have lots of."

Karen nodded. "I just need to find the right one."

Bobby smiled. "I know. Really, it's okay."

"I'm not sure anything will be okay ever again."

Bobby didn't answer. What could he say to that?

Karen looked at him with the hint of emotion in her eyes, but she was determined not to let a single tear drop. She tried to detach herself and just concentrate on Bobby's face—the dark brown eyes; the pitch-black, curly hair; the dimples she knew would appear when he smiled.

She exhaled a long breath and turned back to the headstone. "I wonder what kind of art she practiced."

"Do you want to check? You can Google it on your iPhone. Shouldn't be hard to find if she really accomplished anything."

Karen shook her head. "In a way I'd rather imagine my own truth. I think she loved to put together collages from nature, picking up stray oak and maple leaves wherever she went and then spending hours rearranging them to tell a story."

She knelt and touched the granite stone, feeling the etchings of some of the letters.

"This isn't the one," she said finally.

Bobby joined her as she walked past a few more tombstones. None of them interested her. Only a few had called to her so far.

The sun was starting to set behind them, casting a long shadow through the graveyard. Karen knew Bobby just wanted her to find the right damned stone so they could leave, but it wasn't that easy. It had to be the *right* one.

If she couldn't find it, she'd come back tomorrow, and the day after that.

"Did you know there're two thousand people buried here?" asked Bobby.

She ignored him. A cool breeze blew, and she felt goose bumps rise on her arms. All of a sudden, she moved to her right and fell to her knees in front of an old weathered stone.

"This is the one," she said. "I found her."

CHAPTER 1

KAREN RICHARDSON was one month past her fourteenth birthday when time stopped in the middle of dinner.

It didn't scare her anymore. Not like the first time it'd happened when she was eight. Now, it was just another part of her normal life, different than everyone else—at least she'd been pretty sure of that; however, her perception on that front was about to take a big left turn—but what the heck. It was her life, and the hand she'd been dealt was no better and no worse than her friends'. Just different.

She glanced around the table at Mom and Dad. Tina was out somewhere, probably letting that idiot Jimmy Berenstein cop a feel (or more) at the back of Oak Park, a few miles down the road. Jimmy kept borrowing his dad's beat-up Toyota, even though the old man gave him shit every time. At least that was what Tina told her.

Dad was in the middle of lecturing about some election or other and how it was every citizen's obligation to *VOTE*. Karen could hear the capitalization in his voice. Mom had her head down and was intently studying the mashed potatoes on her plate. Although Dad was supposedly talking to Karen, she knew he was actually including Mom, who didn't give a rat's ass about politics.

Karen didn't either, so she was relieved when time stopped.

Dad's mouth was open, the last words out of his mouth being, "and the sheep in this town...," when his voice stopped like the words had hit a brick wall.

She hadn't been paying attention, but Karen recognized the cone of silence immediately and popped her head up to check Dad's frozen face. She could see a stringy bit of ham peeking out of his mouth. His eyes bulged, which seemed out of character, but she'd never paid much attention to him when he was on a rant.

Mom's head was lowered, her eyes staring at the mushy potatoes on her plate. She looked like she was in prayer, possibly asking the almighty to shut her damned husband up. Her arms hung beside her, and for a moment, she looked off balance, like she could topple over at any second.

The radio had been playing "Payphone" by Maroon 5 when Karen had been mercifully pulled out of the lecture, at least temporarily.

She had been trying to calculate the minimal amount of food she'd have to eat before being allowed to leave the table. Now, she just let go of her knife and fork, which dutifully levitated in midair, not caring that she was giving them a reprieve from gravity.

Maybe Mom's prayer actually worked, but only for Karen, not for herself.

She dabbed her mouth with her napkin, a habit long instilled into her by her mother, who always worried that Karen would leave the table covered in food and that everybody who saw her would stare and wonder what she'd been eating.

Truth was, it'd been several minutes since any food at all had found its way into Karen's mouth, but she used the napkin without even realizing she'd done so and then folded it neatly in half and placed it beside her plate.

"It's been a long time," she said to herself. As she pushed the chair back and slid out, she tried to think back to when time had last frozen for her. Two weeks ago?

"Three," she decided. "Tina's birthday."

She remembered it because time froze while Tina was swinging a baseball bat to smash the ridiculously oversized piñata that Dad had hung in the middle of the back yard. He'd had to rig a complicated set of guy wires, but Tina was useless at hitting it. The display became one of the more boring things Karen had ever had to sit through. When things froze, Karen took advantage, grabbed the bat from Tina's hands, and took a swing herself, ripping a hole in the piñata. When time started again a while later, it looked like the giant stuffed elephant had just decided to shit candy, as it rained down in the middle of the lawn, six feet away from where Tina was swinging.

"This time, I just want out of here," she said. The day had been wasted, listening to several of Dad's rants. She tried to hide in her bedroom at one point, but it was a shared room with Tina, who was there getting everything just so for her hot date with Jimmy.

"Some date," Karen had muttered, but that only got her a glare from Tina.

"You're just jealous, little girl."

"Yeah, right. Like I want that asshole poking me with his dirty little prick."

"Shut your mouth!"

Tina had been prancing around the room in her bra and panties, painting her nails and mucking with her hair like she was the freaking queen of Siam or something.

Karen left to go downstairs, figuring that even being lectured at was better than watching Tina get ready for her fuck-fest.

As she walked downstairs, she could hear Tina singing softly.

Maybe I am jealous, she thought. *Just a little.*

Now she left the house and started to walk down to the beach. It was usually a forty-five minute walk, and it still felt that way to her, but of course no time at all had actually passed by the time she arrived.

"Free time," she called it. Time that nobody else had and she cherished.

Well, nobody else except Bobby Jersey, but she didn't quite know that yet, not in the front of her brain where she did all her conscious thinking; but maybe deep down in some hidden chamber of her stinky subconscious, she had a clue. It's why she kept being drawn to the beach whenever she had her free time show up.

The weather was perfect. The sun was shining on Laguna and the waves were rolling in just high enough to allow kids to body surf.

Now, though, the waves were frozen, random spikes sticking up from the water. Karen kicked off her running shoes (she'd forgotten to change into her flip-flops) and walked to the water.

Out of habit she glanced around, but of course there were only manikins lying on the beach—at least that's what it always looked like. She walked around a group of teenaged boys and glanced down at them.

"Jeff?"

She stopped and stared, but of course Jeff didn't answer back, nor did he glance in her direction. He'd never know she'd been at the beach that day.

Like every tenth-grade student at Central High School, she had a secret crush on Jeff Amsters. He was the guy that everyone noticed. He was tall and had perfect brown hair and a smile that seemed to target any girl nearby. He was the quarterback of the football team and already had college scouts checking him out.

Karen inched closer. She didn't recognize the two guys he was sitting with, and she ignored them. She couldn't help moving closer and finally crouched onto her knees on the sand in front of him.

"You're beautiful," she whispered. She felt guilty, like she was doing something wrong. *I am,* she knew. *I shouldn't be doing this.*

But she moved even closer, so her eyes were only a couple of inches from his. And his lips. She wet her own lips and leaned over to kiss him.

She closed her eyes and imagined him kissing her.

After a few seconds she pulled back.

"That was my first kiss," she said. "Thank you."

Her face turned red, and she stood up and walked away from the threesome. As she walked to the water, she wished that some part of Jeff would remember, but she knew that was just a fantasy.

The water was cool on her toes as she felt sand squish through them. The sun beat down on her, and beads of sweat formed on her forehead.

Should I?

Karen had sometimes walked along the beach on hot days, knowing this was her own personal space and that it was impossible for anybody to ever see her, but she'd never had the courage before.

"Fuck it," she said.

She turned her back to the manikins and pulled her blue I heart L.A. T-shirt over her head. She did it as fast as she could so she wouldn't have a chance to change her mind. Next came her shorts.

As she stood watching the silent waves in front of her, she took a long breath and unhooked her bra. She held it along with her other clothes as she stepped out of her panties.

Can't believe I'm actually doing this.

Out in the water were dozens of swimmers. She could see the ones close to her, but as the water got deeper, she only saw motionless heads rising above the surface. Below the surface were bodies frozen in time but still alive.

Karen turned to face the hundreds more people lying on their beach towels. She stared at Jeff, feeling fear but excitement at standing naked in front of him. She almost pulled her arms up to cover her breasts, but no, she wanted this. She felt a weird desire to show off, to let him and everybody else be near her body. She wanted to exhibit herself and she wasn't going to let the fear win over the excitement.

But she decided not to walk too close to Jeff. Thirty feet away was plenty close enough. The calling would come soon enough. She always had lots of warning when she was going to go back to normal time, but even so, she imagined him blinking and looking at her with that big smile of his. Or would he laugh?

She turned to look south along the shoreline and then back out to the water. The sun felt so nice on her body.

"Next time I'm bringing a towel to sunbathe with," she said. She closed her eyes and looked up, feeling the heat on her cheeks.

"You can borrow one of mine."

She froze, eyes still closed.

Can't be.

Karen wanted it to be her imagination. But another part of her—the lonely part that couldn't share her secret with anybody—had always wished to find somebody else who walked through time.

"I know you heard me."

It was a male voice. She blinked her eyes open and saw him standing in front of her.

"Ohmygod..."

She pulled her clothes to her body, trying to cover her breasts and her groin at the same time. "You can't watch me."

"It's okay. I've been watching you the whole time you've been here."

He looked to be about her age, but she didn't recognize him.

"Turn the fuck around!"

He laughed. "I don't think so. I'm enjoying the view way too much."

Her face colored again, and she turned her back to him. She walked onto the sand and dressed as quickly as she could. The heat she now felt was not caused by the sun.

"Nothing to be ashamed of, sweetie. You've got a great body."

"Ohmygod, I can't believe you watched me. Who are you?"

"I'm Bobby Jersey. Who are you?"

"Karen Richardson."

For a minute neither of them said anything. Then she said, "How long have you been able to slip through time?"

"Since I was a kid. I dunno exactly how long."

"Me too. I think I was eight. I thought I was the only one."

"I thought so, too. Guess we were both wrong."

Bobby was several inches taller than Karen. He wasn't built like Jeff, but he also wasn't butt-ugly like some of the creeps she went to school with.

He wore only a dark blue bathing suit.

"You live near here?" she asked.

He smiled, mouth closed, like he was bored and humoring her.

"Watch this," he said.

Karen no longer was blushing and actually felt curious about this stranger.

Bobby walked over to a middle-aged man standing nearby. Rolls of fat cascaded over his suit, and his back was covered with splotches of black hair. He had been throwing a beach ball with a woman (probably his wife, Karen guessed, though why a pretty, slim woman like that would pair up with that ugly old fart was beyond her). He'd just tossed the ball and it hovered in midair, inches from his outstretched fingertips. He looked like he was grunting from the trivial exertion; he lived in heart-attack territory, and there was always a chance this could be his last trip to the beach.

Bobby glanced back at Karen and held up his index finger. *Watch this.*

He grabbed the fat guy's shoulder and pushed. Jumbo didn't seem to want to move for a moment, but when Bobby kept pushing, the body leaned to the left. Bobby kept at it, helping the guy almost all the way to the ground.

Jumbo stayed on his side, looking ridiculous with his outstretched fingers.

"You can't do that," said Karen.

But of course he could. He just shrugged. "I wish I could be here when time starts again. His wife is going to think he's collapsed, and he'll find himself on the ground without any recollection of falling. He'll think he's going nuts."

"That's mean."

Bobby took a big bow and laughed. "Gotta have a bit of fun. Otherwise, life's too boring."

"Have you done that before or were you just trying to impress me?"

When he walked back to Karen, the smile was gone. He stared at her, and for a second he looked as frozen as everyone around them. Then the corners of his mouth raised a bit, but it wasn't a happy smile. It was a smile full of secrets and lies. He leaned over and whispered in her ear, "You don't want to know all the things I've done, sweetie. At least not yet, you don't."

He put one arm around her shoulder, holding her tightly. He put his other hand on her breast and squeezed, hurting her. She wanted to run, but she was scared, and he was holding her too tightly.

Then just as suddenly, he let her go and backed away.

"See you around, sweetie. Next time I see you, I'll teach you how to fly."

Karen wanted to run away when he released her, but he beat her to it and started racing south down the shoreline.

She felt a bruise on her breast where he'd grabbed her, and she rubbed it softly.

That's when she felt the calling. It started with her stomach lurching, like some interior elf was shaking it like a pair of dice. The shaking stopped, but then Karen felt the calling again, much stronger now. Her body wanted to move away from the beach, and without even having to think about it, she started walking home. The calling had once been scary, when time first stopped for her, but now it was an old friend, reminding her that she had to rejoin the rest of her family, her friends, her community, hustling and bustling a million miles an hour, not being able to stop and appreciate any damned thing.

She moved faster and faster as the calling pulled her home and sucked out anything close to free will. It felt like an invisible magnet drawing her like a bent safety pin, back to where she belonged.

Karen slipped into her kitchen chair (but first enjoyed her last few seconds of freedom by tossing half of her mashed potatoes and all of her carrots into the garbage). Pressure was building inside her as the final moments approached. She sucked in one last breath of freedom as she sat and grasped the knife and fork she'd left suspended above her plate.

"—will just follow the damned idiots who never bother to vote but bitch about the result." Dad stabbed a piece of carrot with his fork.

Karen nodded and looked down to her plate. She took one last piece of ham and chewed it.

"I think I'm full," she said.

"Oh, Karen, you haven't—" Her mother looked at her plate. "Oh, I guess you have eaten enough after all. Okay, dear."

Karen took her dishes to the sink and headed to her room. Tina was gone, thank god, off to give Jimmy a blow job or a fuck or whatever the hell she gave him.

She lay down on her bed and closed her eyes, wanting to think of the kiss she'd given Jeff. Instead, her mind insisted on conjuring up Bobby Jersey, full-blown, pulling her to him and squeezing her breast. He'd scared her, but it'd happened so unexpectedly, she hadn't had time to really think about it. Now, though, she imagined his brown eyes staring at hers, his arms holding her too tightly for her to imagine escaping, and his mouth forming a thin line. It looked like anger or hate, but that didn't make sense.

Did it?

She never wanted to see him again, and she vowed to never go to the beach.

But one more thought rattled around her head, grabbing her attention.

Next time I see you, I'll teach you to fly

CHAPTER 2

KAREN MARIE RICHARDSON was a straight-A student. She had to be or she'd have the wrath of her father to deal with. Although he wasn't a big man, he seemed to grow six inches taller when he was mad, and the one time she'd come home with a midterm C in her math class, he just about blew a gasket.

Getting a C in subjects that were useless, like art, was bad enough, but in science or math... that was like stabbing him in the heart with an icicle at Christmas time. He was a geologist who worked at the university. Every year he published one or two papers researching stuff Karen didn't understand and would never care about. She vaguely understood that her getting bad grades in science was somehow a slight to him, but she never really grasped why.

That all changed once, when time stopped and she snuck into her parents' bedroom and went to the walk-in closet. On the top shelf, she found the box he'd referred to once upon a time after he'd downed a few beers: the old shoe box that held his ancient report cards. The first one she grabbed was grade ten and she almost laughed when she saw the grades.

> Math: D
> English: D
> Science: F
> Music: C
> Social Studies: D

"Oh, man, Dad, have I got you now."

She skimmed through a bunch of other reports, and, although his grades improved through high school, she never found a single A to mark his progress.

Hypocrite.

She had been sixteen when she snooped through her father's belongings, and after she amused herself with the report cards, she found herself wondering what was in the other boxes nearby. They were hidden behind the one she was already snooping in, and she grabbed them. There were three others.

The first box held a gun. She'd never seen a gun before, never held one, but she grasped this one solidly and held it out.

"Do you have any bullets?" She had no clue how to check. It wasn't a revolver, where she might be able to see the point of the bullets hiding in their chambers. Rather, it was a shiny, sleek gun with a clip that would have been smacked into the bottom. She'd seen that done on countless TV shows.

The gun was heavy, and she walked back to the kitchen and pointed it at her mother.

"Oh my god, what am I doing?"

She aimed the gun at the floor and then walked back to the secret box and restored it. A year later she'd realize she couldn't actually fire a gun when time was stopped, but that day she hadn't clued into that yet.

The next box was heavier than the one with the gun, and she hesitated before opening it. A wave of guilt rushed through her as she imagined her father's reaction if he caught her snooping through his stuff.

Fuck it. I bet he snoops through my stuff.

The box lid lifted off easily, and inside was a stack of magazines. She took the top one out. The title was written in fancy lettering. *Asian Girls.* The cover was true to the title, showing a teenaged girl from China or somewhere, naked, holding one breast in her hand while smiling at the camera.

"Jesus, Dad."

She smelled a weird odor and frowned. The magazine had been opened many times, but she doubted he'd read much of the text.

"Bet it's old. Before he met Mom."

She snapped the magazine shut and searched for a date, disappointed to find it was only two years old.

The magazines below the top one were older issues of the same publication. All of them had a naked Asian girl on the cover, and inside all were more explicit, showing girls having sex with other girls or masturbating with vibrators. Karen didn't want to keep looking but she couldn't seem to stop herself. Some part of her wanted to understand why her dad would want these things, but another part of her was... well, just interested.

Finally, she forced herself to stop looking and put the magazines back in the box, shoving it back on the top shelf in the closet.

Part of her was tempted to leave the box where her mom would find it, but Dad would surely figure out it was Karen who'd moved it and there'd be hell to pay.

I guess your secret has to be safe. At least for today.

There was one more box. She opened it and studied the contents.

"Oh my god..."

Karen looked at the items in the box for ten minutes before replacing it.

She'd never look at her father the same way again.

Karen left her father's secret hideaway and walked out of the house. She didn't feel the calling yet, so she went out to wander around her neighborhood.

The silence that surrounded her when time stopped was like nothing she ever felt when the clocks ticked normally. Sometimes she'd wake up in the middle of the night and have to go to the bathroom. The house would be quiet, but there was a type of white noise that permeated any place in southern California. She couldn't exactly hear anything, and anybody else would say it was deathly quiet, but the true quiet, the quiet that resulted from absolutely no movement whatsoever, was so very different. It always creeped her out, and she never got used to it.

Her footsteps made no noise.

If she crinkled a piece of paper in her hand, it was like crunching the softest toilet paper.

Once she used a fireplace poker to smash a window. The poker slid through the glass but not a whisper of a sound came out. She knew that once time started again, the window would shatter and crash, but she had no intention of being anywhere nearby when that happened.

The only sound she'd ever heard in her secret time was when she'd talked to Bobby, and a back part of her mind wondered how that had been possible; no answer was forthcoming.

She walked through the deathly silence and then suddenly stopped.

She'd just found out her father's deepest secret, a secret that she never imagined he could have buried inside him.

What secrets do other people have?

Mrs. Montgomery, her next-door neighbor sat on the rickety old glider on her front porch, perched like she was about to row a boat. She and Mr. Montgomery were old, in their forties, and they were known as the happiest people on the block. They always had ridiculously happy smiles pasted on their faces. Karen hoped she'd be that happy when she was old like them.

She walked into their home and looked around. She'd been there a couple times with her mom, but that'd been years ago. The house was immaculate, as if the Pope were due for a visit. Karen looked around but didn't find much of interest until she snuck into the master bedroom and found Mrs. Montgomery's diary in her bedside table, hidden beneath several pairs of rainbow-striped socks. She turned to the most recent entry, dated the day before.

> The asshole can just eat cold fucking pork chops as far as I'm concerned. I'm sick of just being there to jump as high as he fucking demands. Cold potatoes for him, too. I'll smile for the damned neighbors, but I sure as hell don't have to smile for him.

After rereading the entry, Karen flipped back to find similar nasty thoughts about Mr. Montgomery, and she couldn't help but smile at the two of them pretending for years to be the happiest of clams when in reality they couldn't stand the sight of each other.

As she left the house, she stared at Mrs. Montgomery, grinning like she was the happiest of the happiest, and Karen couldn't help laughing. She knew the truth.

This is fun.

The next house belonged to the Carletons, and the only person in the house was the thirteen-year-old boy, Jesse. He was in his older sister's bedroom, sneaking a sniff from her discarded panties. They were pink, with a faded Minnie Mouse printed on the crotch, right where Jesse's nose was planted.

Jesse was peeking toward the door, trying to be sure that nobody snuck in. The door had been closed, but Karen decided to leave it open when she left. It'd look to him like it suddenly swung open, and he'd just about shit his pants. She wished she could be there to watch.

Bonnie MacDonald lived in the next house. Bonnie was one of Karen's closest friends, and they often hung out together. Bonnie had blonde hair like Karen, but it was longer and silkier, and Karen often thought of just reaching out and touching it. She couldn't do that normally, but now...

Even though it was only about six o'clock p.m., Bonnie's mom was sleeping on the couch. Her dad was out of the picture, having run off three years ago with some young thing. Or so the rumor mill said.

Karen crept to Bonnie's room. She pushed the door open and found the room dark. The tan-colored window shades were drawn and only filtered light crept in.

Must not be home.

After a moment, though, her eyes adjusted to the light, and she could see Bonnie lying in her bed. Karen stared at her.

Bonnie was naked. Her eyes were closed, and she had a smile on her face. Her breasts were much larger than Karen's, who couldn't help stare at them. She then looked down Bonnie's body and saw her hand between her legs. One finger was pressed inside herself.

Karen felt her face turn red, but she was entranced and moved closer. She sat on the bed beside Bonnie, slowly reaching out to touch her left breast. It was warm and the nipple was hard.

Bonnie's smile was wide, and Karen wondered if she was having an orgasm. She moved her hand over Bonnie's belly and placed it on top of her hand. Then she leaned over and kissed Bonnie on her mouth. Her tongue reached in to touch her friend's.

She left one hand on Bonnie's and used her other hand to feel the long blonde hair she'd come in to see. She kissed Bonnie harder, feeling guilt and shame rush through her but having desire and pleasure win out.

She pulled back and once more felt Bonnie's breast. Then she let out a long breath and stood, leaving Bonnie to finish her orgasm in private.

Later, the calling forced Karen to come home, but her mind was filled with her neighbor's secrets. One boy in her class was fucking the history teacher, another liked to dress up in girls' clothes. Major Higgins beat his wife, and their ten-year-old daughter kept razor blades in her bedside table, waiting to gain the courage to slit her wrists.

She started to write a list, and she was surprised at not just the number, but also the variety, of secrets that surrounded her.

Karen had a new hobby.

CHAPTER 3

THE NEXT DAY time stopped again for Karen Richardson. She couldn't recall it ever happening two days in a row, but that didn't bother her. After all, there'd never been any rhyme or reason as to when time stopped. Sometimes it was a couple of times a week over the course of a month, and other times, it seemed like forever. Once she remembered going almost six months, and she'd felt like a normal kid for the first time in as long as she could remember.

At sixteen, she'd now lived with her weird relationship with time for almost a decade, and she no longer questioned how it happened, why, when, or anything else. There were never any answers, and so why frustrate herself by questioning? She might as well ask a fruit fly about faster-than-light travel.

Except...

There was something about that guy—Bobby. He seemed confident. She'd only seen him that one time at the beach, two years earlier. He had hinted at information. He said he'd show her how to fly, and she still thought about that.

Karen enjoyed science, even though she sometimes wished she didn't, and she wondered if Bobby had figured out how to mess with gravity. Force equalled g × mass (Earth) × mass (Karen) divided by the square of the distance to the center of the world. What if somehow her mass was actually zero when time stopped? That would make the force of gravity zero too.

But her mass wasn't zero. If she jumped into the air, she came back down the same as she always did.

God's keeping score.

Well, God or some other freakish cosmic comedian.

Karen had avoided the beach for a year after meeting Bobby. He scared her.

Slowly, though, she started slipping back. Watching people on the beach was one of her favorite hobbies, and walking in the ocean relaxed her.

She went back the day after starting to write her Secrets Journal.

Wading in the water, she thought about going for a swim, but it was colder than normal, and she wasn't really feeling it.

"Hi again."

She froze and tried to pretend she hadn't heard him, knowing how silly that was.

"You can't just ignore me. I'm not fucking blind. You're right in front of me."

She turned. He was only two feet from her. At first, he frowned but then he relaxed and smiled.

"Don't worry. I don't bite."

He laughed and reached out to take her hand. Karen was too surprised to complain, and then she realized that the warmth of his hand actually felt nice on hers.

"It's been a long time," she said.

"Miss me?"

She felt herself flush and stared down at the sand.

He laughed and moved closer, then used one finger to lift her chin.

"You're cute."

Karen didn't know what to say or do. No boy had ever said anything like that to her.

She knew he was the same age she was, sixteen, but somehow he gave off an aura that made him seem much older. If she hadn't known better, she would have said he was at least twenty.

His face was smooth and handsome, his brown eyes staring at her own blue ones. For once, time seemed to stop for Karen, as she looked at the stranger. She couldn't move, as if he held her in a trance.

Then he leaned over and kissed her softly on her lips. Her mind wanted to stop him, but her body wouldn't let her. She felt his mouth on hers and pressed herself to him. His tongue found his way between her lips, and she loved the way it made her feel. Somewhere along the line she had closed her eyes, and she wanted the moment to last forever.

It was her first real kiss. She remembered kissing Jeff and Bonnie when she was free to do whatever she wanted, but that wasn't the same. This was real.

Bobby suddenly pulled back.

"Not bad, kid. You might be worth kissing one day, but not yet."

"What?"

"Besides, you didn't come all this way to kiss me. What are you really here for?"

Karen pursed her lips and felt a rush of anger.

"You're not that great yourself, you know."

He laughed, a long, loud laugh that would have embarrassed her if there was anybody who could hear.

"Actually, I am."

"Modest, too, I see."

He laughed again.

"So what do you want, kiddo? Why are you really here? You want to know how to fly, don't you?"

So he does know.

Her mind imagined her floating over the beach, high above the frozen visitors. There was a way to do it. Somehow, he could use their special talent to soar with the eagles...

Karen tried to say, "Yes, that's what I want," but her mouth was dry, and she didn't trust herself to get the words out. She just nodded twice.

"It'll cost you."

"What?" she whispered.

"We'll get to that."

Bobby smiled. She wanted him to kiss her again,

but he looked away and she knew that wasn't happening again anytime soon.

"You remember my name?" he asked.

"Bobby Jersey."

"And who are you?"

"Karen Richardson."

"Yeah, that's right. You told me that two years ago. I wanted to be sure you didn't give me a different name. Be sure you didn't lie to me last time."

He started down the beach, and she kept pace beside him. They walked around most of the people, and she saw that he stared as they passed. It was like he was looking for somebody but didn't know if it was a man or a woman. He stared at everyone equally.

"You ever do things you wouldn't do if time wasn't stopped?" he asked. "You know, things you'd be ashamed of if anybody knew?"

She thought back to her Secrets Journal and all the times she'd snuck into her neighbors' houses to find what they'd been hiding.

"No. Nothing like that."

"Bullshit. Stop wasting my fucking time. How could you not?"

Karen started looking at the people they passed just as intently as Bobby did, without a clue what she was looking for.

He stopped and said, "You're doing it right now. You'd never stare at people like that if they could see you."

"Well, that's not much."

"You lied to me, though."

"Whatever. So, big man, tell me what you've done that's so damned secretive."

He stared at her and didn't say anything. Then he started walking away again, continuing to look at the strangers.

"Don't need to tell you," he said. "I can show you just as easily."

He kept looking and finally stopped at a man standing beside a lawn chair, his feet ankle-deep in the water. He wore a straw hat and a smile, and both looked ridiculous. He was fat, at least three hundred pounds, with his belly spilling over his bathing suit.

"Looks like an asshole, doesn't he?"

Karen didn't think the guy looked any different than any other guy, but she didn't want to get Bobby off track. "Whatever," she said.

Bobby reached to the guy and pulled down his bathing suit, so it was beneath the water at his feet. It looked like he was naked.

Karen stared at the man's tiny penis and couldn't help giggling, while at the same time feeling horrible.

"You can't do that!"

"You just watched me. Of course I can."

Part of her wanted to be around when time started, to see the man's reaction. She'd never done anything like that before, never imagined it.

A gear clicked in her mind, and she realized that a whole new level of excitement lay ahead of her. Then she took a deep breath when she came back to her senses, knowing she could never do anything to humiliate somebody like that.

Bobby laughed, and she realized he wasn't laughing at the man but at her.

"You're so fucking cute," he said. Then he laughed again. "Have you ever even seen a cock? You haven't, have you? That's not exactly a good example, in case you're wondering."

She shook her head in disgust. "You're just awful."

He turned, looked toward the ocean, and whispered, "I know."

For one split instant, Karen felt sorry for him and realized that she knew very little about Bobby. She had no clue why sometimes he seemed to like her and other times he treated her like shit.

What secrets do you hide, Bobby Jersey?

She'd likely never know the answer. Karen looked at him from behind as he continued to stare out to the water, quiet and lonely looking. She resisted the temptation to reach around and hug him.

Suddenly, Bobby turned to face her. "Come with me, sweetie. You get to pick the next person."

"I'm not pulling anybody's bathing suit down."

"No, this would be different."

"What are you looking for."

"Pick anybody. There must be a thousand people here, so just pick one for me."

For *me*. She liked the sound of that. It wasn't something he was going to expect *her* to do.

She walked slowly, feeling sand mush between her toes.

There was an ice cream stand about twenty feet

from the shore, attached to a pair of washrooms. She turned to move in that direction, although she wasn't really sure why.

Bobby followed her obediently.

"Tell me about flying," she said.

"Knew you'd ask that."

"If you want me to pick somebody for you to humiliate, you tell me about flying."

He grabbed her by putting both his hands on her shoulders and staring at her.

"You're so cute, but sometimes you really are stupid. You believe that shit? Like we need some other piece of magic in our lives, like time stopping isn't enough? I was shitting you so that you'd want to see me again."

"Oh."

"You're old enough to know bullshit when you hear it."

"Yeah. I kind of figured…"

"Bullshit. Pick somebody. Now!"

She looked around and saw a woman lying on a large pink blanket. She was covered with oil and her skin was dark brown, but Karen suspected if Bobby picked off her tiny bikini, she'd see snow-white skin underneath. A lazy bitch who spent all her time in the sun.

The woman was about thirty. Karen wondered what kind of secrets she kept that forced her to want to hide alone among a crowd of a thousand people.

"Her."

Karen and Bobby both stared at the woman. Then

Bobby moved to her and squeezed her neck tightly with both hands.

What the fuck?

"What are you doing? Stop that. You'll kill her!"

Bobby just squeezed harder. "You picked her. This is your fault."

"Stop!"

Finally, he did stop. The woman's neck showed the indentations of his hands where he had strangled her.

"Will she be okay?"

"I doubt it, but I don't really know," he said. "I've never been able to hang around after time started. Called back the same as you. So, I don't know what happens. I think she'll likely live, but she'll choke and wonder what the hell happened to her. Probably have a very sore neck for a while."

"You're cruel."

He didn't reply at first, but then he said, "Everybody can be cruel under the right circumstances. Even you."

"No, you're wrong."

"I'm right."

"I want to get away."

"Away from her or away from me?"

He was looking at her with wide eyes. She wanted to leave him, but she'd never found another person that was like her.

"Just don't do anything like that again."

"You want an ice cream cone?"

"Sure!"

Bobby climbed into the ice cream stand and made

two cones, both chocolate. He handed one to her.

"What makes you think I like chocolate?"

She licked the ice cream, and it tasted great.

"You're a girl."

"Very perceptive of you."

Bobby walked into the girls' bathroom and she followed.

"I like seeing girls when they don't think anybody is looking," he said. Unfortunately, nobody was in the bathroom.

She didn't reply.

"So, it's time for you to tell me what you do when time stops. You've seen what I do, but what do *you* do?"

Karen took another long swipe of her ice cream to buy her some time.

"I like to look in my neighbors' homes, to see what secrets they keep from the rest of the world."

"Ahh. You're a peeping Tom."

"At least I don't hurt anybody."

They both stopped and stared at each other, a familiar feeling lurching through Karen's body. The calling.

Bobby recognized what was happening. "Darn."

"Yeah."

"Come find me next time. I'll be here."

She didn't commit to that as the calling started to pull her back toward her house. She wasn't sure she wanted to see him ever again.

But part of her knew she absolutely wanted to.

Chapter 4

Karen's father was named Parker. Parker Samson Richardson. Her friends sometimes wonder if his parents liked comic books or something, since the name seemed so weird, something out of *Spider Man* or the *X-Men*, maybe. She tried to pretend it was nothing special, perhaps a tribute to some long-forgotten relative or something.

He was forty-one years old when Karen was seventeen. She knew he loved her, even though sometimes it was hard to tell by how he treated her. He smiled and laughed with Tina, but with Karen, he was more reserved and serious. He expected more from her.

One day when Karen was alone with her mother, she asked, "Why does Dad treat me so hard? Why does he love Tina more?"

She immediately regretted the question when she saw the hesitation and heartbreak on her mother's face.

For a moment, there was only silence.

"Truth be told, your dad loves you as much as Tina, if not more. He just knows you're the one who could follow in his footsteps and work in fields that he respects."

Her mom looked around to be sure Tina wasn't nearby.

"He doesn't really expect much of your sister. He still loves her, but he'll be happy if she manages to just find a job—any job—and have a happy life with somebody who cares for her. He wants more for you, and he wants to help you be all you can be."

Karen absorbed this and never spoke of it again. She tried to look at her dad with new eyes, but somehow, he never seemed much different. He seemed so hard to please.

On top of that, she knew his secrets.

On May 30, her world changed. She woke early to the sound of commotion in the living room below. She glanced at her watch: 4:42 a.m.

A gray haze hung outside her bedroom window, waiting for the sun to rise. A hint of bright red lights periodically flashed through the gray.

Police?

Tina was still sleeping.

"Please, help him..."

Mom's tiny voice was full of fear as it hovered and found its way from downstairs. Karen ran to the stairs and saw two men dressed in white, moving her father, who was lying on a stretcher. He was moving a little, but mostly what she would remember later was that he was crying. He moaned from pain and tears fell down his cheeks. Karen had never seen her father cry before. He was dressed in his Frosty the Snowman pajamas, a Christmas gift from Tina two years earlier.

Mom was standing beside the stretcher, one hand on Dad's shoulder.

"Tell me he's going to be okay. Please."

Tears were rolling down her cheeks as well.

"We're taking him to Highland Hills, Mrs. Richardson. They'll do their best."

"I'll go as soon as I get dressed."

The paramedics took Dad outside. Karen ran down the stairs and watched with Mom.

"What happened?"

"I don't know. He woke up and said he needed help. He could barely move, saying the pain was much worse and he couldn't stand it anymore."

"He's had pain?"

The ambulance pulled away with its siren wailing.

"I have to get dressed and go."

"Mom, tell me. What pain?"

They both started up the stairs. "I don't really know. He's had it for a while but wouldn't go to the doctor. Kept saying it would go away."

Mom rushed to her room and called back, "I'll phone you when I know."

Karen watched as her mom got dressed and then after a quick hug, her mom left. Karen sat in her father's favorite La-Z-Boy armchair waiting for her mother to call with any news.

It didn't take long for the diagnosis. Parker Samson Richardson had cancer. A lot of it.

The doctors guessed it started in the liver, but they weren't sure. It had metastasized and spread through his body. His lungs were dripping with the stuff, and when the doctors realized it had spread through his lymph nodes, they told Karen's mom there wasn't much that they could do. It had been too long.

Parker Richardson didn't have a good reason why he hadn't gone to the doctor earlier, but the surgeons seemed to think it wouldn't have made much difference anyway. It was spreading fast and had been for a long time, possibly longer than he was aware.

What caused it?

Nobody had a clue. He didn't drink much, didn't smoke, ate healthier than most people, and had no particular risk factors in his family history.

"He's just an unfortunate random choice," said one doctor. Karen heard him say that, and from his voice, he seemed to be trying to be sympathetic, but the words had the opposite effect on her. They made her angry.

She had been a churchgoer all her life, not every Sunday, but two or three times each month. None of her friends went to church, and when she was younger, they used to tease her; but there was something vaguely reassuring about believing in some crazy old man who lived in the sky and made things happen just on a whim.

Karen once believed those whims were mostly good, but no longer. After her dad went into the hospital, she never entered a church again.

She doubted God cared.

Within a month, her dad had deteriorated into a flimsy excuse of a man. He'd lost weight, so much that his cheeks looked hollow. Karen couldn't believe that she hadn't noticed that he was sick before that night.

Surely Mom noticed.

But she never asked her mother. That would only lead to guilt of one kind or another.

Time stopped for Karen once in that month, and when it did, she stepped away from watching *The Bachelor* with her mom. Chris Harrison was frozen on the screen, a huge smile on his face as he talked to the man who was picking the most eligible girl in America to be his wife.

"Stupid show," Mom said.

"I know," Karen said.

They never missed an episode. Now, though, in Karen's private time, she wanted to see Dad.

In his semiprivate room, he was on his back, his eyes staring into empty space, his mouth wide as he gasped for breath. His lungs didn't work very well, and he couldn't seem to get a good deep breath.

She sat on the edge of his bed and put one hand on his cheek.

"Hi, Daddy..."

She reached down to hold his left hand with her

right.

"It's been a long time since I called you Daddy, hasn't it? Sometimes I miss that. I miss how close we were when I was a little girl and you were my hero. You were always there to chase the monsters away from under my bed and to sneak me a cookie when Mom said I'd had enough treats for one day. You helped me with my homework when I couldn't figure out how to multiply or couldn't remember the names of Christopher Columbus's ships."

She thought back to those days, memories flooding through her. Daddy helping her to build sandcastles, teaching her how to fish, and even how to hopscotch. None of her friends had a father who would jump rope with them. Only she had that.

"I miss you, Daddy."

Karen leaned over and hugged her dad, wishing that he could give her a hug in return. She knew she'd never be able to do this when time wasn't standing still; they hadn't hugged for many years. Now there was an additional gulf separating them—the box in the closet.

"I've got a secret, too, Daddy. I wish I'd told you about it, but I knew you'd never believe me. Who in their right mind would believe it? But with your love for science, I just wish I could have told you and convinced you it was true.

"Maybe if I told you about finding *your* secrets—the gun and the magazines, and... you know, the other thing. Maybe if I told you about what Mrs. Montgomery writes about her husband and all the other hidden gems on our street. Maybe I could convince you, but I doubt it. It's too freakish."

She shrugged and wiped her nose with a tissue from his bedside table.

"I love you, Daddy."

Part of her hoped that some of the sentiment might sink in and that his soul would feel a little better after she was called home. Who knew?

She stayed with him for what felt like two hours, but of course there was no way to measure time when clocks didn't tick.

Later, when she settled back to watch the silly TV show with her mother, she felt a tiny bit more at peace.

One week later, she was at the hospital again, in normal time.

She was alone with her dad, sitting beside him, telling him about her day. She tried to visit every day, knowing any particular day could be his last, wanting to give her mom a break. Mom sat with Dad twelve hours every day, with never a hint of complaint, but Karen knew she appreciated it when she spelled her off. Tina also took her fair share of time sitting with him.

The gasping for air was much worse, and everybody knew the end was very close.

"I still hate broccoli, you know." Karen was trying to make light conversation when she realized Dad had stopped breathing. She jumped to his side and saw his mouth move, trying to get just one last breath, but nothing was working anymore. His eyes pleaded with her.

"I love you, Daddy. I always have."

She held tightly to both his hands and stared directly into his eyes. He blinked one last time and then stopped even trying to get any air. He was as frozen as when time stopped for her.

After a few moments of just being with him, Karen called for a nurse and then phoned her mom to tell her.

CHAPTER 5

IT WAS MORE THAN a year before Karen saw Bobby again. She didn't miss him. In fact, he almost never crossed her mind. Her mind and her heart were with her dad. His death had left a hole in her soul that she struggled to fill. When time stopped for her, she walked through some neighbors' homes, but she didn't feel the same excitement. She didn't even bother to write down what she found in her Secrets Journal.

Her reaction in her free time wasn't much different from normal time. For almost six months, she didn't crawl out of the hole that consumed her.

Early in the new year things changed.

She woke in the middle of the night. Time was stopped. It rarely happened in the middle of the night, and the combination of enough time having passed and the relative rareness of a night-time stoppage shook her mind free; she felt positive for the first time since the funeral.

Excitement. Curiosity. Freedom.

Her special feelings flooded back to her, and she jumped out of bed. She never knew if she'd have ten minutes, an hour, or half a day to herself, but she didn't want to waste a single second.

She knew it made no sense to say she had "an hour" to herself, because with time stopped, the concept had no meaning, but it *felt* like time was passing to her, and that's what mattered.

Curiosity. Her favorite emotion. She loved the itch inside her that wanted to know what was going on in the houses down the street.

She decided to head to a small shopping area nearby. She called it "downtown," but really it was just a group of stores that happened to have opened in the same general area: a Starbucks, a used bookstore, a bakery, and a half-dozen others.

Homes surrounded the stores, and those homes commanded her attention tonight.

The first two were locked tight.

The third was different. It was a small, wooden, two-story house with faded brown paint and a sagging appearance that made her expect to find an old husband and wife sleeping soundly.

The clock had stopped just after midnight.

The main floor was quiet and dark. Karen could see a light upstairs and she carefully climbed up. Even though she knew that nobody could *catch* her, she felt a rush of excitement at the prospect of somebody turning and saying, "Hey, what the hell are you doing here?"

The light was coming from a bathroom. She opened the door and saw a guy a little older than her, maybe twenty or twenty-one. He had long, greasy hair, and he stood naked in front of the sink. He had one hand on his fully erect cock. He seemed to be watching himself in the mirror.

She wanted to leave but couldn't. She stared at the guy. He was standing with his feet spread apart, gritting his teeth. He needed a shave, but she only barely noticed that. She reached out, moved his hand away, and put her own hand on him. She felt warmth and wetness. There was a tube of lotion on the counter. She had never touched a man before, and she wanted to know what it felt like.

Karen had turned eighteen the month before with little fanfare and had never been close to having a serious boyfriend. She sometimes fantasized about being with somebody who would make love to her and give her the kind of pleasure she only ever felt from herself.

She touched the skin of his penis and rubbed it a bit, but as she did so, an image formed in her mind... her friend, Bonnie MacDonald masturbating. She had wanted to catch her again but even though she'd snuck into Bonnie's room several times, she'd never had any luck.

Karen replaced the guy's hand and left, but she left the bathroom door open. That'd give the guy a bit of a shock.

She walked over to the Starbucks. It was closed but she stared in the window, knowing there'd be nothing much to see.

"You don't seem much like a coffee drinker."

Karen saw his reflection in the plate glass

window, and of course she immediately recognized his voice.

"I suppose you drink coffee all the time," she said.

"I do, but that's because I'm much more mature than you are."

She turned and faced Bobby Jersey. In the year since she'd seen him, he'd grown bigger, filling out. She knew that some girls at her school would consider him quite handsome.

But he scared her. Not a lot, but a little.

"You're the same age as me, remember?"

"Oh, I remember."

"Hey," she said. "What are you doing here? You don't live near here. Do you?"

"I was looking for you. I want you to show me where you live."

"Why?"

He didn't answer right away. He just looked at her with the bright eyes that she remembered from the times they'd met at the beach. After a minute, he smiled and said, "We're normally on different schedules. Sometimes time stops for both of us simultaneously, like now, but sometimes it's just me or just you."

"I know. So?"

"So, I thought I could come and visit you when time stops and you're frozen there, ready for me to do whatever I want to you."

Karen wanted to laugh, hoping it was just a joke. He was smiling and he made it sound light, like he was poking fun at her.

But... why was he here? Why *did* he want to know

where she lived?

"You tell me where you live," she said. "What's your address?"

"16 Sunnyside Lane."

He'd answered too fast. She knew he was lying.

She wanted to run away but couldn't. He was her only link to whatever power they shared.

He leaned over and kissed her on the mouth. His tongue pushed into her, and she couldn't help responding. She put one hand on the back of his head to pull him closer.

Then he pushed one hand roughly up her shirt and pushed her bra off one breast, grabbing her and holding her tightly.

"Stop!"

He didn't let her go, squeezing her breast again, laughing.

Then he let her go but he grabbed one wrist, stopping her from running.

Fear pulsed through her. She used her free hand to put her bra back. She wanted to get away, to scream for help that couldn't possibly come, to kick him in the balls, to slap him, to yell at him for doing that, but mostly she just wanted him to go away.

"Please leave me."

"No. Not until you tell me where you live."

"No fucking way."

"Oooh, the little girl swore."

"Fuck you!"

He laughed at her. "When I'm free to move around and you're frozen in time, you won't be able to stop me from doing whatever I want with your body."

"Leave me alone!"

He laughed once again, and she couldn't help but look at him.

"It's okay," he said. "I was just screwing with you. I wouldn't do anything. I just like to press your buttons."

"Doesn't really seem like that's all it is."

"Listen, I'm sorry. I went too far." His voice softened, as if he really was sorry. "I promise I won't do that again."

She listened, not knowing what to believe.

"At least not without your permission."

Finally, the smile got to her. She knew he was playing her now, that the smile meant nothing, and yet somehow it meant a lot. No other boy paid any attention to her, and part of her was excited by the groping.

"So tell me where you live," he asked again.

"No."

He shrugged. "There's a fifty-fifty chance you'll be called back before me. I'll just follow you."

Karen knew he would do exactly that. And would he follow through on his earlier threat? One day, would she be reading or watching TV and suddenly realize he'd been there? How far would he go if he did? Would he just play a practical joke on her or would he hurt her?

She started to walk away from Bobby, not wanting anything to do with him.

"Watch this," he said.

"What now?"

"Just watch."

There was an old man walking across the street. Bobby pulled something out of his pocket and showed it to Karen. It was a box cutter. She saw the razor-sharp blade and watched as he walked over to the old man.

"Bobby, don't hurt him."

The man was between steps, so he appeared to be balanced on one foot. He was intent on where he was walking, and part of Karen briefly wondered what business he had this time of night. Nothing was open. Maybe he was just going for a walk in the fresh air.

Bobby didn't hesitate. He took the box cutter and slashed the old man's neck.

Karen froze, not believing what she'd just seen. The cut was deep, very deep, and although no blood flooded out, she knew that as soon as time started again, the man's life was going to spurt away onto the sidewalk.

"Oh, my god... Why?"

Bobby put the box cutter back in his pocket. "Why not? For fun, of course. I just wish I could be here to see it."

"You're a monster," she whispered.

Once more, Karen wanted to run away from him, but instead she found herself walking closer to the man, staring at the thin slice that crossed his neck. She patted the man's cheek and said, "I'm so sorry."

Bobby pulled her around to face him. She saw triumph in his eyes, laughter in his soul, and power radiating through every part of him.

She wanted to kiss him.

"Leave me alone," she said. Her voice was shaking, and she didn't know anymore what she really wanted.

Then his face went blank. "Shit. I have to go."

He pushed her away and ran fast down the street. She guessed that he had a long way to go, and not a lot of time to do it.

The old man stared forward, nothing in his eyes but determination to meet his destination.

Chapter 6

That night, Karen had trouble sleeping. Everything seemed normal (well, as normal as any day could be for her), but when she went to bed and turned the lights off, her mind wouldn't stop.

Bobby had gone to a lot of trouble to track her down today. In some ways it was flattering and fun, in other ways it was fascinating and suspenseful; but now that she lay alone in her bed and the night spooks of her mind woke up, all she felt was dread and fear.

He'll rape me one day.

I'll be sleeping in my bed, and I'll wake up feeling hurt and bleeding, and I'll know he's found me.

But would he? She struggled to pull back the funny parts of Bobby that she liked so much, the jokes and the ability to not take anything too seriously.

Then her mind would turn back to the old man, surely dead now.

I can never let him find me.

She'd stay away from the beach and keep a closer eye on things when she walked around town, but that was no guarantee.

Karen knew that everyone left footprints wherever they went. Did he snoop on her Facebook page? Did he know her cell number? There was lots of opportunity to follow her home from school or church.

I told him Dad's name.

When her dad had died, she remembered talking to Bobby, telling him how lost she felt. She tried to make a joke about her dad's name, but now that comment was haunting her. If Bobby remembered Parker Samson Richardson's name, it'd be easy to find where she lived. Easy as slicing an old man's neck.

She didn't have to be sleeping when he found her, of course. If time stopped for her, and he had his freedom, it could happen anytime at all. He could attack her at dinner or in the middle of English class, and she would just feel pain hit her out of the blue.

Only she would know what had happened.

Karen tossed and turned with worry, not falling asleep until after four o'clock. When Mom woke her by jostling her arm, she cried out in fear, pulling away from the only person in the world that she could totally trust.

Two weeks later time froze in the middle of English Lit, with Mrs. Frey rambling on about the theme of

Hamlet. Although Karen had enjoyed reading the play, she hated the way Mrs. Frey would dissect every little bit of it and ask the class, "What does this scene *really* mean?"

Karen never got it, so she was thankful for a break.

She gave a mock salute to Mrs. Frey as she walked toward the door. Her desk was at the back of the class, because the teacher liked to have all the troublemakers near the front.

Bonnie MacDonald was two desks over and one up from Karen; she went to look at her friend. She only hesitated a second before running her hand through Bonnie's hair and touching her cheek. She thought about watching Bonnie masturbating and wished she could find a way to make that happen again.

Reluctantly, she left the class and passed through the halls to the closest exit. Cautious, she looked around but couldn't see Bobby Jersey anywhere.

There were several houses nearby that she'd never visited so she went inside the first one.

She found Alexander Michaels sitting in his bedroom. Mr. Michaels was a forty-year-old chubby guy who worked the evening shift at Starbucks. Karen had been served by him several times and was always a bit creeped out when he handed over the proper change and grinned at her. She always felt weird.

He had his pants pulled down to his ankles. His penis was flaccid, but she suspected it wasn't going to stay that way for long.

Karen was pretty sure he lived alone. The bed was unmade, and the closet door was open. Only a few men's shirts hung there, no dresses or women's clothing of any kind.

"Can't say I'm surprised at that."

Michaels was at a desk staring at his laptop. He was in a chat room, and when Karen read through the notes on the screen, she felt awful. He was talking to a fourteen-year-old girl, pretending to be a boy her age.

Beside him was a stack of printed paper. She flipped through it, shocked to see dozens of transcripts, each one with him talking to a young girl. They all seemed to end with him asking to meet her.

She took the papers, and shoved them in a manila file folder, and carried them with her as she left.

"Gonna stop you, pervert."

She wanted to slap the guy—or worse—but she thought it would suffice to mail the printouts to the police and let them take care of things. Alexander Michaels would wonder how his precious papers disappeared, but he'd soon enough find them waved in front of his face.

When Karen was outside, she stopped, realizing that this was the first time she'd done anything while time was frozen that would significantly affect somebody's life.

"Feels pretty good."

She walked to the next house. A woman was in the bathroom scrubbing a toilet with a toothbrush.

Presumably not her own.

Karen didn't recognize her. She was in her twenties, skinny, dressed in floppy gray jogging pants and a matching sweater.

The bedroom was messy here, too, and a framed photo of the girl and a man, both smiling brightly at the camera, lay on the floor. The glass was cracked.

Karen left, not feeling good about things. She couldn't do anything to help the girl.

Why would that matter? I've never helped anybody before.

She walked past several houses, wondering why the hell she should start caring about the people she spied on. All she'd ever wanted to do was learn what they hid and add to her Secrets Journal.

She had a lot of entries now, including her priest, who she watched reading pornography online; several people who took illegal drugs when nobody was watching; thieves; liars; adulterers; and many others. Her little town was full of the seven deadly sins... and more.

If she believed the bible (and really, some days, she didn't pretend to believe it, even to herself), all her friends and neighbors were doomed to rot in hell.

She sat on a bench beside a bus stop and thought about her family. She missed her dad, and her mom didn't have any secrets that Karen had ever found. She might be the one exception to ascend to heaven one day.

Tina?

Karen's older sister was just dumb. One day she

would realize that giving blow jobs and probably screwing her boyfriend wasn't going to help her accomplish anything. One day Jimmy Berenstein would see some other girl and dump Tina without a minute's thought.

That morning, Tina had been getting ready for school with Karen, but there was something different. She was too happy, too perky, and Karen realized now that she hadn't seen Tina at school after all.

She knew where Jimmy lived and walked in that direction. It wasn't far from Karen's home, which Tina thought convenient.

The house was a dump, a duplex, where Jimmy lived in one half with his dad. Karen had no idea where his mom was, since she was never mentioned.

Jimmy's car was parked in front of the house, and Karen wasn't surprised that the front door wasn't locked. She walked in as if it were her own home and looked around. The living room stank of stale smoke, with several half-empty glasses on the coffee table. A big stain covered much of the rug. Four bottles of Miller Genuine Draft were discarded in the middle of the stain.

She looked around but didn't see anybody on the main level, so she climbed the stairs. The master bedroom was empty, as was the bathroom, but Karen found what she was looking for in the other bedroom.

Tina sat on a bench and Jimmy sat behind her. They were both naked. He had an erection.

In his hand, he held a razor blade, and he was using it to slice lines into Tina's back.

There were dozens of other cuts in various stages of healing, left over from previous sessions.

Tina's face was full of tears, and she looked like she wanted to scream, but Karen imagined that that was the very last thing she would do.

She knew that Tina would do anything for Jimmy, but this was worse than Karen could have imagined.

She stared at them, anger rushing through her. Even though she wasn't on the best of terms with Tina, she *was* her sister, and she wanted to protect her.

Karen didn't hesitate.

She grabbed the razor blade from Jimmy and sliced into his penis lengthwise, like gutting a trout. Of course, nothing changed, but when time started, he'd never again hurt her sister. All he'd care about would be getting to the emergency ward and making sure they stitched him up.

That night, after time started again and Karen had listened to the last of Mrs. Frey lecturing on metaphors, she waited for Tina to come home.

Tina was quiet and declined dinner. She went to her room, claiming she was tired from not sleeping well the night before.

Karen followed Tina.

"Are you okay?" she asked.

Tina frowned. "Why would you care?"

Karen kneeled in front of her sister and looked

into her eyes. "It's okay. He won't hurt you again."

Tina opened her mouth, but nothing came out. She looked to the side, not able to meet Karen's gaze.

"It's okay," Karen said. "I know what he does to you. But it's over now, right?"

For a moment the room was silent and neither girl moved. It was almost like time stopping, but Karen could hear background noise, including her own breathing, so she knew she was in normal time.

"How do you know?"

"I saw."

Tina didn't ask how or when or why or any of the questions Karen expected. She just hugged Karen and started to cry.

Chapter 7

Three months went by without time stopping for Karen. There were days when she felt normal, as if there was nothing different between her and Tina or any of Karen's friends.

She worried about Bobby and whether he would find her and hurt her, if she'd be in the middle of laughing with her mom over some funny scene on *Modern Family* and suddenly double over in pain from whatever Bobby might inflict upon her.

More often, though, he didn't cross her mind.

What did cross her mind was a blur of wants and desires and regrets, most of which skirted the edges of her consciousness. She thought of her dad and the secrets he had hidden in the closet, of the knowing smile on Mrs. Montgomery's face as she faked to the world how happy she was, of her sister's gaze that she sometimes felt trained on but when she looked was aimed somewhere else, of the guilt conjoined with pleasure when she remembered slicing Tina's boyfriend's cock. Most of all, she pushed the image away that refused to leave: the time she visited Bonnie MacDonald in her bedroom. None of her other silent visits struck her as strongly or as frequently.

Mid-April. L.A. didn't really have four seasons, but in Karen's mind, spring was in the air. She sat on a picnic table in Munson Park, about two blocks from school. It was a Saturday, and she was reading an old science-fiction novel, *Rendezvous with Rama*, by Arthur C. Clarke.

Dad's favorite book.

Halfway through, she put the book away and lay down on the picnic table with her eyes closed. It was just over eighty degrees, and a slight breeze made it the perfect spring day for Karen.

She had almost drifted off when she heard, "Hi, Karen. Sleeping?"

For a second, she thought she was just daydreaming, but the voice was too real. She blinked and sat up.

"Hi," she said.

Bonnie MacDonald smiled but did not seem to know what to say next.

"Wanna sit with me?" asked Karen.

"Sure."

Bonnie sat beside her, and they stared toward a distant baseball diamond, where a bunch of little leaguers excitedly ran through their paces.

"You know..." started Bonnie. Her voice trailed off into silence.

Karen felt fear rush through her. She wanted to be anywhere but here. *She knows. She's going to tell*

*me to stop looking at her out of the corner of my eye.
She's going to tell me to piss off and that if I want to
have freakish fantasies, to leave her out of them.*

Bonnie tried again. "I sometimes feel like I'm different than other people."

Karen swallowed, trying to slow down her mind so she could understand what she was hearing.

"Really? What do you mean?"

Bonnie turned to her and stared into Karen's eyes.

"I think you know. I think we're a lot alike."

Karen didn't know what to say. A sense of relief flooded her, but at the same time she felt guarded. She'd never admitted anything to anybody, barely even to herself. She tried to nod, but it only looked like her face was shaking in the breeze.

Bonnie touched her hand, and after a few seconds Karen returned the grasp. She smiled.

Two weeks later, Karen brought Bonnie home when both Mom and Tina were out. She'd never hinted about her secrets to anybody... until now. She led the way to Mom and Dad's bedroom. She could never stop referring to it as her father's room, even though he'd been dead for close to two years.

Karen was nineteen now.

She held Bonnie's hand as they snuck into the room. The closet was a walk-in, with a shelf near the top. The four boxes were still there. She went to the bathroom to grab a small stool and climbed up.

"I'm sure Mom hasn't looked at these. There's a

bit of dust on them from them sitting here.”

“Pretty freaky. You sure had balls, looking in here in the first place. I’d never be able to do that.”

“You’d be surprised what you can find courage for when you know you won’t be caught.”

“Well, there’s always a *chance*.”

Karen laughed. “Well, I’m sure most people would agree with you.”

She lifted one lid. “Here are the report cards I told you about. And these,” she said as she moved the first box aside, “are the porn magazines.”

“God, that must have totally been yucky.”

Karen nodded and pulled down the third box. She opened it and took out the gun, holding it carefully, not wanting to scare Bonnie.

“Whoa... that’s... well, I’m not exactly sure what it is.”

Bonnie laughed, and Karen soaked in the sound. She moved to Bonnie and kissed her on the mouth. It was an act she was getting used to, but she liked it better every time. Bonnie put her hand through Karen’s hair and then hugged her.

“You know, we’re all alone... we could be doing something else with our time,” said Bonnie.

She smiled, and Karen’s heart jumped. She’d wanted to hear Bonnie say something like that since their conversation in the park.

It took all of Karen’s willpower to say, “I really want that, but I need to show you the last box. I’ve never been able to talk to anybody about it until now.”

Not even Bobby.

The box looked the same as the other three: off-white, formerly used to hold five hundred standard-sized envelopes. The top fit snugly, and Karen had to pry it open.

She pulled out a newspaper article and then a small notebook.

"That's her," she whispered.

Bonnie took the newspaper carefully. It was more than twenty-five years old, discolored to a sickly yellow brown.

Local Girl Found Dead

The article described how the body of eight-year-old Tammy Preston had been found in a small park near her home.

The girl grinned from the newspaper. A couple of her teeth were missing, and she looked like she was full of joy and hadn't a care in the world. Although the photo was black and white, Karen knew that her copper-colored hair fell past her shoulders and that her eyes were blue.

The article said that she had been shot by a .45 caliber revolver and that the police were combing the area. So far there were no suspects.

"Such a pretty girl," said Bonnie. She turned to Karen. "You're sure?"

Karen nodded and handed Bonnie the notebook. It contained only a few pages of handwritten notes.

"That's Dad's handwriting. It's dated at the top, and he would have been thirty-two when he wrote it. I was eight—the same age Tammy Preston was when she was killed.

Bonnie read the notes:

It's been fifteen years now, and there's rarely a day I don't think about Tammy. I never knew her until that night, but since then, she's been part of me, like a conjoined twin, locked together forever. I killed her, and now she haunts me. Maybe that's a fair trade.

I've never told anybody, never written it down, never asked God or any other entity for either forgiveness or understanding. How could I? I haven't forgiven myself yet, and I sure as hell don't understand why I killed her.

It just felt like something I wanted to do. And when I did it, I enjoyed it. I liked pulling the trigger and watching her life seep out of her.

Even today I feel the same rush of joy I experienced that day. I feel the pleasure, and I know how easy it would have been to kill others after her.

But... even at seventeen, I knew I was lucky to have gotten away with it. I didn't live nearby, and my gun wasn't registered or anything, so there wasn't any obvious way to track me down. If I left fingerprints, there was nothing to compare them to, since I've never been arrested or joined the military.

Nobody saw me, nobody heard her screams, and if anybody did have any suspicions, they were always about the drunken fool who lived two doors down from Tammy. I read the news stories and heard the gossip, and there was never anything I needed to worry about.

But I always *have* worried.

I worry that I might feel that urge again and need to follow it. I've got two girls now, and they depend on me. I can't end up in jail.

I know it's wrong but I'm writing this for my own benefit. I wish I could say I'm sorry, but when I face myself in the mirror, would I really believe my own lies?

"Holy shit," said Bonnie. She'd read only the first couple of pages and flipped through to see how many more there were.

"The rest just talks about the same stuff. You've read the important pages."

"I don't know what to say."

Bonnie leaned over and hugged Karen.

"It's okay," Karen said. "I don't know what to say, either."

"Did your Dad seem crazy or anything?"

Karen shook her head. "Strict and a bit condescending, but pretty normal."

"You should tell your mom."

"I can't. She thinks he was a wonderful person. What good would it do to tell her the truth? I thought maybe one day she'd stumble across this stuff herself, but so far, she hasn't. Or maybe she *has* and just doesn't want to deal with it."

Karen put the box back in its secret place and took Bonnie's hand.

"Let's go for a walk. Fresh air will help."

Bonnie smiled and gave Karen a quick kiss. "Kay!"

The next day, time stopped for Karen. It'd been a while, and it took her by surprise.

She was an intern at the Mayberry Care Center, which mostly meant that she spent time reading books or talking to terminally ill patients.

"My Lord, girl, you never know what pain is like until you're being called home to God."

It was Mrs. Thompson talking to her. The old woman was wheezy and took a long time to finish her thoughts. She had liver cancer and was hooked to a morphine IV drip, which was the only thing that stopped her from screaming in pain. Most of her white hair was gone, and wrinkles scratched across her face. She looked like a child's vision of the wicked witch in Hansel and Gretel.

But she was kind. She tried to smile for Karen and did her best not to show the pain that wracked her body. She never had visitors, so when Karen came to see her, it was like the sun shining after a terrible hurricane.

"I wish I could help you," said Karen, holding the old woman's hand.

"I know that you—"

Time stopped.

Mrs. Thompson's face froze, and Karen could see the pain in her eyes trying to squeeze out. Silence dropped around her. Karen hadn't realized how much sound there was in the clinic ward until it stopped.

"I'll be back," she said.

She left and walked down Maple Street. There weren't any maple trees around, and she wondered if the street was named to make the Mayberry Care Center feel more welcoming. It was a short street and led only to the center.

As she looked for houses that she wanted to walk through, she realized she hadn't worried recently about Bobby Jersey, and she wondered what he was up to. She no longer thought about him hurting her when she was frozen, and he was free to do as he liked. It'd been too long. If he wanted to do something, he'd have done it already.

A sickening truth came to her: she missed talking to him.

He was still the only other person she'd ever met who lived the same life she did. As much as she loved Bonnie, she could never tell her about what she thought of as her *real* life. Her *free* life.

She'd think I'm fucking nuts.

Bobby's the only person who understands.

There was one other reason she felt safer from Bobby. She knew exactly where to find him, and if he ever messed with her, she'd mess back, only a whole lot worse.

Karen worked her way down the street, wandering inside the homes that looked the most interesting. Her Secrets Journal was now crammed full of things that nobody imagined would ever see the light.

She knew of dozens of men who were cheating on their wives or girlfriends, and an equal number of women doing the same.

She had seen every possible sex act, between every combination of a man and a woman, and sometimes with three or more people involved.

She watched people hurt themselves and those they loved, over and over.

She saw most of the Ten Commandments broken without much thought by the sinners, and she saw people treating other people horribly, while in public smiling as if they were the nicest people in the world.

Karen realized that she could never like most of the people in her neighborhood. They lied, they cheated, they stole, they fucked each other over like there was no tomorrow, and they didn't seem to feel a hint of remorse.

On the other hand, remorse flowed like blood through her veins. She would often visit the secret boxes in her mother's bedroom, looking at her dad's .45, hefting it in her hands, rereading his confession and then looking at the face of the innocent girl whose life he had stolen.

And she'd cry.

Karen shook her head to try to shake out the demons that haunted her. For some reason they worked more on her when time stopped, as if the worldly issues slid off her body and left her shrouded in her father's guilt.

"Stupid," she chided herself. There was nothing

she could do about the past.

There was a party in the house down the street from the Mayberry Care Center, about twenty people scattered around the basement and plumes of marijuana smoke hanging motionless in the air. They looked like college students. Karen was a sophomore, and even though it was a long shot, she checked each person to see if she knew anyone.

Nope.

The bathroom door was shut but not locked. She opened it and saw a girl about her age bending over the sink. Her pants were off and her legs spread apart. A guy was fucking her from behind. He had a grizzled black beard and a joint in his mouth. His expression showed that he was only concerned about his own pleasure and didn't give a rat's ass about the girl he was using. She was grimacing and gritting her teeth.

Karen moved closer and saw that he wasn't using a condom. She doubted they'd known each other before the party, but the girl wouldn't likely forget him anytime soon.

Karen felt anger rush through her, and for a second, she thought about slicing Tina's boyfriend's cock. Surely this guy deserved the same.

Didn't he?

Then a thought hit her: *What makes me so perfect a judge?*

She wondered if she might turn into a vigilante, roaming the streets to take revenge for the sins she discovered.

She left the building and walked away, trying to

forget the party.

"You're back."

"You're very observant."

"Still as cute as ever."

Karen didn't really want to talk to Bobby Jersey, but then again, she did.

Fuck, I'm messed up.

"I guess I just miss talking to somebody who understands."

"Yeah," he said. "I'm glad you came back. It's been a long time."

"You ever wish you were normal?" Even as the words left her mouth, she knew she really was asking herself that question, not him.

"Nah. I figure I can have a lot of fun and nobody's the wiser."

She nodded, not wanting him to elaborate on the kind of fun he was talking about. She'd seen some of it and didn't need to see any more. He was one more asshole in a sea of assholes.

"Can you come with me?" she asked.

"Where to?"

"Just a mile or so away."

He shrugged and laughed. "Why not?"

On the way, Karen told Bobby about the secrets her father had kept, including the murder. He didn't interrupt her, just listened. Karen kept looking straight ahead while they walked, so she never knew if he glanced over to her during the story or not.

When she finished, he put a hand on her

shoulder. "Sorry you had to find that out. Must be hard."

"I want to make it right somehow."

They walked through the gates of Blue Ridge Cemetery. It was midafternoon and the sun was bloody hot. She didn't care. She needed to find Tammy Preston.

Karen looked down at the closest tombstone. She'd been walking for almost an hour and still hadn't found what she'd been looking for.

For that matter, she wasn't sure she even knew for herself exactly what she was seeking. The one she was looking at now had a woman's name followed by:

> Born July 4, 1960, Died December 10, 1999
> Beloved Mother and Artist
> She Brought Life to Those Close to Her

A gust of wind blew some loose strands of Karen's long blonde hair so they covered her view. She pushed them back behind her ears.

"Is that the one?"

The voice behind her was gentle but insistent.

"Are you getting tired of looking?"

Karen smiled as she turned to face Bobby. He stood a respectful two feet behind her, as if he were trying to give her all the privacy she might need while still being there to offer any emotional support.

Not bloody likely, she thought.

Bobby was nineteen years old, just like she was. Somehow, though, he looked older. If she didn't know better, she'd peg him at about twenty-five. He was tall, rugged, and handsome, exactly the kind of guy who would turn girls' heads wherever he went. His deep voice made her wonder if he could have had a future in radio.

Karen, on the other hand, knew she barely looked seventeen, let alone nineteen. She was slim and short and never seemed to fill out like other girls her age.

"Sorry, I didn't intend to sound impatient," he said. "Take all the time you want. Time is the one thing both of us have lots of."

Karen nodded. "I just need to find the right one."

Bobby smiled. "I know. Really, it's okay."

"I'm not sure anything will be okay ever again."

Bobby didn't answer. What could he say to that?

Karen looked at him with the hint of emotion in her eyes, but she was determined not to let a single tear drop. She tried to detach herself and just concentrate on Bobby's face—the dark brown eyes; the pitch-black, curly hair; the dimples she knew would appear when he smiled.

She exhaled a long breath and turned back to the headstone. "I wonder what kind of art she practiced."

"Do you want to check? You can Google it on your iPhone. Shouldn't be hard to find if she really accomplished anything."

Karen shook her head. "In a way I'd rather imagine my own truth. I think she loved to put together collages from nature, picking up stray oak and maple leaves wherever she went and then spending hours rearranging them to tell a story."

She knelt and touched the granite stone, feeling the etchings of some of the letters.

"This isn't the one," she said finally.

Bobby joined her as she walked past a few more tombstones. None of them interested her. Only a few had called to her so far.

The sun was starting to set behind them, casting a long shadow through the graveyard. Karen knew Bobby just wanted her to find the right damned stone so they could leave, but it wasn't that easy. It had to be the *right* one.

If she couldn't find it, she'd come back tomorrow, and the day after that.

"Did you know there're two thousand people buried here?" asked Bobby.

She ignored him. A cool breeze blew, and she felt goose bumps rise on her arms. Suddenly, she moved to her right and fell to her knees in front of an old weathered stone.

"This is the one," she said. "I found her."

The grave marker was hard to read but once she was close to the ground, she could make it out easily enough:

> Tammy Preston
> Died Too Young
> Never to be Forgotten

Karen ran her fingers over the etchings and tried to imagine the loss Tammy's parents would have felt. She couldn't.

"I'm so sorry, Tammy," she whispered. "I wish I could have helped you."

She wiped a tear from her cheek, closed her eyes, and said a silent prayer. Even after distancing herself from her church, she needed to do that.

It wasn't long afterwards that she felt the calling; she had to hurry back to work before time started again.

As she ran back, she knew Bobby was following her, but she couldn't do a damned thing about it.

CHAPTER 8

KAREN GOT BACK just as she felt the tension rising to a ridiculously high degree. Her body was tingling and every cell was shouting at her to *get back into the fucking right place!*

The calling had never been this strong. She wondered what would happen if she somehow found the courage to ignore the un-ignorable and stay where she was, out of time, out of place. She'd never been able to resist the calling, though; and if she'd been unable to do it while knowing that Bobby Jersey was following her, she surely never would.

He knows where I work.

The thought was followed by: *He can find where I live anytime he wants to.* The hospital had records that would be easy for him to find if he chose to.

But then, why would he bother? He already knew where to find her. The next time that he was free, and she was frozen, he could come over and do whatever he wanted.

Bobby was evil. She knew that. She knew it as

surely as she knew her own name, and although his smile said otherwise, in her heart she knew that he'd happily do whatever happened to cross his mind. She'd seen that side of him, and she was frightened of it.

"Go see Mrs. Jenkins."

Karen snapped out of her thoughts and realized that her supervisor, Maggie Kincaid, had had to repeat her request.

"Sorry, Maggie. I'm on my way." She smiled and hurried down the hall to Room 217.

Mrs. Jenkins had only been admitted for a few days and was already close to death. Karen felt anger whenever she visited, because Mrs. Jenkins was thirty-two, much too young to be dying. Her husband visited her every morning and every night, and when Karen saw him, she saw confusion, fear, and anger on his face. She understood because she felt the same way. No fair God should ever allow some disease Karen had never heard of to take away such a young woman.

"Hello," she whispered. She took the patient's hand. *The patient,* she reminded herself. *Not "Mrs. Jenkins."* Dehumanize them as much as possible. That was part of her training.

Every day when Karen left work, she felt lonely and frustrated.

But she felt an amazing sense of tranquility by the time she got home. Every day she made somebody's life just a tiny bit better than it would otherwise be.

She wanted to work at the Mayberry Care Center

for the rest of her life.

"Thank you," said the frail woman. She tried to squeeze Karen's hand but could only manage a tiny pressure. Tubes ran from her nose and arms. There were others beneath the covers.

"Would you like me to read to you?"

Mrs. Jenkins shook her head, a gesture Karen barely noticed. "Just..."

Karen waited for her to finish the sentence, but the woman couldn't get the words out. Her lips moved but no sound emerged.

"What did you say?"

Karen leaned close.

"Just kill me."

Karen pulled back in shock.

"Please," whispered the woman. "It hurts so much."

"I can't."

Mrs. Jenkins stared at her, her mouth clawing in bits of air. Her eyes were like accusing spikes.

"Please let me read to you. Last time we started a Danielle Steel novel. Should we continue?"

The woman just stared at her. "Please," she whispered one more time.

Karen picked up the paperback novel and flipped it open to Chapter Four, where she'd left off the day before and she started to read.

Forty-eight hours later, Mrs. Olivia Jenkins was dead. In those last two days, she suffered immensely. She couldn't catch her breath and felt as if she was breathing through a straw. Her guts were full of shiny glass fragments that churned and ripped her insides, her brain assaulted by lightning bolts. Even the morphine drip did little to dull the eternal pain.

Karen wanted to help her, but there was nothing she could do. She had little control over the medication the patients were given. After all, Mrs. Jenkins wouldn't be at the clinic if she weren't a terminal case waiting for death.

That didn't make Karen feel better. Suddenly, she realized that many of her patients wanted her help, to ease them away from the horrible last days ahead of them into a peaceful sleep. Most didn't ask with their mouth—they asked with their eyes. She now knew the meaning of the wide-eyed stare that greeted her so often. Until now she'd thought it was fear, which made total sense to her; but now she realized it was also a plea for help.

One night when she was twenty-one, she lay in bed with Bonnie, both naked. Karen needed to hold her tightly, wanting to feel the love of her girlfriend, hoping the feelings they shared would help remove the memories of her day job.

She kissed Bonnie passionately and rubbed her back from the shoulders down to her ass. The two girls pressed their bodies together, and Karen felt herself getting wet, the memories of the waiting dead finally falling from her mind.

Suddenly, her arm was wretched down to her side

with a sudden jerk, and she was slammed onto her back as if an invisible giant plucked her off Bonnie and tossed her like an old Barbie doll. It happened without warning and both girls were stunned.

"What happened?" asked Bonnie. Her voice was full of confusion. "I thought you were enjoying it."

"I was. I didn't pull away. My body just slammed down."

"That's impossible."

Karen realized what happened. She felt her belly and found a sticky spot.

Fucking Bobby Jersey. Ohmygod, he was here.

She knew without even having to consciously work it out. Time had frozen for Bobby, and he used his secret time to come to her. He'd found her making love with Bonnie, pushed her aside, probably fondled both, and masturbated on her.

Fucking pervert.

Tears spilled down her cheeks. "I'm so sorry, Bonnie."

"But what happened?"

"I—I'm not sure how to explain."

"It's okay. I'm here for you. You can tell me anything. You know that."

"Yes. I do."

And she did. She told her everything about being able to move when everybody else was stuck in time. She told her about Bobby and about her dad and her sister's loser boyfriend. She told her about all the buried secrets she'd found over the years, and she pulled out her Secrets Journal to help convince Bonnie what she'd seen.

The only thing she didn't tell her was the time when Karen had spied on Bonnie herself.

It took two hours to get her story out, and during that time Bonnie barely talked. She nodded occasionally and let the story unfold. As Karen revealed more details, she was convinced that Bonnie thought she was a freaking nut case. By the end of the story, she was sure she'd ruined the only true love she'd ever felt.

When she finally stopped talking, though, Bonnie smiled and just said, "I love you. I want to hear everything from this point forward. No more secrets between us. Pinkie swear?"

Karen grinned and held out her smallest finger to connect with Bonnie's.

Thirteen days passed before time stopped again for Karen. In that time, three of her patients had died, and she'd had no further visits from Bobby.

She had planned her time-freeze this time. It was the middle of the night. She snapped awake and saw Bonnie curled up beside her, like a cute little snail.

Karen was wearing pajamas and didn't bother changing. Nobody would see her. She went to the kitchen and picked out a sharp carving knife.

It had taken very little effort to find out where Bobby lived. Unlike her, he was outgoing and wanted everybody to know everything about him on Facebook, Twitter, and a few other sites. Once Karen decided to track him down, she had his address within a few hours.

He lived in the basement of an apartment owned by his mom. She broke a window, not caring if there was an alarm system. If there was, she'd be long gone before the first ring of the claxon.

He was sleeping naked (no surprise to her). Karen pulled the covers off him and used the knife to slice a very thin line on his belly, the same place he had defiled her with his semen.

She'd already written a note that she left propped beside him: *Leave me alone, you fucking creep. If I ever see you again, I'm going to cut your cock off. You know I'll have no qualms about doing it.*

She left and walked to the Mayberry Care Center. The building was mostly dark so the patients could sleep, but there were still a half-dozen employees keeping track of things.

Carlene Jameson was in Room 173. She was an old woman, close to eighty, who'd been waiting to die for more than two weeks. Like most of the others, she was in pain every minute of every day and just wanted it to be over.

Karen walked into the drug room and filled a hypodermic with morphine. She took it to Carlene Jameson's room and inserted it into her IV, depositing the deadly dose so it would bring the rest that the old woman desperately wanted. She'd begged Karen for help several times, and Karen no longer feared helping. She'd just needed to have time stop so she could take care of things without being caught. She'd never be allowed in the drug room normally without authorization. This way, she could help Carlene and leave no indication she had even been in the same building.

"Good-bye," she whispered. She kissed the old woman on the forehead and then took her time as she left the building. She walked around downtown until she felt the calling and smiled as she went back home to sleep with Bonnie.

Chapter 9

Four years passed.

Karen was twenty-five, and it seemed that she'd always lived with Bonnie. Any secret insecurities Karen had felt about her relationship were long gone; she knew they'd be together forever.

Long gone also was Bobby Jersey. After threatening to hurt him, Karen had not heard from him again. She rarely thought of him, since she no longer needed him. Once he had been the only person she could share her secret life with. Now, Bonnie shared that part of her, even if it wasn't something she could directly participate in. It didn't matter.

Karen loved her work at the care center. She loved being able to soothe her patients, but when they had that special look in their eyes, she could help them with that too.

Carlene Jameson was the first, but there'd been many after her. Karen knew in her heart that she was truly helping them. They suffered and had no chance of recovery. Waiting in pain to die is something few people were equipped to do gracefully. Karen only helped when time stopped for her, so there was no way to tie the murders to her. As far as she knew, nobody ever really suspected anything unusual had happened. Terminal patients die. No surprise there.

Only one area of her life nagged at Karen. She sometimes woke late at night and thought of her father. She remembered the four boxes he'd squirreled away in the closet and the words in his confession, written so many years later: *I wish I could say I'm sorry, but when I face myself in the mirror, would I really believe my own lies?*

Part of her tried to forgive him, to say that she was just as much a murderer as he was, but that didn't hold water for her. She was killing to help people. He took the life of an eight-year-old girl who had her whole future ahead of her.

Tammy Preston had been dead in her grave for close to thirty years. She would have been in the prime of her life right now. No punishment could be doled out to her father anymore, but there was still one thing that Karen had struggled with since finding her father's secrets nine years earlier.

"Hey, Mom," Karen called when she walked into the house. Even though she hadn't lived there for years, it still felt like home to her.

Her mom was in the kitchen, baking bread. It was a hobby she'd picked up in the past few years, when she found a cooking group organized at her local supermarket. She smiled when Karen walked in, and they hugged.

"How's things?"

"I'm good," said Karen. "We're both doing great. One piece of news for you—we're looking into adoption. It'll take a long time, but you always told me good things come to those who wait."

"That'd be so wonderful! It's been a long time since I've heard little footsteps padding around this place."

After a pause, Karen said, "Mom, I need to show you something. It's kind of a big deal."

She took her mom by the hand and started up the stairs to the master bedroom.

"What is it?"

Karen sat on the bed with her mom beside her. Both of them could feel tension in the air.

"A long time ago, I found some things that Dad had been hiding away in the closet."

Her mom stared at her, clearly surprised Karen had snuck into their bedroom closet.

"I know I shouldn't have gone in there, but I did. I think you need to see what he was hiding. You need to know because you have a view of Dad that you may have to modify. I've been haunted by the boxes in the closet for years, and I just need you to know they're there."

Karen went to retrieve the boxes and placed them on the bed beside her mom. She suggested they be opened in the same sequence she originally had opened them: the report cards, the magazines, the gun, and the note.

Karen hugged her mom, who just looked

confused. Then she smiled and said, "I'll be down in the living room. I'll make us coffee for whenever you're done."

She bit her tongue as she left, wondering if she'd done the right thing.

Thirty minutes later, Karen's mom came down and sat with her, smiled as if resigned to the truth found upstairs and gave Karen a long hug. They never spoke of the boxes again.

The last of Karen's stress points melted away, and she smiled as she thought of her future.

Chapter 10

Two years passed. Karen and Bonnie had the perfect life. They loved each other, they enjoyed their jobs, they enjoyed their home, and they found time to travel a little bit each year.

They hoped to adopt but so far that hadn't worked out. That was okay; they were patient. They knew it would happen one day.

Karen was twenty-seven. She had helped a dozen terminally ill patients find the peace they wanted so badly, and she'd made the final days of a hundred others easier by reading to them, listening to them talk about the events that shaped their lives, or just smiling and holding their hand while they watched television.

Even that part of Karen's life felt perfect to her.

Bonnie came up with the idea.

"Hey, let's go to the Halloween party at the Micimac this year."

"Really?" The Micimac was a pub a couple of blocks from their home. They dropped in from time to time, but Karen had never thought of joining the regulars there. "Like get dressed up and everything?"

"And everything! Of course!"

Karen wasn't sure, but Bonnie hugged her and said she knew Karen would love it.

They dressed up as characters from a recent movie, both men, both wearing fake beards and army gear. To her surprise, Karen loved the party.

At midnight, they were dancing with a dozen other couples. Karen would always remember the D.J. was playing "Mermaid" by Train.

All of a sudden Bonnie let go of Karen and grabbed her throat. She started to choke.

Karen felt like time had stopped, but this time it hadn't. She was frozen with fear and confusion as she looked at Bonnie.

Blood gushed between Bonnie's fingers, spurting over the dance floor. Her face was white with shock and her mouth opened and closed, but Karen couldn't hear any words. The noise of the music drowned anything she might have gasped.

When Bonnie sank to the floor, somebody screamed. The music stopped suddenly, and the lights all came on. Somebody yelled, "Call 911!"

Bonnie looked at Karen, who was still frozen, her mind unable to comprehend what was happening to the woman she loved.

Finally, Bonnie rolled onto her side and that broke the trance. Karen dropped beside her to see what was happening. Bonnie's hands fell away, and Karen saw more blood dripping from her neck. There was a thin slash line cut horizontally through Bonnie's throat.

"No! No, don't take her from me, Bobby!"

Karen looked around and saw a woman dressed as a genie. She grabbed one of her scarves and placed it around Bonnie's neck, hoping to stop the bleeding; she was afraid to pull it too tight, though, for fear of choking her.

It seemed forever before the ambulance arrived. Two men pushed her aside to work on Bonnie. They put her on a stretcher and took her away. Karen ran after them, and they let her ride in the ambulance to the hospital.

The paramedic kept her away. "Don't get too close. She needs air."

His eyes told a different story, though. *Somebody sliced her throat. If it was you, you're not getting close enough to finish the job.*

Karen waited three hours while they performed emergency surgery. In that time, she was interviewed by a female cop, who looked at her with disbelief in her eyes when Karen said she had no idea what happened.

"You say you were dancing with her, though. She was holding you and facing you. How could anybody slice her throat without you seeing it?"

Because time was stopped for him.

"I don't know."

She knew she sounded like she was hiding something, because she was. It never crossed her mind to tell the truth about what had happened.

The cop told Karen to go to the police station the next day and sign her statement. She warned her there would be further questions.

They let her see Bonnie a little after three a.m. She was unconscious, and the surgeon gave Karen the news.

"She has severe brain damage from lack of oxygen. The flow of blood to her brain was stopped for quite some time."

"Will she recover?" Karen knew the answer even as she asked the question, but she had to be sure.

The doctor sighed. "Miracles do happen from time to time."

Karen felt tears running down both cheeks. She took Bonnie's hand and held it, not letting go until the sun came up.

The next two weeks were the hardest of Karen's life. She spent most of her time at the hospital, talking to Bonnie, wanting her to hear her voice and know she was there. Sometimes Karen didn't know what to say, and she started reading to Bonnie, the way she'd done for so many patients.

Every day it seemed less and less likely that Bonnie would recover. The doctors weren't sure how much to tell her, because she had no legal standing. They weren't married, they weren't related, and there was little legal recourse from them living together, regardless of how committed Karen said their relationship was. Bonnie had never filled in any paperwork that would identify Karen as her next of kin.

Eventually Karen found out the truth: Bonnie was brain-dead. There was no chance of recovery. Her body was breathing because of the machinery forcing air into her lungs, but otherwise she was just a lifeless husk. The woman Karen loved more than life itself was gone and would never return.

After those two weeks, Karen finally turned her attention to Bobby Jersey.

"You fucking bastard," she said to her empty living room. "I'm going to kill you for taking her from me."

Karen had never understood why Bobby did the things he did and she hadn't much cared. Now she realized that she should have done something to stop him earlier, but the things he did had never directly affected her and she couldn't bring herself to interfere. Now she'd give anything to be able to go back in time and stop him before he'd had the opportunity to take Bonnie from her.

She knew his address.

It was a Saturday when time stopped for her. She knew exactly where to go. Electronics didn't work when time was stopped, but she could still ride a bicycle. She hopped on her bike and cranked it as hard as she could. Bobby currently lived about three miles from her, and although she hadn't been to the house, she'd studied the maps, knowing one day she might need to go.

When she arrived, she dropped the bicycle and strode into the house.

Sitting in the living room was a middle-aged woman, watching some mindless television. A balding, skinny man was in the kitchen making a tuna sandwich. She ignored them and searched the rest of the house. There was only the master bedroom and one other. It had been converted to a reading room, with a couple of armchairs and a set of wall-to-wall bookcases.

"Shit," she said. *He doesn't live here.*

The address Bobby had allowed her to find was fake.

She felt empty, unwilling to believe that she couldn't find him, that she'd never have the satisfaction of revenge for what he'd done.

She rode her bike slowly home, winding around town, looking uselessly for any hint of Bobby. She headed down to the beach in case he was there, but no dice.

And then the calling came to her and she had to ride back home.

Two days later, Karen had checked everything she could think of. There was no entry for anybody with a last name of Jersey in Laguna Beach in any online directory, no new address or hint of anything from his Facebook account (in fact she found a recent entry with the fake address she'd previously seen), and it slowly dawned on her that he'd lied to her from the first day they met. Bobby Jersey likely wasn't even his real name.

She continued to go see Bonnie every minute she could. The love she felt never diminished, and she sometimes wished she could crawl into the hospital bed with her, holding her like she would have in their own bed.

Karen had finished reading several novels to Bonnie

and was close to the end of another when she went to visit one night.

Bonnie's room was empty.

Karen panicked and ran to the nurse's station. As usual it was hard to get information, but the distress written on her face was enough to convince the nurse to tell her, "They've moved her to a long-term care facility."

"Where?"

The nurse looked around. She knew the life Karen shared with Bonnie, but rules were rules. She hesitated and then whispered, "This never happened." She scribbled the name of Bonnie's new home onto a Post-It note and handed it to Karen. The nurse turned her back and walked away.

Bonnie's quarters were nice but more crowded than in the hospital. Six patients were crammed into one small room. Karen knew that Bonnie didn't care, but *she* cared. She wanted Bonnie to have the best. Unfortunately, there wasn't much she could do to help.

She held Bonnie's hand, kissed her cheek, and pulled out the book to continue reading while a machine forced air into Bonnie's lungs.

That night, Karen woke up at a little after 2:00 a.m. with a sense of purpose and inspiration. She went to her computer and pulled up the website for the *Los Angeles Times* and searched for unexplained deaths caused by slit throats—Bobby's normal method. She had no reason to think he'd do something different.

There were three stories in the past few months, all about mysterious injuries to throats that seemed to be caused by box cutters or something similar. None of the victims had been connected to the others. She mapped out where they occurred and found them centralized near Union Street and Casper Avenue, nowhere near where he'd led her to believe he lived.

Time stopped a week later, and she spent a few subjective hours searching the area. Finally, she found him. He was using the computer in a small back apartment. The room was a mess, with plates of rotting food scattered around. Posters of recent science-fiction movies were stuck on a couple of walls, and a large flat-screen TV dominated the room.

Bobby was hunched over his keyboard, typing something into Google, but he'd only gotten as far as "How do—?" before she'd arrived.

He looked the same as the last time she saw him. Tall, handsome, trustworthy.

She wanted to kill him right then, but that wouldn't be enough. She left, went home, and thought about her options.

When time started again, she knew what she had to do.

The next day Karen called in sick. She went to a park nearby and sat on a bench, watching the birds as they chirped and pecked at food tossed to them by other visitors. She enjoyed the feel of the sunshine on her face and smiled as little children played hopscotch and tag.

She walked through her neighborhood and said hi to some of the people she knew. It occurred to her that she hadn't had a vanilla milkshake in years, and she ducked into the Dairy Queen to order one. Karen tried not to think about anything except what was in front of her eyes at any particular minute.

The day went by. She tried her best to enjoy it. As the sun fell, she walked to Bobby's house. By the time she got there, the sun was gone, and only hints of scattered light paved the way.

She knocked and waited. After a minute, Bobby opened the door, staring at her like she was a ghost.

"Hi," she said. "Aren't you going to invite me in, Bobby Jersey? Or should I say Bobby Jameson?"

He stepped back. Karen walked into his house without giving him a chance to change his mind.

"You found me."

She looked around the room like it was the first time she'd been there.

"Robert Peter Jameson. Born in Newark, New Jersey, liberating the name of your home state as part of your new persona." She looked around at the computer. "In reality, of course, you're just a pathetic loser, a murderer, and a freak."

Bobby had recovered enough to say, "Good to see you, too. You can leave now."

Karen looked at him and shook her head. She wanted to cry, but she forced herself to concentrate on the business at hand.

"You killed the wrong person."

Bobby shrugged. "I hear she's not dead."

"That's a technicality and you know it."

In spite of herself, a tear dropped down her cheek. "You fucking loser," she whispered. "Why did you do it? *Why the fuck did you do it?*"

His face hardened, but a small smile lifted the corners of his mouth.

"Why? Because I met you more than a decade ago, when you were just as pathetic and freakish as me." He looked like he wanted to spit at her. "But you changed and left me behind. That bitch changed you. She made you happy, and you didn't want anything to do with me. You were too damned good for me. I was back to being a freak."

"You slit her throat because I loved her..."

"Damned right."

Karen felt drained, guilt rushing through her.

Concentrate, she told herself.

She opened her purse, pretending to look for a tissue, but she pulled out a knife instead and didn't hesitate. She rushed to Bobby and buried the knife in his chest, pushing him to the wall.

He screamed, but that just hardened her resolve and she pushed the knife harder. The blade slid against ribs as it punctured the lung behind them. She had no idea if anybody had heard him scream, but the sound didn't last long. He stared at her and moved his mouth, but no noise came out.

"No more secrets, Bobby. I wanted you to see me," she said. "Doing it when time was stopped wasn't right."

He reached to her but had no strength in his arms. He started to slide to the floor.

Karen watched the life ebb from him but felt no real

satisfaction. It was a job, a job long overdue, but one that was finally finished.

When she was sure he was dead, she left the apartment and closed the door behind her. She didn't bother taking her purse with her.

The walk away seemed to take forever. She half-expected a police car to come screaming toward her and armed officers to take her into custody, but nothing happened. She just walked and walked, and eventually found herself at the care center where Bonnie was housed.

She couldn't say "where Bonnie lived" because she wasn't alive. Not really. The machines might cause her body to breathe, but that wasn't living.

The caretakers had come to know Karen and trust her. She signed in and went to Bonnie's room, where she closed the door behind her.

"Hello, my love."

She knew how all the machinery worked, from her job at the Mayberry Care Center, and she was able to disable the monitors, so no alarms would be raised at the front desk.

She sat on the bed beside Bonnie and gently rubbed her hair.

"You always had such beautiful blonde hair," she said. "I loved touching it. I loved our life together."

Karen leaned over and kissed Bonnie on her cheek one last time. She wanted to kiss her lips, but the tube allowing her to breathe snaked down her throat.

Then she put her hands around the frail neck and squeezed. At first, she didn't do it hard enough, and Bonnie's body kept breathing. She squeezed harder and harder, and she finally felt Bonnie shaking a little bit... at least she thought she did. She kept it up, finding it hard to see through the tears but telling herself she needed to release the woman she loved.

Eventually, the monitors showed Bonnie's vital signs at zero. She had no idea how long it took. Time was standing still in a very different way for her.

Karen lay down beside her beautiful angel and kissed her cheek one last time. She closed her eyes and tried to remember all the good times they'd had together. She held Bonnie, whispered "I love you," and waited for the police to arrive. ⚭

Second Chance

I love writing stories about time. If you're a long-time reader of mine, I'm sure you know that. I love thinking about obscure things to do with time, and that ends up with stories like Placeholders, Miranda, Secrets, and so on.

Well, here's another one.

I wrote Second Chance with the thought that it would be the first of a series of stories. As you read it, I think you'll see what I was imagining: a few (or maybe more than a few) stories set with the Second Chance corporation creating all kinds of interesting problems for my characters.

It hasn't happened yet. After writing this story, I ended up working on novels and when I did have a chance to come back to shorter works, I never came up with the second story in the series.

One of these days, I hope to revisit this universe. I think there's a lot to be said yet, if only my mind would figure them out.

Michael Bailey asked me to write a story for Qualia Nous 3, and I was thrilled when the book came out with my story.

Mᴀʀᴋ Sᴛᴇᴠᴇɴsᴏɴ sat in his car on Center Street in Aynsville in upstate New York. The town only had a little over twelve thousand residents so there was never a serious traffic jam, but today it seemed like it was taking forever to get anywhere.

Beside him on the passenger seat of his eight-year-old Camry sat a wooden box.

Mark glanced at the box every few minutes, crazy thoughts passing through his mind. Chief among those thoughts was whether he should have put a seat belt around the box.

He shrugged as the car in front of him inched forward. Now he could see that there was construction in front of the First National Bank and Trust. Oncoming traffic was being diverted and the cars in front of him waited in various measures of patience for their turn to move through the intersection.

"We'll get there soon enough," he said. "Not much of a hurry anymore."

He looked at the box again. It was a dark brown with a very nice hand-carved swirl pattern on the top.

He hoped Kim would have liked it.

The box was about a foot wide and another foot long and about six inches high. It was heavier than he had expected.

"We'll be home before you know it."

He reached his hand over and caressed the top of the box. It felt warm, so he clicked the air conditioning on.

"I miss you."

His heart hurt as he said those words, but he didn't cry this time. It felt like he'd been crying all week and maybe he just didn't have any tears left to leak out.

Traffic was still snarled, so he put the car in Park and rubbed his eyes.

A new song from Maroon 5 was playing on the radio but he had barely been listening. They had been Kim's favorite band and now he wished he'd been able to take her to that concert at Madison Square Gardens last year. It was about the tenth thing he'd regretted since he'd woken that morning.

He'd never gone ice skating with her.

They'd never had kids.

He'd never even officially proposed marriage to her, but they both knew that was only a matter of timing.

He'd never taken her back to her home town. For that matter he didn't even know the town name. It was somewhere on Trinidad (or maybe Tobago, now that he thought of it).

They'd had the whole rest of their lives to do these things. Unfortunately the rest of Kim's life was over, since she'd been run down by a crazy drunk driver a week earlier.

She'd been twenty-six years old, same age as him, and she was the only girl he'd ever loved.

"You'll still be with me forever, babe," he told the box.

Mark had already cleared a place on his book shelf for Kim. It was the bedside table on her side of the bed. He'd moved the book she'd been reading, along with the couple of home decorating magazines she'd kept there, down into one of the drawers. He'd see her every night as he crawled into bed.

He knew he'd say good-night to her each night and tell her he loved her, and every morning he'd wake up with a "Good morning" for her.

Nothing could ever change how much he loved her.

The cars ahead of him continued to stand still, as if they were all sleeping. Mark craned his head and could see a couple of workers directing a small earth-mover into position.

"Won't be long now, babe." He caressed the box again.

The radio was playing some commercial, and suddenly he realized he needed to listen.

"...so, if you've made a mistake or need a do-over, come on down and see us at 193 Central Avenue. You really can have a second chance."

Second chance...

Of course he'd heard the commercials before but never really paid attention. His life was perfect as it was, because *Kim* was perfect.

Now she was gone.

He remembered the first time he saw that amazing smile of hers. It was at the public library. Almost nobody ever borrows books at the library anymore, but Mark loved the feeling of just wandering through the stacks and smelling the musky odor of the thousands of books waiting patiently for somebody to pick them up. The library seemed like his private realm, and he went there every few weeks, just to wander around and pick out a few mysteries to read.

Free was a good price. He couldn't really afford to buy books.

He'd finished perusing one aisle and walked around the end of the rack, turning to go up the next, when he almost bumped into her. He jumped back in shock, not having realized anyone else was around.

Mark must have looked pretty goofy because the girl burst into laughter, her wonderful broad smile filling her face.

He started to laugh, too, and stuttered an apology.

"No worries. I get lost in books, too," she said.

She may have been the single most beautiful girl he'd ever seen. Her black face was full of laughter and had a constant smile for him. Her hair was an intricate pattern of braids and beads, and he knew in an instant that she was miles out of his league.

But, it didn't end up that way. Three months later they were living together in his small apartment in Aynsville.

Now, two years after that, she was dead.

193 Central Avenue was a small building just on the edge of town. He'd driven there almost with no thought, and with no serious hope that the ads he'd

been hearing could be true.

What did he have to lose, though?

Nothing. He'd already lost everything.

Second Chance. He studied the sign over the door and entered, carrying Kim inside her box. He wasn't sure if he was taking the box because he wanted her to hear what was happening or he didn't want to take the risk of leaving her in the car, alone.

The receptionist asked him to wait, and he did, sitting with Kim's box on his lap. After about ten minutes, the receptionist escorted him into a back room and closed the door. The room reminded him of a doctor's office. There was no examining table, but there were a few devices that looked like they could be used to probe inside you. Mark wasn't really sure, but in his imagination, aliens could use them for probing their kidnapped victims.

"You're Mark Stephenson?"

The man came in wearing a white cloak, also like a doctor might.

"Hi," he said. "Yes, that's me."

"I'm Peter Smythe."

They shook hands.

"Are you a doctor?"

"Umm... no. I'm more of a lawyer by training, actually."

"Oh."

Smythe walked around a desk and pointed at a chair for Mark.

"You want to go back in time to fix something?"

"Yes."

He held the box up. "This is..."

Now the tears started to roll out from his eyes. His throat was constricted and all he could do was sob. He shook his head in frustration and almost decided to walk out. It was a stupid idea anyhow.

Smythe moved a box of tissues toward him and said, "Take your time."

Mark wiped his eyes and blew his nose, then took some deep breaths until he felt he could talk again.

"This is my girlfriend. She died last week. Killed in a traffic accident."

Smythe just nodded.

"I couldn't really afford to bury her, so she was cremated. I think that's better anyway, because she can be with me all the time."

"You want to change what happened?"

Mark looked at he man as if he had three heads. "Of *course* I want to change it! I love her!"

"It's a common reason for people to come here."

"It can't possibly work, though."

"Oh, but it can." He shrugged. "Most of the time. There's cases where the procedure doesn't work, but our success rate is ninety-seven point nine percent. The technology gets better every year. When we opened five years ago, we were only about eighty-nine percent, so things are much better."

"You can send me back in time? Really?" Mark's voice made it clear he didn't believe it.

"Well, yes and no. Do you know what quantum entanglement is?"

Mark had no clue what that meant so he just shook his head.

"Well, it doesn't matter. Let's take an example. You

wake up one Saturday morning and you wonder if you should get out of bed. You can either get up and go make a coffee or you can roll over and go back to sleep. Okay?"

"I'd go back to sleep."

Smythe laughed. "Well, in quantum theory, you actually make both choices. The universe splits into two. In one of them, you go back to sleep. In the other you get up and make your coffee."

Mark shifted the box on his lap and subconsciously rubbed the top. He didn't really know what to say.

"The universe is constantly splitting into duplicates, due to the choices we make all the time. There are an infinite number of universes with *you* in them. In some of them, you've gone off and done wildly different things in your life. In some you've died. In some you're married and in others you're divorced. In some, maybe it was you that ended up being killed in that car accident." Smythe glanced down at the box in Mark's lap.

"All of the universes where you are exactly in the same situation that you are now are connected through something called quantum entanglement. And we can send you to one of those other universes."

"That all sounds like magic."

"Oh, it's not magic. It's pure science. Quantum mechanics has been the most important branch of physics for the past century. This is just one offshoot of it."

"How does going to another—what—universe? How does that help me? Wouldn't I be in the same situation?

"If that's all there was, then yes, but we can insert you into that alternative timeline at any point we want. Just part of the technology. We can insert you a week ago, so you can stop your girlfriend from being killed."

Mark looked down at the box again.

He didn't believe it. But he really wanted to.

"Why haven't I heard more about this?"

"Our clients end up in an alternative timeline, so they're not around to say how fabulous the experience is."

He pulled out copies of *Scientific American*, *Discover*, and a few other magazines and spread them out. The cover stories of all of them were about Second Chance.

"It's real?"

He felt like he was pleading, but he wanted so much to have Kim back.

"Yes, it's real."

He stared at Smythe, afraid to ask the next question. He knew he ran the risk of being disappointed.

"What does it cost?"

Smythe took off his glasses and nodded. "It's a tough decision for all our clients, Mark. Our price is simple. It is everything you have. Absolutely everything. That's why I'm a lawyer talking to you and not a doctor or scientist or businessman. I have to be sure you completely understand. We'll take everything you own. If you own a house, we get that. Your car. Bank accounts. All your furniture and any other possessions. Even your clothes. Everything."

He glanced down at Kim's box. "Even her."

Mark couldn't believe it. He resisted even the

possibility of giving Kim up, grasping her box closer to himself.

"Why would you possibly want her? No!"

"Think about it, Mark. You'll be going to somewhere else. You can't take all your stuff with you. Your girlfriend will be alive there. You will have all the same possessions over there that you have here.

"You'll disappear from this timeline, and everything you have would normally be divided among your heirs. For all intents and purposes you will be dead here, but still alive in the timeline with her. You won't notice any difference at all, except she'll still be alive. What can it possibly matter to you that we have all your stuff here? We'll sell it all and that will be our fee."

Mark took a week before returning to Second Chance and signing the contract and all the necessary documents. The lawyer just smiled, having known he'd be back.

For the procedure, Mark was sedated. He was allowed to keep twenty dollars in his wallet, his credit cards (because he would need them in the new timeline), his ring of keys, and the clothes he wore to the clinic. He surrendered the box holding Kim but it was a very hard thing for him to do. All of a sudden he understood what a person who had an arm amputated called a phantom limb, feeling the loss of something that isn't really there any more.

He didn't ask any more questions about the process, and specifically he did not ask what happened if he was one of the two point one percent of people for whom things didn't work out. He hoped he'd be dead but he didn't really care. Whatever happened, it was worth it if he could have a chance, any chance at all, of saving Kim's life.

When Mark arrived in the new timeline, he woke as if from a long sleep. His head was cloudy and he was lying on the ground. He pulled himself up to a sitting position and recognized Central Park in downtown Aynsville. He licked his lips and stood. He felt dizzy for a moment but that passed soon enough.

Did it work?

He walked a block to where he knew his car was parked and passed a newspaper box. He knelt down to read the date: August 5.

Oh my god...

He stared at the paper, trying to convince himself everything was really true.

"Hey, there you are!"

His legs felt weak as Kim came running over to him and hugged him. He hugged her back and kissed her cheek and held onto her head, staring into her eyes.

"I love you," he said. "I love you. I love you!"

"And I love you." She added, "Is everything okay?"

"Everything is perfect."

He hugged her closely again.

She laughed. "Let's go. We have to get to the market before it closes.

Her words sounded ominous and he clenched her hand as she started to walk out to the street. He pulled her back just as the drunk driver roared by in his stolen pickup truck.

For a moment, neither of them said anything. Kim

looked up at Mark and then out to the road. Her eyes were huge, and all he could think of was how beautiful she looked.

"I could have been killed," she said. "You saved me."

They hugged one more time and Mark felt a huge relief wash over him. He silently thanked Second Chance, grateful beyond words.

That night they made love. It was intense and fierce and hot and wonderful, and when they were done, they lay together in the bed, touching each other and whispering "I love you" to each other as they fell asleep. It was one of the best nights of Mark's life.

The last thought as he drifted off was a promise to ensure that every day with Kim was always better than the one before.

They woke the next morning to the sounds of birds chirping outside the bedroom window. It was a Sunday morning and Mark had decided they should go for a picnic later that day.

He smiled when he looked at Kim, and she smiled back. He stared at her face, loving the sight of her, but a tiny shiver ran down his spine. He didn't know why.

She gently punched his shoulder. "Cheerios again?"

He nodded. It was their normal Sunday breakfast.

They made their way to the kitchen. She filled the bowls with the cereal while he got the milk from the refrigerator. He watched her out of the corner of his eyes, and he noticed she seemed to be moving a little slower than normal.

Or was she? Was he just imagining it?

They ate in silence, enjoying each other's company and the occasional bird chirps. Sunshine cascaded into the kitchen and Mark couldn't help but reach over and touch Kim's hand halfway through their breakfast.

"I cherish you," he said. "I always will."

She nodded while munching on her Cheerios. When she finished her mouthful, she said, "I will always cherish you, too."

But it didn't sound right. It sounded like her voice was just a tiny bit different from how it should be.

He hoped his smile didn't look fake.

Kim had a shower while he rinsed off the breakfast dishes and he followed and had his own shower when she was done.

Almost invisible little flecks of dark skin were on the bathtub when he got in. Bits of Kim down the drain. He wanted to look closer but he just started the shower instead.

What the hell is going on? he asked himself. *There's absolutely nothing unusual about her today.*

He tried to think of something else. Anything else. The weather, the local baseball team (of which he knew almost nothing), the new action movie he'd heard of, the impending end of summer, but every time he tried to deliberately distract himself with all these things that he didn't really give a crap about, his mind would wander back to the growing feeling that something just wasn't right.

He knew what it was.

Kim should be dead.

And part of his mind insisted that she was. He knew

differently, because he'd just finished touching her warm skin, had made wonderful love with her last night, and was the recipient of her amazing, disarming smile, and he knew that nobody got to see that smile the same way he did.

It didn't matter, because the rotten core of his brain continued to insist: she should be dead.

Monday morning arrived and there were no birds chirping. The clock radio woke them at six o'clock and Mark felt like he hadn't had any sleep in a thousand years. His eyelids didn't want to stay open and his body kept screaming at him to just fucking stay in bed.

Kim hopped out of bed immediately, like she always did, and headed to the bathroom to go pee.

"Nothing is different," he whispered.

He ordered his body to co-operate and help him get out of bed.

By Thursday, he was watching her every second he was with her.

He wondered if the way she blinked her eyes was the same as always.

He knew that she didn't lick her lips as often before. She did it a lot now. She was different.

And maybe her scent was different. He wasn't as sure about that and wanted to kick himself for not paying as much attention to that before.

Kim finished her shower—surely faster than normal —and he followed her. As she dried herself off, she looked at herself in the mirror. Mark couldn't recall her ever doing that before.

The next day, she fell asleep while they were watching *Big Brother*. They'd recorded the show on the DVR and were waiting to see which houseguest would be evicted, when he heard the tiny snores beside him. They'd been holding hands but Kim's head had lolled to the side.

It wasn't that she'd never fallen asleep when they'd been watching TV before, but it sure wasn't common.

He took the opportunity to look at her... well, examine her, as he knew that's actually what he was doing. He studied the tiny lines that branched out from her eyes and her beautiful black skin and the tiny cracks on her lips.

She was still (and always would be) the most beautiful girl he'd ever seen, and he knew there was no way somebody like that should ever be with an average Joe like himself... but there she was.

He touched her hair, and it felt—

(poisoned)

—different somehow. It wasn't as soft as he remembered. He wanted to pull a clump to see if it would just fall out, like it should if she was a corpse.

He took his hand from her hair and stopped holding hands with her.

You're not my Kim.

He wanted her to be Kim, but she wasn't. He was living with a stranger that was like an identical twin in every possible way. She had the same DNA, the same fingerprints, the same memories, but it wasn't *his* Kim. He didn't know who the hell this girl was.

He waited until the following Wednesday, to see if his feelings would change, but they didn't. If anything, the sense of loneliness increased, the feeling that she was a zombie or some other kind of animated corpse grew more and more pronounced, to the point where he could barely stand the sight of her.

Last night, she'd moved to him in bed and reached over to rub his belly. He didn't react, just lay still, not wanting her. She soon reached down to feel his flaccid cock, and he still didn't do or say anything. There was no way he could do that with her. Fucking a cold, dead person who was rotting away. It was a disgusting idea. Eventually she took her hand away and rolled onto her side, away from him.

When he arrived at Second Chance, the same lawyer was there, but of course he didn't recognize Mark. They'd met in Mark's original timeline, not here.

"You're Mark Stephenson?"

"Yes. And you don't need to tell me anything. I'm a returning customer. I'll sign."

Peter Smythe smiled.

"I'll have the documents prepared."

"I'll wait."

Two hours later, he signed over all of his worldly possessions.

He awoke in Central Park, very groggy, and it took a moment for his mind to clear. He walked a block to his car and checked the date at the newspaper box: August 5th. Again.

"Hey, there you are!"

Kim ran over to him and hugged him. He resisted the temptation to push her away. He wanted her, but he knew this Kim would change and eventually be no more like *his* Kim than the other one had been. Right now, though, she was the woman he loved.

"Is everything okay?"

"Yes," he answered. "Everything is going to be perfect."

She laughed. "Let's go. We have to get to the market before it closes.

Her words bounced off the walls of his head over and over, and before he knew it, she'd stepped out onto the street just as the pickup truck came screaming by.

The box sat on the sacred spot he'd planned for it: the bedside table Kim had always used for her reading material.

Every night he sat on the edge of the bed and talked to her, telling her about his day, no matter how boring and uneventful it was. He loved her and he needed to always be sure she knew what he was doing.

"I love you," he said each night as he caressed the box and leaned over to kiss it good-night.

And every morning, his first thought was to say good-morning to her. He never missed a day. ✕

The Goldilocks
Zone

At first glance, this isn't a story that twists time in knots, but it is a time travel story from a different perspective.

This one was also commissioned by Michael Bailey, for his great anthology, You, Human. Michael wanted stories that showed what it was meant to be human.

Well, that just called to me. I do my best to make emotions a bit part of every story I write, and what better focus could there be about an ultimate "human" story that emotions?

*B*ARB:

I love being in the water, especially when I'm exploring with Punky and the gang. They know the San Diego shoreline better than any human I know, and even though they're dolphins, they treat me better than most people do.

They're so beautiful as they glide through the water and show me their secrets. I'm the only person they've shown their secret stash, where they've dropped little trinkets they've found while exploring the ocean: bones, pieces of lost jewelry, and a nice collection of shells.

Now, though, I've been with them an hour and it's time to climb back in the little motor boat and head back to shore. I dropped off my scuba tanks and got changed before going back to my office at MBRD.

I'm the luckiest girl in the world. This morning I woke up before Darrell and counted some of the things that make my life so worth living:

> 1. Well, the most important thing is Darrell himself. We've been engaged

for ten months, and although we haven't set a wedding date yet, I feel the day is getting closer.

2. My job at the Marine Biology Research Division at Scripps. How many people get to swim with dolphins and study their habits for a living?

3. I'm totally healthy and expect to live a long and happy life with my best friend.

So, yeah, who could ask for more?

Back at my desk, I skimmed through my e-mail, which was mostly administrative minutia that nobody really cared about, along with a few Internet jokes and memes that were spreading around the campus. I didn't bother looking at most of them. I wanted to get to my research.

My work is all about dolphin communication. I feel in my soul that they can talk to each other just as easily as humans can, but we just can't break their code and talk directly to them.

One day.

A new e-mail popped into my inbox, and I smiled when I saw it was from Darrell.

Hey! I have something exciting to share with you. Tonight, we deserve a nice dinner out. Candles, wine, soft music, the whole thing. I'll make reservations for 8:00.

Love ya, babe!

Something exciting?

I stared at the screen and tried to imagine what it could be. I knew what I *wanted* it to be. I *wanted* it to be Darrell suggesting a wedding date, but that's not really the way his e-mail read. It sounded more like something he'd just found out today. News from work?

Of course he only worked a few buildings away from me, in a more isolated section of MBRD, and he could have just walked over and had lunch with me. I liked that he was excited and wanted to have a romantic dinner to spill the beans.

A promotion? Maybe, but he's already the chief researcher for micro-biology, so I don't think there's many positions he could be promoted *to*.

Tonight can't come soon enough!
Sigh... I love my life.

I'm not sure San Diego is the restaurant capital of the world, but I like eating out no matter what. Darrell made us reservations for The Seafood Factory, which he knows just might be my favorite. Their menu is three pages, all different types of seafood, and even though I always study the list as if I'm going to be tested on it, I usually gravitate back to have a linguini with white wine sauce topped with fresh mussels, clams, and whatever fish is the catch of the day. Today it's catfish.

The only music was some soft harmony in the background that we would have to really pay attention to in order to hear, but that's okay. I didn't care about that.

Darrell was dressed in jeans and a T-shirt that had

a bunch of splotches in different colors splattered on it. There's a circle surrounding them, and almost nobody would recognize it was the image of bacteria growing in a petri dish.

Although we didn't deliberately match clothing, I'm wearing jeans and a blouse with a faint image of dolphins leaping out of the water.

We both wore our jobs.

Darrell deferred to me when the waitress asked about wine. I ordered red for a change, a nice five-year old French Merlot.

When we'd arrived at the restaurant, I could see he was excited. His eyes were bright, and he was bursting with... well, something. I knew he wanted to do this right, though, and I didn't press him for anything until we had our wine glasses ready to toast.

"To you and your big surprise," I said.

He grinned and we clinked glasses. The wine was very smooth, and I wondered why I don't drink red more often.

Darrell licked his lips, and seemed to be taking a long time, so I finally said, "Well, are you going to tell me?"

I reached out and touched his hand.

He nodded and put his glass on the table, then leaned closer to me.

"I've been asked to join the Starcraft team."

That's the last thing I was expecting. At first I wasn't sure I heard him right.

"Why? There won't be any results coming back to Earth for... actually I'm not sure how long. But not any time soon, right?"

"It's not to analyze results." He took another sip of his wine and then added, "They want me to go."

"Go?"

It was like he was speaking dolphin-ese or something. It didn't make any sense.

"To a planet called Gliese 163c. It's been known for decades now and was recently bumped up to be number four on the list of planets that could support life."

I didn't know what to say about this. I'm sure my mouth was hanging open in disbelief or shock or astonishment or some other stupid thing. I certainly felt all of those things. Darrell sensed me feeling lost and added more details.

"They told me the news first thing this morning. It's amazing, Barb! This planet is in the Goldilocks Zone, so it's not too hot and not too cold. If it were any closer to its sun, the water would evaporate. If it were any farther out, it would freeze. Instead, it's just right. The surface is covered with a massive ocean, and they told me a shit-load of other technical stuff, but the bottom line is that they think there's likely some kind of life there. Possibly microbiological, and that's why they want me to go."

He paused and I could tell the worst was yet to come.

"It's fifty light years away."

And there it was.

I don't know much about spaceships that go to those faraway stars. The Starcraft ships only started leaving Earth a few years ago. Have there been five of them now? Six? I don't know.

What I *do* know is that if it's fifty light years away, Darrell will be gone for the next century.

And I'll be here, alone.

What was I supposed to say to that? I couldn't help the tears that started to fall from my eyes.

Darrell came around and knelt next to me.

"Oh, babe, I'm so sorry."

He held me to him, but I had trouble holding him in return. My mind is on fire. How is this even possible in my perfect life?

"Can I go with you?" I somehow blurt out.

I cried on his shoulder, and I have no clue if the other people eating their dinners noticed or cared about what was happening.

"No," he said. "I asked, but the extra weight of adding partners for all the crew members... it's too much."

Finally, after what seemed like forever, I hugged Darrell back. I squeezed him and pulled him to me, as if I could stop him from leaving with the force of my puny arms.

I grabbed his face and kissed him. I didn't know when he would be actually leaving, but I felt like this might be the last perfect kiss.

Later, we were back in our seats and I finished off my wine, then poured more.

"You won't age," I said.

He didn't want to talk about that part of things. That got me angry.

"You're thirty-two now, same as me. What happens?"

He spoke softly.

"If I understand it right, it takes the ion thrusters about two years to get the ship close to the speed of light, then the trip there takes fifty years, then two years to slow down at the other end. The mission will stay there for one year."

I waited. He knew the math already. The longer he avoided telling me, the madder I got.

He finally blurted it out.

"On Earth, a hundred and nine years will pass. Our spaceship will be spending most of that time at relativistic velocities, so only nine years will pass for me."

I only knew as much as the next lay person on how this stuff works. It felt wrong to me that by going so fast, they age slower. I know it won't feel to them like time is slowing down, but those are the rules. Einstein set everything in motion for this more than a century ago. How it works? Who knows.

"I'll be dead when you get back," I whispered. "And you'll be forty-one."

He didn't reply. He didn't have to.

DARRELL (OUTBOUND):

It's been a month now, and the ship is accelerating at 0.03c now. That's one-thirtieth the speed of light for those of us (like me) who don't know crap about this. There's a monitor in the main recreation section of the ship that tells me that number and also tells me our relativistic factor is now 1.00045. For every second we fly, a tiny bit more than a second passes on Earth.

By the time we reach our cruising speed in twenty-three months, our speed will be .9996c and our relativistic factor will be 35.35887. We will travel to the Gliese 163 system in what feels like no time at all, but everyone on Earth will be aging like crazy.

Including Barb.

I felt so heart-broken when the ship took off. Even though it's been a few months since I broke the news to her, it was so hard to leave.

But how could I turn the opportunity down? It's the chance of a lifetime.

I worried that it would be boring, but so far so good. The acceleration makes the ship feel as if it has near-Earth gravity, there's lots of room to wander around, and there's a dozen other people going along for the flight, so I'm not lonely.

Well, except for bedtime, when I pull the covers over me and think of Barb.

Best not to dwell on that.

Everyone on board is a scientist of one sort or another, half men and half women. I wonder if that was deliberate, and I've been meaning to check the other Starcraft teams to see if it's the same.

It would make sense. None of our partners will be there to greet us with open arms when we return.

When we left, they told us not to bring photographs of our loved ones, letters, or memories of any kind. Psychologically, it makes it worse. We need to try to forget them.

So, I have no photos of Barb. I regret that now. I want to see her.

Sometimes I think I'm making the biggest mistake of my life.

DARRELL (INBOUND):

Earth fills the wall of the projection room. It's hard to believe we're almost back home. Harder still to believe more than a century has passed there since we blasted off.

It's like time travel. To me, it's as if it's only been a few years. The time dilation didn't feel like anything. Instead, it feels like somehow the Earth has sped up its rotation and everyone there aged prematurely, dropping off one by one...

I looked at the view of our home planet with Elli. The ship didn't have the image projected while we were far away, but it's back now, so we're trying to find what's different from when we left.

My hand slid over to hers and grasped it. I loved holding her hand. Somehow it showed the strength of our relationship. Over the past few years, we've grown so close, and it makes me once again thank whatever gods decided I should be on this mission.

"Do you see anything?"

We were both staring at North America, because we know that the best.

"Is California different?" I asked.

I could feel her shrug. "Don't know," she whispered. "Maybe."

We could have asked the Machine, of course, but where's the fun in that?

Elli thought Florida looked a little thinner, but it looked the same to me.

"Who cares?" I asked suddenly. "We're almost

home!"

At that, Elli jumped up into my arms and wrapped her legs around me. She kissed me long and hard, and I loved every second of it.

"Still six months till we arrive," she said when we broke the kiss. "But it feels like home already."

Those six months went crazy fast. There wasn't a lot to do work-wise, because we'd all filed our reports from Gliese 163c long ago. The long and short of it: we couldn't identify any form of life at all. It was a completely wasted trip.

Well, that's not exactly fair, is it? It's the nature of science to propose a theory and then run experiments that either support the theory or disprove it. Science wins either way.

The working theory of life on Gliese 163c was disproved, but that's still valuable information. It just doesn't quite feel like it.

Elli is a physicist, specializing in testing gravity fluctuations. No matter how often she's explained that in detail to me, I'm still not sure I get it.

That's okay. I get *her*.

After a few more months, the ship had braked enough to remove all relativistic effects and we could see Earth with the naked eye.

Then it seemed like the blink of an eye and we were home.

We got taught some basic history lessons during the last month. There were still 51 states, the two political parties still traded the White House, and although there were lots of small changes, there was nothing enormous. We could have slipped to ground without the lessons and not have been out of place.

I felt a little disappointed with the lack of change, but neither could I decide what differences I would have really liked to see.

After leaving the ship, we were quarantined, the same as the eleven other Starcraft ships that made it home before us.

None of them found life anywhere.

I was placed in a kind of quarantine, which seemed ridiculous. How could I be contagious if there wasn't as much as a virus on Gliese 163c?

It was after a week in quarantine that the message arrived that changed everything.

People no longer used e-mail, not exactly, but some kind of thought-transmission process accomplished pretty much exactly the same thing. The difference was that I sensed the message in my mind, clear as a bell, rather than on a computer monitor.

> Dearest Darrell,
>
> If you're sensing this, you're about to make me the happiest woman alive. Yes, alive!
>
> When you left, I was so unhappy. I missed you terribly and thought my life no longer worth living. I somehow trudged along toward the rest of my unsatisfactory life. I continued my work on dolphins, of course, but it was like the spark of life had left me.
>
> Then, everything changed.
>
> Has anyone told you about stasis yet? It's a technology that allows people to be, well, I suppose paralyzed is the best word. I'd say "frozen" but there's nothing cold involved.

Our bodies are just stopped.

Of course I jumped at the chance to volunteer and I was one of the first test subjects. I had myself stopped until three months ago.

And, other than some minor side effects, I'm here, waiting for you, wanting you so much... and I hope you still want me too.

I know you expected I'd be dead. Far from it. I'm here, I'm still young like you, and I want us to spend the rest of our time together.

Miracles do happen.

Please contact me when you are ready.

With all my love, Barb.

Barb?

Barb?

My mind went numb, I think. I sat and stared into infinity, not knowing what to think.

"You were supposed to be dead," I said.

I'd steeled myself to know without a doubt she'd be gone. That's what the psychologists told me to do, because there was no chance she'd be alive. People didn't live to be a hundred and forty years old.

But, she cheated death.

I stumbled to the bathroom and threw up into the toilet. The acidic taste in my mouth somehow felt deserved.

I cleaned myself up and then went back to the bedroom portion of my quarters to lie down. I closed my eyes and pulled at the threads of memory I had for Barb. It was such a long time ago.

I remembered how we met, at the Scripps Research

Institute. She was just joining the staff and going through orientation. Her eyes were wide and taking it all in. I was passing her group, and I think I fell in love with her the minute I saw her. She had that amazing smile she always wore for me, beautiful blonde hair, and her eyes... that's what always got me. They could see into my soul.

Our first date was one of the singular most perfect days of my life. We danced and laughed and ate... and then we made love.

From then, every day was a new adventure, and my mind seemed to want to show every one of them to me all together, so that the memories were all mashed together into a giant chaos of love.

I'd destroyed all that.

Elli was my life now.

But how could I abandon Barb after she'd risked her life in stasis just to be with me?

I knew I had to see her, no matter where it led me.

BARB:

He's actually coming to see me.

Everything is going to work out after all. I was so happy to get the virtual invitation to get together, I almost just glossed over the fact that it was all done telepathically. At least that's what it feels like to me. I know the geeks have some weird scientific way it works, quantum neuro-whatever, but it feels to me like Darrell just reached out with his mind and mentally slipped an invitation into my mind.

Who cares *how* it happens, as long as it *did* happen.

And there he was, walking up the sidewalk to my apartment.

My heart was racing, and I knew I was breathing hard. God, I missed him so much...

When the door opened and he stood there, I could see the shock in his face.

"Hi."

My voice was almost non-existent. It was only a wisp of a whisper.

"It's really you," he said.

Then we ran the few steps that separated us and melted into each other's arms. It felt like the past ten years (or the past century) hadn't interrupted our love.

I wanted to kiss him, but he just held my cheeks and stared into my eyes.

"I can't believe it," he said. "They told me you'd be..."

"I know. The stasis engineers told me you'd have trouble believing I'm here. Nowadays, it's nothing special. People stop their clocks whenever they want, but for me it was, well, it was brand new."

He just continued to look into my eyes.

"I love you," I said.

He looked like he was going to cry. I didn't understand because we were finally back together. I wanted to kiss Darrell, but the expression on his face held me back.

"What's wrong?"

"I'm just confused."

"It's me, Darrell."

"I know. I just... I found somebody else."

"Oh."

"I don't know what to do."

Darrell looked exactly the same as the last time I saw him. He had thick dark hair, strong features that were almost craggy, and a deep voice that just carried me away. Those weren't the words I expected to hear, though.

I stepped back and wondered why it hadn't occurred to me. I'd been so concerned about *our* relationship, *our* love, *our* future, that I never considered Darrell might not imagine himself in that picture.

Somebody else.

"Who is she?"

He shrugged. "I'm not sure it matters." Then he added, "Tell me what you've been doing."

So I led him to the couch, and we sat down, side by side. I poured us each a glass of wine. Merlot, like we shared the day he told me he was going to leave. Somehow, I thought it would be like the other bookend, bracketing the time we were apart.

I felt like guzzling the whole bottle.

We talked. I told him about how I was back studying. My understanding of marine biology was a century out of date, but I was a fast learner and I hoped to be useful again one day.

One day, one day, one day.

"You mentioned there were minor side effects to the stasis. What were they?"

I avoided the question. "Nothing much. We can talk about that sometime. Not now. What about you?" I asked. "What are you planning on doing?"

He took a minute and then said bluntly, "I have no

clue. I'd always expected to be busy working on follow-up from my trip. Categorizing the new life forms, researching their DNA... but there's nothing to do now."

We both sipped our wine.

"I still want our life together," I said. "I understand about the other girl, of course. It makes total sense you'd find somebody. But, I want you back."

He took a deep breath and nodded. Then he locked eyes with me, and then he leaned over and kissed me. It was one of the most memorable kisses of my life, soft and sweet and then turning to passion and love.

Darrell spent the night with me, and I hugged him in bed as I slept. I refused to ever lose him again.

DARRELL:

How could I have *not* chosen to be with Barb? No matter that I love Elli today and Barb is more a series of wonderful memories, the fact is that she sacrificed everything for me. Being a guinea pig for stasis must have been a stunning risk for her.

Am I supposed to just turn my back on her after that?

No. I didn't really have a choice. I needed to be with her, regardless of how I felt about Elli.

I went back to my "home" the morning after finding Barb, and I spent hours just staring at the walls. At some point I'd have to find a place to live outside of the facilities connected to the quarantine area. Barb and I would have a home together.

I'm still not sure how I feel about that.

I neuro-synched with Elli and told her Barb was still alive and that I would be going back with her.

There was a lot of crying on both sides of the conversation. I knew I could flip on the textile switch and touch a synthetic version of Elli's face, but the holograph was about all I could manage to do without falling to pieces. I felt like a coward, but Elli was as understanding as possible. That helped. A little.

When we ended the chat, I felt more lonely than when I'd first set foot on the starship. This time, it felt more personal, more real somehow.

I felt like crap, but I was determined to make this work. Barb had given too much to me, and I had to find a way for us both to be happy.

Over the next few weeks, Barb and I spent a lot of time together, me trying to re-find the love that had been lost a hundred years ago.

And it worked. I started to fall in love with her again as if it was the first time we'd met. She still had her playfulness, her laugh, and those amazing eyes.

I tried to ignore the nagging guilt and aching desire for Elli.

It wasn't long, though, that I noticed something unexplained. There were crow's feet pulling out from Barb's eyes. I'd spent a lot of time looking into those eyes. This was new, almost overnight, which was a ridiculous thing to think, but it was true. She hadn't had them earlier.

Looking more closely, I saw small liver spot on her face, and wrinkles that stretched along her neck. I could see her chin sagging, which was also definitely recent.

I don't think she noticed, but some strands of her hair were turning gray.

"Barb?"

"Yes, sweetie?"

"You never told me about the side effects of stasis."

She pulled back from me. We were sitting in her kitchen, drinking coffee.

"It's nothing."

"You're aging," I said. "Incredibly fast."

There it was, out in the open. Somehow, I must have noticed it subconsciously, but I needed those crow's feet to knock me into realizing it consciously.

She looked down at her coffee.

"Tell me what's going on." I knew I'd raised my voice, but whatever was happening was too important. I should have just researched the early history of stasis myself, but I hadn't thought to do that.

She shook her head. "I just can't..."

"Tell me!"

I found myself grabbing her wrist.

"You're hurting me!"

I let go. I stared at her and said slowly, "Tell me what is going on. I can see it on your face, so you've got to stop lying to me!"

She started to sob, and a tear fell down her face. She wiped it with a napkin.

"I just wanted to have as much time as I could with you," she said. "The early trials didn't perfect the process. That's what guinea pigs are for, I guess. Most of the early stasis attempts stopped people for only a short time. I was the first one to go long-term. Not long after I was stopped, they found a problem."

"You'd be aging when you were re-started."

"Yes. I'd only have a short period while my body adjusted, and I wanted to have that time with you."

"But now?"

"Now, my body is going to catch up very quickly to the age I should have been."

"How fast?"

"I'll be ancient within a month. My chronological age will have caught up with me by then. I was hoping to have longer, but it's starting already. There's no way to stop it."

I leaned back and stared at her, not knowing if I wanted to hug her or yell at her.

Then I remembered Elli.

"You made me give up the woman I loved just so you could have one last fling?"

"That's cruel. I love you."

"You knew this was going to happen."

Another tear fell as she nodded.

"I can't believe you deceived me that way."

"I need you. I love you."

I stood up and stared at the woman who once meant the world to me. Now, all I felt was disgust.

"I never want to see you again," I said. "I can't believe anybody would be that selfish."

And then I left.

Elli didn't answer my attempts to connect with her for a week. I couldn't blame her. Although she finally agreed to have coffee with me, her face was stone. She hated me, and I totally understood.

When I left her, she never talked to me again.

BARB:

Every part of my body hurts. My face looks like it's been through a shredder, with wrinkles crawling all over it. Much of my hair has fallen out, and the parts that remain are brittle and white. I'm just so tired all the time. I can barely walk.

Even the pain-killing wands can't take all the problems away from me for more than a short while. I waved it over myself one last time, though, and caught a taxi to the shore.

I still love the ocean. It was my first love, and Darrell was my second. I might not have him, but I still have the water.

I walked out, not bothering to change into a swim suit. Who wants to see an old hag in a bathing suit, anyhow? Jeans and my old dolphin shirt suit me just fine, thank you very much.

Nobody is walking on the beach today. It's sunny, warm, and I see nobody for miles around.

That's good, too.

I don't know how long I have before the wand wears off. An hour or less, most likely.

I walk out to let the waves splash my body, and I look out to the great sea.

Punky isn't around, of course, and in fact, I'm too close to shore to have any dolphins at all join me for a swim, but that wasn't going to stop me from hoping.

The water is rough and splashes against my body as I walk out deeper. Already, the muscles in my arms are complaining, but I don't care.

I'm only forty years old and the whole rest of my life has been sacrificed to be with the only man I ever loved.

As I dove into the water, I remember the wonderful kisses we shared when he loved me just as much. The memories calmed me as I swam away from shore. I smiled. ⚹

The Exchange

For a long time, I had an idea I wanted to work into a story: what if there was a way to buy and sell time?

I had no idea what that looked like, but I sent myself an email with that thought. I often do that with unfinished ideas, so that I don't lose it. Just a single-line email saying, "What would it be like to buy and sell time?"

The email sat in my in basket for several years before I finally found an idea of how to use it.

At the time, I had a different email show up, a request from Christopher Paine, publisher of Dark Discoveries magazine. He was hoping I might consider submitting a story.

Well, the stars seemed to align, since the entire story of The Exchange came to me, and I loved it.

Fortunately, Chris Paine did as well.

"WHAT WOULD MAKE you steal ten thousand dollars?"

"What? Who is this?"

"That's not important. Tell me, what would it take?"
"Don't be ridiculous."

"What would it take, Barry? What would turn you into a criminal?"

"I'm going to hang up now."

"Don't do it, Barry. You *really* don't want to do that."

"Who the hell is this?"

"Everyone has a pain point, my friend. Everyone. Tell me what yours is. Tell me what you wouldn't want to lose. What's so important to you that you'd commit a crime to keep it safe?"

Barry Holder hesitated. He really wanted to just hang up. The call display on his phone just said Private Caller so that was no help. He didn't recognize the voice, but it had a hint of a Brooklyn accent, so it was likely somebody local. Barry lived in an apartment in Manhattan, the Dakota, famous for being the place John Lennon once lived and where he was murdered.

"Let me be clear. Nothing could make me steal any

money. There's nothing you can say that would make me do that. Our conversation is over."

He hung up the phone without waiting for a reply.

Stupid crank call, he thought.

Barry took off his glasses and dropped them on the kitchen counter and swept his sparse white hair back with his hands.

"Nobody knows who I am," he whispered. "It was just a freak call."

Although Barry hated to admit it, whoever it was had gotten to him and he was feeling a little rattled. He put his glasses back on and went back to check on the steak he was broiling in the oven. He poured himself a glass of white wine (a Sauvignon Blanc he'd picked up the weekend before) and drank half of it in one gulp.

Without thinking much about it, he walked to the apartment door and made sure it was locked. He couldn't help glancing out the peephole, but there was nobody there.

Of course, nobody's there. Get hold of yourself, Holder.

He picked up his phone and checked again, but there was no way to find out who had called. His phone was a state-of-the-art smart phone with all the gizmos any technophile would love, but it had no way to trace the call.

"Just a stupid asshole." Barry knew he was just trying to convince himself, but deep down he knew it wasn't going to be so easy. He expected the phone to ring again any moment, but it stayed silent.

He clicked on his television and switched it to a channel that played continuous soft classical music, hoping it would soothe his nerves a bit.

Before he knew it, the bottle of wine was empty and the sun had set, casting darkness throughout his apartment. He clicked the light on in his bedroom and almost considered popping the cork on another bottle, but he knew he'd regret that in the morning.

9:30 p.m.

He yawned and decided to check his e-mail one last time before bed. There were several pieces of spam that his filter hadn't funneled directly to the trash can, and other than that, there was only one other message.

> To: Barry Holder, Director of The Switch
> From:
> Re: My Phone Call
>
> Barry, the next time I call, do *not* hang up. That would be a big mistake. To help you understand how serious I am, you should check on Jake's welfare. In particular his friend, Aaron. I suggest you do that right now.

"Sarah?"

"Dad?"

"Is everything okay?"

"Umm, what do you mean? It's been quite a night, but..."

"Is my little grandson okay?"

Sarah hesitated and sighed. "Jake's okay now. It took him a long time to calm down. He—Dad, how do you know?"

"What happened?"

"His friend, Aaron. It looks like somebody strangled

him. Jake was the one who found him. God, he screamed so loud and so long. Aaron's mom ran out, but—"

"Somebody strangled an eight-year-old boy? Who in God's name would do such a thing?"

"The police don't have a clue so far. It's still early, though. It just happened a couple of hours ago."

Silence hung on the phone between them.

"Dad, I've got to go. I don't want Jake to be alone right now."

"Sure, sure, honey. I'll call you tomorrow. Or soon."

"Bye, Dad. Love you."

"Love you, too."

Barry didn't sleep well that night, expecting his phone to ring at any time, but it never did. He stared at the ceiling and tried to imagine who could be trying to blackmail him, and more importantly, what he was going to have to do to call him off.

Hopefully, it really *was* only about money.

At a little after four o'clock, he finally drifted off to a sleep filled with sleazy little nightmares.

The clock radio burst alive at 6:15 a.m. as it did every morning, seven days a week, three hundred sixty-five days a year. Barry Holder had no weekends, no vacation, no Christmas or Thanksgiving, and sick days were considered only in extreme cases. He'd been the Director of the Exchange for fourteen years and nine months, and in three more months, he'd be retired. His retirement would consist of full salary for the rest of his life, and that could be a very long time, indeed, due to the fringe benefits of his job.

He never regretted the grind, because there was always that carrot dangling out there, reminding him that he would be a very wealthy man and potentially live forever.

This morning, he was dead tired, after the lack of sleep, but he still climbed out of bed without hesitation and staggered over to check both his cell phone and his e-mail. There was nothing unusual at either.

The shower felt unusually cold, but Barry knew it was just his imagination. He dressed in one of his dark blue suits and picked out a lighter blue tie to go with it. He had a massive closet that held several dozen suits. Once a month, The Exchange sent a shopper in to replace any suits that were no longer in fashion or were wrinkled. They wanted the Director to always look his best, and of course he had no time himself to take care of such things.

His normal limousine was waiting at the front of the Dakota. Frank Chambers had been his driver for his entire tenure at The Exchange, and Barry breathed a sigh of relief when he saw Frank behind the wheel.

The Exchange's official name was *The New York Time and Life Exchange*, but nobody ever called it that. The most important commodities market on the planet was always just called by its two-word nickname.

The limo was customized with bulletproof glass and was reinforced with an extra thick body and floor, so that even explosives wouldn't cause any damage. The security Barry commanded was like the President's, but to many people his job was even more important.

He traded people's lives every day.

The next phone call came that evening, only a few minutes after he got back from work.

"What would make you steal ten thousand dollars?"

"Leave Jake alone."

"Would you steal ten thousand dollars to keep him safe?"

"Listen, you son of a bitch. I can have you thrown in jail for threatening me."

"You try any such thing and Jake is dead. I swear to god I'll kill him the same way I killed his rotten little friend. Don't push me, Barry. *Don't fuckin' push me!*"

Barry hesitated, not knowing how to react. He'd thought of calling the FBI throughout the day but had always backed down. The thought of Jake being killed was too big a risk to take.

The voice on the other end of the phone was dead serious. Of that, Barry had no doubt. He could hear it in his voice, and he'd proven his point by murdering Jake's friend the night before.

"What do you want? I know it's not about money."

"You know damned well what I want."

"I can't. There's too many controls in place."

"I don't give a rat's ass about the controls. I just want you to get me five years. Just five. You do that and your little shit of a grandson lives to see another day."

Barry squeezed his eyes shut, wishing for some magical solution that might suddenly appear.

The voice continued, "You do anything stupid and Jake is dead. It can happen in minutes, Barry. You can't protect him, so just fuckin' concentrate on what you need to do."

"When?"

"You tell me the best time. This week, though. No screwing around."

Barry tried to think but his mind felt cloudy, as if all the neurons in his brain were just running around in circles.

"I'll have to think about it. I just can't come up with anything right now."

"I'll call again tomorrow." Barry heard the Brooklyn accent again, stronger than the night before. "Remember, Barry, don't do anything stupid. I'll know."

Barry believed him.

That night, he felt every one of his 53 years. Muscles throughout his body ached from being so tired after having so little sleep the night before. He thought of opening another bottle of wine, but somehow the thought didn't appeal to him very much.

His couch seemed to call to him, and he sat with his legs up on his glass coffee table. His own face stared back from the three-month old issue of *Time* magazine that he kept there. It was a bit of vanity that he hadn't been able to keep in check.

On the magazine cover, he smiled broadly with his arms folded in front of him. The Exchange was behind him. He remembered the security concerns of having the photo taken outside on Wall Street, but really, until that issue of the magazine was published, not many people would have been able to put a face to his name.

The caption on the cover was blood colored and

read, "The Most Trusted Man in America?"

The focus of the article was about his upcoming retirement and who might take his place. Of course, the article implied nobody could, when in his heart, Barry knew almost anybody had the skills. His career had been built on trust, but the actual work was minimal. America didn't really know much about that. They just knew he was the king of Telomeric Stasis Transfer. Most people assumed he'd invented it, which was nonsense.

He picked up the magazine and flipped to his favorite page, which had an old photo of him and his wife, Kathy, on their wedding day. They were young and full of hope.

Kathy died of leukemia when Sarah was just two years old. After a year of grieving, Barry decided to devote his life to stopping such unnecessary deaths, joining a DARPA project looking at the biochemical reactions of telomeres, the tiny ends of DNA strands that looked like the little plastic things on the ends of shoelaces. As DNA replicated, the telomeres grew shorter with each copy, and that gradually weakened the person built from that DNA, allowing disease to creep in.

Private industry hoped to find ways to capitalize on telomeres, but the Defence Advanced Research Projects Agency beat them to it.

Barry had wanted to find a way to stop telomeres from shrinking, but instead, his team found out how to use nanotechnology to mine enzymes that controlled the telomeres.

They found how to move them from one host to

another, taking time from the end of one person's life and transferring it to another.

"I miss you so much, Kathy..." He rubbed his thumb on the photo, as if he were caressing her cheek. "I wish you could tell me what to do."

The phone rang. He wanted it to stop, wanted more than anything for it to be silent again. He knew it was the man who wanted him to cheat the system, but he felt paralyzed to do anything.

After three rings, Barry finally moved and grabbed the phone. Then he could see it was Sarah calling.

"Sarah? Is everything okay?"

"Oh, god, Dad. He's gone. Somebody took him." Then she broke into a long crying session. Barry's heart sank.

"Sarah! Tell me what happened!"

She cried a moment longer and then was able to compose herself. For the first time in many years, he wished he lived in Boston with her.

"Somebody took Jake. It was at the playground. We were there and I was reading a novel and Jake was playing on the swings. Oh, god, I didn't take my eyes off him for more than a minute, but then I heard him scream and a man was running and carrying him in his arms and they got to a dark car and the man got inside with Jake and they drove off. Somebody else had the car ready to go and there was no time. They stole him, Dad!"

Sarah started crying again, but softer this time.

Barry was stricken silent. Everything was more real now.

"Did you call the police?"

"Of course I called the police. They're looking but they don't have much yet. The car didn't have any license plates. I don't really know what kind it was... a big black car with tinted windows. I don't know cars, Dad. Oh, god, they have to let him go. They can't—"

She bit off the end of the sentence, but Barry heard it in his mind. "They can't strangle him like they did Aaron."

"God..."

"What am I going to do?"

"Is Pete there?"

"He's coming home now. He was in San Francisco on a business trip. He got the first plane."

Barry didn't know what to say. He couldn't say, "It's because of me. They're using Jake to blackmail me." And he couldn't tell the police. That would seal Jake's doom.

"I'm going to try to come down to see you on the weekend, sweetie."

Unexpectedly, Sarah laughed. "Yeah, right. Like you'd miss time so close to your retirement. Don't patronize me, Dad. I just need you to listen, not make commitments you can't keep."

Maybe I can, he thought.

Sarah had to get off the phone a few minutes later, as the police lieutenant had more questions for her. She'd only been able to take a quick break to call him.

There was one thing she hadn't asked: "Yesterday, when you called, you seemed to know something was wrong. How'd you know that, Dad? How'd you know something was very wrong? What are you hiding?"

She hadn't asked, and part of him wondered if she

really had forgotten, but he knew better. Sarah was a smart cookie who noticed everything. That was really why she'd called tonight—to see if he'd volunteer anything he might know. He felt like he'd let her down.

It took an hour for the kidnapper to call him.

"What would make you steal ten thousand dollars?"

He didn't answer at first. He felt a million years old. He just wanted to curl up and cry, and he was surprised that tears were actually leaking from his eyes.

"Are you there, Barry? Don't fuck around."

"I'm here," he whispered. He grabbed a tissue to wipe his eyes.

"Jake's asleep. He was crying a long time, so I drugged him. He's going to stay drugged until he's either tossed back safely to his dear old mama or I strangle him and toss his useless body in the dump. What's it going to be, Director?"

"I'll do it."

"Tomorrow."

"Yes, tomorrow. Come at 3:00. Trading is over then, and that's when I do the transfers. I only have two scheduled. I'll cancel one of the recipients."

"Five years, Barry. You understand?"

"Yes. It'll be five years. But I need Jake free."

"Not until after we're done. He's been blindfolded the whole time, so he can go free. You just have to do your part."

Barry Holder nodded, not sure he could speak. The most trusted man in America was about to commit first-degree murder.

The clock radio woke him at his normal time, 6:15 a.m. No surprise there, no magical awakening to find that the whole mess was just a fanciful nightmare. It was all just as real as the night before.

Barry wondered if Jake was still drugged. He wondered if he'd ever see his wonderful grandson alive again or if the next time they were together would be for the funeral. He wondered how Sarah was doing and whether she'd mentioned anything to the police about Barry calling out of the blue the night that Aaron was brutally murdered. He wondered if he could just go back to sleep and pretend the whole awful mess had never happened.

But he couldn't.

He showered and got dressed in a light brown suit with a tan shirt and a matching striped tie.

He tried to eat some toast for breakfast, but he had no appetite.

Soon, he climbed into the limousine and said good morning to Frank Chambers, who talked about the Yankees game the night before. Barry didn't follow baseball, but he always let Frank talk.

The Exchange started trading at ten a.m. Barry was in his office, where several computer monitors huddled in a semi-circle on his desk. He could see the bid and ask prices change through the day.

At the opening, the lowest ask for a year's worth of time was $3,000,000. As always, he wondered who would want to sell a year of his own life for any amount of money. Most of his sellers ended up being young, under thirty, and he supposed it was the standard belief of the young that they would never die. What's one year off a life that would be stretching far into the future?

Except it wasn't always the future. Kathy proved that. She died when she was twenty-six, and Barry would have given any amount of money for one more year with her.

The highest bid was $2,950,000. That was the most anybody was currently willing to spend to buy a year that would be added to their normal life span.

It didn't seem like that much to Barry, but then, he couldn't have afforded it. Only the obscenely rich could afford to buy time.

America didn't care. America was proud that they'd found a way to extend life, even if the vast majority of the population would never be offered the chance.

As he watched, a match was made. A new buyer agreed to pay the three million dollar fee and the buyer/seller combination was filed away in the central computer system. Later that day, Barry would contact them both to start working out the arrangements of the transfer.

The money left the buyer's bank account immediately, of course. There was never a chance that the deal could go south. As both parties understood, five percent of the fee would go to the government as their commission, while the remaining 95% would stay in escrow until the transfer was complete.

Five percent of the time would also be stored away for Government use, so the buyer was really only adding three hundred forty-seven days to his life, not a full three hundred sixty-five.

The buyer wasn't guaranteed to live that extra year, of course. Just guaranteed he wouldn't die of natural causes. He could still die in an accident or other un- natural way.

Barry continued to watch the monitor as trades were completed during the day. By the time the Exchange closed trading for the day, sixteen deals had been consummated. The final year was sold for $3,675,000.

It was three o'clock.

One of the computers (the one on the right, which was used for non-essential everyday administration purposes) listed four people in his waiting room.

Two donors, one legitimate receiver, and the blackmailer. Barry clicked an icon on the computer and saw the image from the camera mounted in the waiting room. All four were men, but it was easy to tell which was the blackmailer. He was older than the other men, late forties, and he clenched his teeth and kept looking furtively around the room. The others were more relaxed, not fearing anything. After all, they knew they were in perfect hands.

He clicked on two names and watched the receptionist send the two patients into the operations room. He deliberately wanted to get the evil deed out of the way first, so he left the legitimate couple waiting.

After a couple of minutes, Barry took a deep breath and went into the clinical room to join them. The support staff had gotten the donor and recipient stripped to the waist and the two men were lying on comfortable raised cots.

"Mr. Joseph Brown?"

The donor smiled and nodded. "That's me."

Barry turned to the other man. "You'd be John Smith?"

"I would."

The blackmailer stared up at Barry, with eyes that looked like beacons of evil. Barry could almost read his mind: *You only have one chance to save Jake, pal.*

He locked eyes with his enemy and nodded. A lump formed in his throat. His breathing felt heavy and he could feel his own heartbeat.

He told them both, "It's really a very straightforward procedure, as you know."

"Then get on with it," said Smith.

Ahh, there's that Brooklyn accent.

Barry wanted to hear him say one more time that he would let Jake go when they were finished, but he knew he couldn't say anything like that, not with Joseph Brown there to listen.

The procedure was very simple, and Barry had performed it tens of thousands of times. He'd never had a mishap, and every single customer had left satisfied, either because they'd had a year added to their life or they had just turned into a millionaire.

The most trusted man in America.

First, he would inject the donor with a solution containing billions of atomic-sized nano-machines. They had only one purpose: to search out telomeres and attach themselves to the enzymes nearby, essentially forcing the telomere to contract in size by a tiny fraction.

Second, Barry would extract as many of the tiny machines as he could and inject them into the recipient. The machines worked slower with the recipient, taking several days to go through the entire body, lengthening the telomeres with the stolen enzymes.

Once that was done, the job was complete. It looked as if Barry was just extracting a magical life force from one person and giving it to the other.

"This won't hurt," he said.

And it didn't. Both men stayed resting for a few minutes after the transfer, but they were then able to leave. They didn't experience any side effects.

After they left, Barry completed the transfer on the other two patients, and then closed up for the night. As always, Frank Chambers drove him back to the Dakota.

"Dad! Jake is home!"

"Oh, thank god! Is he hurt?"

"No, he's fine! Oh, I'm so relieved. He says he doesn't know who took him or why, but it doesn't matter. He's home now and I'm never going to let him out of my sight again."

"What a relief!"

"Dad?"

"Yes, Sarah?"

"You didn't have anything to do with this, did you?"

Barry stared at the phone, not wanting to lie to his daughter. But, then, he realized, he'd done much worse today.

"No, of course not. Why in the world would you ask that?"

Sarah didn't say anything for a moment. "Forget I said anything."

They talked a bit longer and then said their good-byes.

Barry wondered how "John Smith" was feeling tonight. He likely felt on top of the world, having had an extra five years of life surging through his body. Everyone felt that way at first, even though research had shown it was purely a placebo effect. There was nothing in the transfer itself that would cause euphoria, but they all felt it.

He popped the cork on a bottle of Merlot, feeling like celebrating. A smile crept across his face as he took the first sip and he toasted the empty room.

He opened the *Time* magazine one more time to see his beautiful wife.

"Here's to you, Kathy. You're still my inspiration."

He wished he could tell Joseph Brown the truth. The man had come to The Exchange expecting to lose a year of his life in exchange for a lot of cash.

Instead, he got the cash, and five years was added to his own life instead of any being subtracted.

John Smith, who was likely out celebrating his newfound youth, would never know his life expectancy had actually been decreased by the same five years.

After all, nobody knew when the grim reaper would come calling for them. It was the business of The Exchange to move time and life around, but in the end, nobody really knew when their time would be up.

Not even Barry Holder. He finished his glass of wine and yawned, knowing he'd be able to sleep soundly tonight. As he walked into his bedroom, he clicked the alarm on his clock radio off. For once, he planned on being late to work.

As he fell asleep, he decided he really was overdue to take a few days off and go visit Sarah and Jake.

Life's too short, he thought as his eyelids drooped.

The First
Lunar Halloween

I am a very proud and very long-time member of the Horror Writers Association (HWA).

The HWA does tons of great work for all writers of horror and dark fantasy. One of the best is that they publish terrific anthologies, giving every member a solid chance to be included. These anthologies are always readily available in most bookstores.

One of the recent anthologies was Haunted Nights, which was themed around Halloween. At first, I didn't think I had an appropriate story, but then the idea hit me about Halloween on the moon. What would that be like?

I think I wrote this one in a couple of days, with me chuckling a lot of the time. I knew it was different and fun and nobody else had ever thought of the idea (as far as I know).

The story was accepted by the editors, Ellen Datlow and Lisa Morton. I was thrilled, since Datlow is one of the finest, if not the finest, editor of short fiction in the business. I'd never had the opportunity to be published by her, and it was very meaningful to me that she loved the story.

The other editor, Lisa Morton, is a close friend of mine, which was one of the reasons I almost declined to submit. Fortunately, I know she is one of the most ethical people in my life, and she wouldn't have taken the story if she didn't love it.

Haunted Nights remains one of my favorite anthologies I've appeared in.

OCTOBER 1, 2204

The discussion topic was buried in the last part of the Tranquility City Council monthly agenda: Halloween Celebration.

It was brought forward by Susan Sauble, after she'd been inundated by requests from her students. Susan was the 149th Cohort Group Leader and had been in that position through all their school years, since they were five. Now the fifteen kids in the cohort were all twelve Earthies old (or nearly so).

The Mayor read the agenda item out loud and called on Susan to speak.

"Thank you, Mr. Mayor.

"Here in Tranquility, we've always encouraged our kids to research their heritage on Earth. Nobody remembers all the details, of course, but we all feel the ties we have to our homeland."

She paused so that everyone could use their own imagination however they wished. She herself had only ever seen Earth directly twice. It was a bright, shining white sphere hanging above the moon's surface, totally wiped of life but a constant reminder on video screens of their original homeland, before the aliens destroyed it.

"This year, one of our students found a reference to an ancient holiday tradition called Halloween. It is full of fun, laughter, delightful costumes, mock fear, and other attributes. The holiday seems quaint, while allowing our cultural roots to shine through. I'd like our cohort to be the first annual class to re-create Halloween here on the Moon."

She paused before adding the tough part. "And, I'd like it to be on the surface. The kids are ready to go out and see the face of Earth above them. Of course, I'll supervise, and we have a Surface Leader who will be with me, Jonathan Petty, to ensure all safety precautions are followed."

At first there was stunned silence in the chamber. There'd never been a situation where that many kids ventured up to the surface at one time.

The Mayor broke the silence. "You know the risks."

"Yes, of course."

"The surface is so harsh... and..."

He looked to the other Council members for help, but they all seemed to be busy staring at their desks.

Susan decided to finish his sentence, "The aliens?"

He stared at her.

"We all know the rumors," she said. "Jonathan assures me the trip will be totally safe."

In the end, though, Susan convinced them that this was a perfect opportunity. In her mind, she had the perfect field trip planned, and she wanted it to be the most memorable event the kids would ever experience during their school years.

The motion passed seven to two.

OCTOBER 31, 2204

Susan had spent much of her spare time the past couple of weeks researching information about Halloween, and she was fascinated with what she found. She and Jonathan worked together to plan the field trip.

The documents she could find were few, though. When the Earth was destroyed, so too was the vast repository of data that Tranquility relied on. Now, the Internet seemed like a vague myth. All that survived was the random pieces that happened to be downloaded when the Earth-Link was severed as well as memoirs and journals from the original Tranquility residents. These were the ones she pored over.

"Susan?"

She looked up from her monitor. Jonathan. She smiled at him.

Jonathan was forty-two Earthies old, compared to her own thirty-nine. Tall, even for a Moonie, wide infectious smile, full of confidence. She liked him.

"Ready?" he asked.

"I'm not sure, but I suppose I'm as ready as I'm going to be."

She could feel herself getting anxious, and she took some deep breaths to try to calm herself. Going up to the surface was still a big deal to her.

Jonathan took her hand and half-pulled her along.

"It's going to be fine. They're going to have a blast."

"I know."

She didn't know any such thing.

Over the past few weeks, the pair had planned the trip. Well, if she was honest, it was mostly planned by Jonathan. He was the surface expert and took Susan's ideas and made them practical.

The kids were all waiting for them at Groundport. Their parents were helping them into suits. Most of the kids were taller than Susan, and it was sometimes a challenge to find a suit that fit each person perfectly, but after a while, everyone seemed happy.

First step: decorations.

"Okay, parents, you can leave now. Kids, you need to decorate each other's suits with your markers. Remember, the costumes used to be scary. Monsters, aliens, ghosts, whatever you like."

The decorations took about an hour. Susan decorated the front of Jonathan's suit with a big mouth with two legs sticking out. She remembered seeing pictures of long-extinct giant fish when she was going to school herself, and she tried to remember what they might look like.

"I love this idea," Jonathan said to her. "I *get* this thing. Halloween. It's a chance to pretend to be somebody else for a little while. You can use the occasion to become somebody frightening or someone who aspires to greatness. It's a temporary do-over, a break from the boredom of our everyday lives."

Boredom? Susan knew Jonathan spent several hours every week up on the surface. Hard to imagine that being boring, but who could tell?

The costumes would all disappear from the suits when they came back, cleansed with the normal re-entrance routine.

She stared at the PETTY marked at the top of Jonathan's suit. It was bright green, as was everybody else's name. Once outside, there would be no other way to tell everyone apart.

"Okay, it's time," she called to the class. The suits were starting to get warm, but they couldn't activate the cooling system until their helmets were in place.

"Can I ask a question?"

Susan looked over and wasn't surprised to see it was Matt Wiley. He was always asking questions. "Of course," she answered.

"What about the Aliens?" Aren't they up on the surface?"

She hesitated and looked to Jonathan. He nodded and answered, "There's no reason to believe the Aliens are on the Moon. That's an old myth with no facts to back it up."

"Are you sure?"

"I've been topside at least fifty times, and although there's a lot we don't know, we've never seen a single sign of any Aliens here. As far as we know, they're all on Earth."

A tiny voice carried from the back of the class, a voice Susan recognized immediately as belonging to her own daughter, Selene.

"What if you're wrong?"

Susan said, "Nobody is wrong. This is totally safe, so you just need to enjoy your first Halloween!"

They finished up and started to gather around the

tube. Only five people at a time would fit, so Jonathan went first with four kids. The next two trips took four kids each, while Susan waited for the last trip with the final two teens, including Selene.

As they rose up the two hundred meters to the surface, Susan felt like she was leaving her life behind. Going upside never felt normal to her. It was leaving the safety of the underground city for the vast expanse of the surface.

Nobody liked it. People belonged underground.

When she left the tube, the Earth was almost full, and it blasted enough light to cast shadows.

She tried to ignore it. She had to watch the kids.

"Testing. Can everybody hear me? Raise your hand if you can."

Everyone raised an arm, some slower than others, but that was normal kid behavior. She knew they wanted to run and jump and explore, as she had the first time she herself visited the surface all those Earthies ago.

Soon enough.

There were surprises ahead, and she wanted them to enjoy them.

"So, remember, this is Halloween! It's intended to be scary and fun and thrilling and... well, mysterious. I know you all want to go run around and jump, but we're here to follow the Halloween Path."

Even though most of their helmets had darkened due to the bright Earth-shine, she could see the kids staring at her in wonderment.

"Look at Earth," she said. "That was where our ancestors came from. Humans lived there for thousands of years."

She didn't add, "Before they were all killed in a single day."

She stared up, too. Earth was an extraordinary mystical globe high above, a brilliant gem stretching out above them, four times wider than the sun.

Jonathan added, "It used to be blue. The aliens killed everyone and the planet ended up covered in bright white clouds. Nobody knows if it'll stay that way forever."

"When we get back," said Susan, "you need to write a report, so pay attention."

Jonathan took the lead and started half-walking half-hopping ahead. Everyone else followed, with Susan at the end. She didn't mind. It was Jonathan who'd come out the day before to set up the Path. She was just happy to see the kids on the surface, not freaking out, and being part of the day.

It was time.

Jonathan led the way to Station One, as they had planned. Everyone except him was skittish and had difficulty controlling their movements, but they were all having fun. Susan knew the suits were completely safe, so even if somebody fell onto a sharp rock, no damage would happen. If it was her, all she would feel would be embarrassment.

The Halloween Path was set up in the shape of a diamond with three stops before they would head back to Tranquility. Altogether, the trip should take an hour. Everyone had enough air for three hours.

The group hopped and skidded their way to the first stop. Jonathan had planned the route to navigate around any large rocks or craters. His foot prints were still there from when he'd set everything up. All their foot prints would be there the next time anybody took the same route. Nothing changed on the moon.

When everybody arrived at the first stop, Susan checked the time. All good.

The kids all formed a semi-circle around a flat rock that had a holo-projector set up. When they crowded around, the projector started automatically using a technology nobody understood. They could hear the narration clearly in their suits.

Susan lost interest, having seen the show a dozen times already. The visuals showed an old-fashioned home as it might have existed on Earth, with kids showing up shouting "Trick or Treat!" before a witch answered, screamed at them, and sprinkled candy into their bags. She hoped it was close to being accurate, but they'd never know for sure.

Instead, she looked back to the sky, to the amazing Earth.

Even though the sun was below the horizon, it barely mattered. Earth was the moon's bigger sun now.

Looking away from the homeland, the sky was pitch black, sprinkled with a million tiny stars. She felt an urge to reach up and scoop the stars in her hand, like she imagined humans scooping grains of sand from a beach.

A sense of nostalgia grew in her, the loss of humanity's roots, and she wondered about the most common mystery in Tranquility: Were the Aliens still on Earth, and if so, what were they doing?

The Halloween show finished with a loud clap, and the kids all jumped. So did Susan. Even though she knew it was coming, she'd been lost in thought.

"Time to go to Station Two," said Jonathan. "Susan will be leading this time, so get in line behind her."

As she led the way, Susan remembered some of the things that she'd found out about Halloween that she hadn't managed to incorporate into the three projection shows. There just wasn't time to include bobbing for apples, Halloween kisses, razorblades in candy pumpkin pie, orange and black, egging houses (whatever that was), theme parks, and a hundred other topics that she'd dug up. Who knew how many were real and how many were myths? That was part of the fun.

Besides, she needed to leave some things for the class to research on their own.

She glanced back to be sure everyone was following her.

It took another ten minutes to get to the second stop, and Susan was starting to feel a bit winded. She wasn't used to traveling this way.

When she got to the stop, the kids gathered around and started watching the second holo-cast. This one talked about traditions related to fortune tellers and diviners as well as people telling ghost stories to scare younger children.

Her favorite was how unmarried women sitting in a darkened room on Halloween night could look into a mirror to see the face of her future husband. If she saw a skull instead, she would die before marriage.

She could remember the script word for word, since

she'd written it, with Jonathan's help of course.

Suddenly she looked around and realized Jonathan was not there. She blinked and looked again, sure her mind must be deceiving her.

But, no.

The tension that had been building up inside her made Susan feel like she was going to explode. She gulped and tried to not react, so that she wouldn't scare the kids.

"Jonathan?"

No reply. Matt Wiley turned to look at her and then joined her as she hopped a bit in the direction they'd come.

"Jonathan!" Susan knew that there was panic in her voice, but she couldn't help it.

"Miss Sauble?"

Matt was beside her and had put a gloved hand on her shoulder.

"It's okay, Matt. I think he just went to get something."

"I know," Matt said. "He's the expert."

The other kids were staring at them. Susan subconsciously looked for the girl with SAUBLE in bright green letters on her helmet. After another minute of no response from Jonathan, she said, "Let's back track a bit. Maybe he's nearby."

They all started following along the messy footprints they had left. As they did so, Susan changed her frequency and asked Tranquility Central Communication if they'd heard from Jonathan. They had not.

It was a stretch to call Tranquility a city. Only two

thousand people lived there, all the people left alive in the solar system. The outpost had started as a mining camp before the invasion, pulling out a surprising amount of raw diamonds. Every woman on Earth had wanted an engagement ring with a diamond from the moon.

Now, Tranquility did no mining. Its sole purpose was survival of the remaining humans.

About two hundred meters back, they found where he'd left the path. Two grooves led off to one side. They hadn't been there earlier. Susan felt dread, knowing with a weird certainty that the parallel grooves were from Jonathan's boots as he had been dragged.

"Stay here," she said to the kids. Matt wanted to go with her, but she held out her arm to him, too. "I won't go far."

The grooves curved back behind a crater that rose high above her head. She shuffled along slowly, and her heart jumped when she saw a helmet ripped apart, lying on the ground.

On the faceplate, she could see PETTY in the now-familiar bright green color.

Blood covered the whole area, a giant splatter of darkness. It had flash frozen in the frigid temperatures.

The helmet itself had a giant jagged rip in it, like a ridiculous monster had taken a bite from it.

Aliens.

She wanted to scream, but she couldn't. She wanted to run, but it felt like her feet were nailed to the moon's surface.

"Jonathan...?"

Whatever she said, the kids would hear.

There was no sign of the rest of Jonathan's space suit, nor of his body. There was a wide path that she could see that continued to move around the crater into the wilderness beyond.

She had to get the kids to safety without panicking them.

Susan moved back to the front of the path where the kids stared silently at her.

"It's okay," she said. "Mr. Petty needed to go back because of a minor problem with his suit. We're going to go back now, too."

One of the kids asked, "Why did he just leave without telling us?"

Susan didn't know for sure who asked, but she just snapped, "Because he didn't. Let's go."

But where?

She knew the general direction to get to Station Three on the Halloween Path. They would have to go there, and then she could figure out the direction back to Tranquility.

"This way," she said.

Susan started walking and realized she needed somebody she trusted to bring up the rear. Not Selene, though. She needed her up front, close to her.

"Matt, you make sure everyone follows. Okay?"

"Sure."

Susan had never felt so alone in her life. She knew only a general way to the third stop, and she worked to get there. Every few minutes she stopped and hopped around to face the kids to be sure they were all following.

It took twenty minutes to get to the third stop.

When she got there, the holo started playing, but she just ignored it. The Halloween trip was the very last thing on her mind.

It'd been an hour since they'd left the city. Two hours of air left.

She counted the cohort members in her head... twelve, thirteen, fourteen...

Fourteen.

"Oh, no."

Matt Wiley was missing.

"Matt?" She waited a beat and then yelled, "Matt!" She knew the yelling would do no good. If he was alive, he would have answered the first call. Safety was drilled into every Moonie as soon as they could crawl.

Aliens.

No, it couldn't be. They weren't really on the moon.

Were they?

Nobody knew for sure, but the old stories that had been passed down for a half-dozen generations told of how the aliens destroyed Earth and then left an outpost on the moon, not realizing that humanity's only remaining habitat was there.

Maybe they found out today.

She looked up at the blazing Earth, shining brightly in the sky and wondered as so many others did before her, what exactly happened up there?

They would never know. She looked back at her 14 remaining kids.

"Stay here. Move closer together, so you can watch each other. I'll be right back."

She hopped back along the way they'd come,

pursing her lips from fear. If something happened to her, what would happen to the kids?

She had to get them back.

There was no sign of Matt as she tracked back for several minutes.

If he was hurt somewhere and she left him, he would likely be dead before a rescue team would find him. Time was their enemy now as much as anything else.

If she didn't leave him, who knew what would happen to the other kids?

She stopped and tried to think, but her mind didn't seem to want to work. She didn't know what to do.

"Mom?"

Selene's voice shocked her back to reality. "I'm coming back," she said.

"We're scared."

"I know. I'm almost there."

The trip back to Groundport was the longest walk of Susan's life. She kept imagining Matt calling to her, but she knew it was never real. None of the remaining kids heard anything.

She took the trailing position this time, and she kept constantly chatting which direction to go, so the kids would know she was still there.

When they got back to the Port, she once again counted the kids. Fourteen.

Oh, god, how can I tell Matt's parents that I left him out there?

She blinked away tears and forced herself to just

work on the task at hand. She waited for the shaft to open and she loaded the first five kids inside. She made sure Selene was in that first group.

Shortly, everyone was back inside in pressurized rooms. As per normal protocol, they were scanned and cleansed, and then they waited in a holding area.

Susan thought about aliens.

All the kids were chattering to each other, now that they were safely home. She knew they'd all been terrified on the surface, and she wondered if they'd ever feel comfortable going back again.

As the mandatory hour-long quarantine period ended, a door slid open and they were free to leave.

Standing in the doorway was Jonathan Petty.

She thought she was hallucinating, or maybe that aliens had somehow entered his brain and were controlling his body.

"Hi, everybody!" he called. He was grinning widely and two techies that walked into the room with him laughed along with him.

"What the hell?" Susan stared but didn't know what to say.

"It's Halloween, remember?"

The kids all stared at him, as confused as Susan.

"Remember what I said about Halloween? It's a chance to be somebody you're not. Sometimes that's a scary person, and this year I wanted to make you all feel like you were experiencing a real Halloween up on Earth. I wanted to be an alien for you, and scare you a bit."

"You mean... your helmet? The blood?"

"All fake. Prepared ahead of time. I thought the

blood was a nice touch."

It still wasn't sinking in to Susan. "It wasn't real?"

She looked at the kids, and she could see them all starting to smile and grin, mostly at her own discomfort. After all, they hadn't seen the site where Jonathan's helmet and spilled blood were.

Fake blood, she corrected herself.

"I really think this is what Halloween was like," Jonathan said. "Kids going out trick or treating and the people in their homes scaring them. Isn't that right?"

Susan couldn't help but nod. That sounded right to her, too. She just hadn't expected to live through a real Halloween.

Why had the people on Earth done this year after year?

"Halloween must have been awful," said Selene.

Jonathan smiled. "We'll never understand, but the good points much have outweighed the bad."

In spite of herself, Susan ran to Jonathan and hugged him. She'd never done that before, but she still needed to be convinced he was real.

"Where's Matt?" she asked.

"Matt?"

Susan looked through the door Jonathan had come through. "Isn't he with you? He'd want to..."

She snapped her head back.

"Tell me he was part of the trick."

Jonathan shook his head. "I don't know what you're talking about."

He looked at the kids, scanning them all, and then he said, "Oh, god, what happened?"

"He was there one minute and then he wasn't."
"He's still out there?"
Susan couldn't reply. She felt sick and frozen.

The rescue team suited up quickly. Susan and Jonathan went with them. She led them to the last place she knew for sure Matt had been with them, and then to the third leg of the Halloween Path, the first place she noticed he was missing.

They never found a trace of him. A week later, they held a remembrance service for him.

In her heart, Susan blamed herself. She should have been the one at the end of the line, not Matt.

When she was back in her cabin that evening, she cried.

She never wanted to think about Halloween again.
⅍

JOHN R LITTLE

Demon Air

This is the second Halloween story in this book, and it was published almost the same day as "The First Lunar Halloween."

This time it was Cemetery Dance who invited me into an anthology, Halloween Carnival. I was thrilled to participate alongside some of my own favorite authors. Sometimes readers think that writers take other writers for granted, but that's not the case, at least as far as the writers I know (and I know quite a few).

We all love reading, and we all love meeting the authors whose stories have enriched us. That's one of the reasons I enjoy going to horror conventions, following authors on Twitter, listening to podcasts featuring the writers I like, and of course emailing them.

Most authors love hearing from their fans, and again, I'm no different. I love answering emails, talking to fans at conventions, signing my autograph. I am grateful for anyone who enjoys my work, and I hope I never disappoint any of them.

Halle Barry's mother used to tell her all the time how she was named after the famous black actress. After all, Michelle Barry absolutely loved Monster's Ball and the X-Men movies.

But Halle knew that was a crock. After all, when you looked at it, the math didn't add up. Those movies were released a couple of years after Halle was born. No, she wasn't named after the actress.

Halle Michelle Barry was born on October 31st, and Mom was a die-hard Halloween fan. She'd decorate the house every year starting on whatever weekend immediately followed October 10th, since that was close enough. Any earlier, and she might be considered a quack, so until that point, she only planned things out in her mind.

On the first Saturday after October 10th, though, the plastic ghouls and giant pumpkins with macabre faces painted on them would be dragged to the front porch. Tombstones would pop up on the lawn and so would arms that seemed to be reaching up from their graves.

It happened every year until mom's early death, nearly five years ago.

Halle's mother loved everything about the holiday. She dressed up at the door with a new costume that she'd design each year, each more ghoulish than the year earlier.

Having a baby born on her favorite day must have been quite a thrill for her, even if Halle had her suspicions, since mom once let slip that she had been three weeks premature.

Mom never admitted it, but Halle always knew she was named for Halloween.

The only other person she'd ever heard of who was named for a holiday was Chrissy Snow from the old sit-com Three's Company. Halle was delighted to find out that Chrissy was in fact short for Christmas.

"Welcome to Diamond Air Flight 194, departing Los Angeles on route to Sydney."

Halle barely listened to the loudspeaker. Her seat was cramped and uncomfortable. The flight was only half-filled, mostly with fat, old white men, and she wondered how they were managing, stuffed into the tiny spaces.

That's what you get for a bargain fare, she thought.

The flight attendant went through the normal talk about safety. Halle watched, just wanting the plane to take off so she could have a nap.

The plane had three seats by the left window, three by the right, and three in the middle. The two aisles were narrow enough that she wondered how they would be able to push a serving cart up and down.

A glass of red wine might be good. Help her sleep on

the long trip.

Halle was on the leftmost seat of the middle section. She was afraid of heights and so didn't want to be anywhere near a window.

"Supposed to be nice in Australia this week."

She looked to her right. The boy who'd spoken was on the other side of the middle section, an empty seat between them. He was Asian but had no accent. Maybe seventeen.

Great, a talker.

She just wanted to be left alone, but neither did she want to be rude. She smiled and nodded and then turned her attention back to the flight attendant, suddenly riveted by the seat belt demonstration.

It was October 30th, late afternoon, and Halle Barry was flying to find out who she really was.

She snapped awake without even realizing she'd fallen asleep. The airplane cabin was quiet and dim. She heard the low hum of the engines carrying her across the Pacific Ocean.

Halle's mouth was dry and she looked around for a flight attendant to ask for a bottle of water.

Never did get that wine.

She checked her watch. It was just after 8:00 p.m. She'd slept for several hours. Most of the window shades were pulled down so passengers could watch the in-flight movie, but a couple still peeked out to the water below. The sun had already set.

Halle yawned and stretched.

"Good sleep?" asked the teen sitting over to her

right.

She nodded but only glanced briefly at him. She pulled a book out of her purse and opened it up, as if to read, but she really wanted to just think about how her mother had lied to her for her entire life.

And, honestly, why hadn't she noticed?

Halle's face looked nothing like the rich, curving coffee color of her mom's. Mom had a wide smile that melted anybody she looked at. Halle's face was full of sharp angles, and she was the skinniest girl she knew.

Her mother blamed the differences on Halle's father, who was nowhere to be found.

"He was a skinny bastard, too. You take after him."

She didn't like that her face was blotchy and dark, her bone structure so odd, and her gait very gangly. She sometimes felt like an alien in her own home.

But she never imagined that she'd been adopted, until two months earlier. Her mother had died years ago, but it took a DNA Ancestry test to shock Halle out of her comfort zone.

> 68% Australian Aborigine
> 21% New Zealand
> 11% Scottish

She'd expected to see 95% African with a pinch of other heritage tossed in for good measure. After all, that's what Mom was.

The last thing she expected to see was Scottish, but almost stranger was that she the lion's share of her ancestors were natives from Australia.

Certainly cleared up a lot of why she looked so different from her mother.

"Why did you lie, Mom...?"

It was the question she'd asked over and over again, but she'd never get any answers.

Instead, she decided she needed to celebrate her heritage by finding out more. That's why she was flying to Sydney right now, connecting on a flight to Uluru via Virgin Airlines to then trek to Ayer's Rock. She needed that connection with her roots.

After a week in the outback, she'd be heading to New Zealand and finally to Edinburgh, Scotland, to finish her ancestry tour.

Maybe she'd learn something about herself, maybe not. Either way, she was looking forward to a great vacation.

"Ladies and gentlemen, we've just passed the International Date Line, so welcome to October 31st. Happy Halloween, everybody!"

The flight attendant waved at the passengers as if she were a cheerleader at a college football game. Nobody else seemed to notice her except Halle.

It felt odd to be thrust into a different day at the snap of her fingers.

It reminded her again of being thrust into a new life, a new way of looking at her family, her ancestors, her everything.

There were three flight attendants, two women and one man. They all huddled near the front of the plane and were shortly joined by the pilot and co-pilot. The five of them whispered together.

What's wrong?

There were no passengers in the front row. Otherwise, they'd be infringing on their personal space. Halle was glad she was seated halfway to the back.

"What are they doing?" asked the teen to her right. She could hear an edge in his voice. "Shouldn't somebody be in the cockpit?"

Just as he said that, the pilot and co-pilot stared at Halle. She wanted to say, "I didn't say anything," but she was shocked by their stares and felt afraid. She had no clue of what.

They continued to stare at her for a couple of minutes before the pilot and co-pilot finally stomped loudly down the aisle. They each went into one of the bathrooms, which were at the back of the plane.

"What was just too weird," said her seat-mate.

She looked at him and couldn't disagree. She nodded and could feel her heart pounding in her chest.

The three flight attendants all went into the cockpit and shut the door behind them.

That added a new level of weirdness to things.

Halle looked around. Nobody else seemed to have noticed anything. Most of the passengers were watching movies on tablets, reading, or sleeping. Only she and her mystery seat-mate seemed to have seen anything.

"What's your name?" she asked.

"Carter."

"I'm Halle."

He nodded. "Do you fly much? This is my first time, but it feels odd."

"Odd to me, too."

The male flight attendant was the first to emerge

from the cockpit.

When he'd gone in, he'd reminded Halle of a beach bum. Long, blonde hair that would blow in the wind, a happy smile, handsome, rugged, looked to be in his early twenties. He'd be right at home at a Malibu beach party.

Now...

She stared at him; he was wearing a Halloween mask. The face was dark red, almost burgundy, and it looked rugged and abrasive, like she'd scratch her finger if she caressed his cheek.

His blonde hair was now blackened, shorter, and somehow animated. It reminded her of a million thin worms crawling up from his scalp.

He smiled at Halle, and the mask moved perfectly well. It was unnerving and made her sink lower into her seat.

The two women followed him out and stood behind him. They too had the same kind of mask on, as realistic as the other one.

"Is that real?" Carter asked.

"Of course not. It's Halloween now."

He didn't answer. She wasn't sure if that was because he realized it was obvious, or if it was because he didn't believe her.

She wasn't sure she believed herself.

One of the women crossed her arms and stared at Halle. She felt her gaze bore into her and had to turn away. The other passengers were finally noticing.

After a couple of minutes, the pilots walked back from the bathrooms. They had also put on masks that were the same burnished deep red color.

The five crew members stood at the front of the plane, a united front apparently ready for whatever might happen.

"Shouldn't somebody fly the plane?"

Halle glanced over at Carter. Surely he knew about automatic pilots, but even so, she felt as unnerved as he.

She whispered, "I don't think this is a very funny joke."

The pilot was an older man, about sixty. His hair had been white earlier, but now it was the same wavy black as all the others.

They were nothing if not well coordinated.

"Could I have everybody's attention?"

The pilot was talking, and his voice carried over the intercom. He wasn't using a microphone, but that didn't seem to matter.

A few passengers were still asleep. A flight attendant walked to each in turn and slapped them hard on the face. Some cried out in pain and surprise. Everyone turned to stare and wonder.

When he had everyone's attention, the pilot continued. "Welcome to Demon Air. We will be taking most of you the rest of the way to Sydney."

Most?

A drunk woman somewhere behind Halle called out, "Fuck you! Just get me another drink!"

The pilot stared at the woman, and Halle could almost feel a laser beam strike her down dead. Nothing of the sort happened, but she was convinced it could.

"If we can continue without interruption?"

One of the flight attendants had moved to the drunk

woman and glared at her. She no longer looked like she wanted another drink.

"You are some of the fortunate few to ever fly Demon Air. Of course, it's because you're pathetically cheap and refused to fly a more, shall we say, conventional airline. Diamond Air is about the bottom of the barrel. But, on Halloween, we come alive, and now we're going to show you a flight you'll never forget."

The co-pilot went to the cockpit and came out carrying a large green bowl. In other circumstances, it might have been a salad bowl. Halle had no desire to see what was in it, but he started walking down the aisle beside her. She wanted to hide under her seat, but she was trapped.

He stopped by a passenger two seats in front of her.

"One of my favorite Halloween traditions is to bob for apples."

The passenger shook his head when he looked in the bowl.

"Do it."

"No, it's not..."

"I don't like to keep asking."

The passenger lowered his head but then shook it and pulled himself back.

"No. You can't make me."

Bobbing for apples didn't sound like the worst thing in the world to Halle.

The co-pilot thrust his arm forward and grabbed the man by the throat, squeezing tightly. He fought but it looked like he was trapped by a vice grip. The man struggled for a moment but then collapsed in his seat.

"Who's next?"

The co-pilot stared at Halle.

"Ahh. You."

He brought the green bowl toward her, and she could see water sloshing. When she looked down, she saw that the water was tan-colored and had patches of fuzz floating in it.

The apples were rotten.

Not just a little. They were mostly brown patches with worms squirming in and out. There were so many worms that she couldn't see any spot on any of the apples that were clear.

How am I supposed to get one?

"Bob for the fucking apple, lady."

Halle glanced ahead of her but couldn't see the passenger who had refused.

Is he dead?

The co-pilot leaned over to her. "Now!"

She stared into his face, not believing what she was seeing. It wasn't a mask, at least not like any mask she'd ever seen. It was too perfect. She's swear the demon face was real. His tongue was forked, and his breath smelled like rotten eggs.

"Last chance."

His eyes were yellow orbs filled with black bits. Real.

Halle lowered her head, trying not to smell the putrid water and disgusting apples. She closed her eyes and took a long breath. Finally, she found the courage to lower her head even further and her chin touched an apple. Before losing her courage, she bit into it and pulled her head back. She opened her eyes, and resisted spitting the apple out, even when she felt a worm crawling inside her mouth.

She nodded quickly, asking if she was done.

The demon smiled. "Good job."

Then he moved back past her and she spit the apple out to the floor.

She wanted water to clean her mouth but she didn't have any, and there was no way she was going to ask.

The other demons were walking around the cabin, but she tried to ignore them.

They're real.

"Carter?"

He looked over to her, his mouth clenched. He was afraid.

From the front of the plane, she heard, "What other kind of Halloween fun can we have?" It was one of the flight attendants. She was waving her arm to get all the passengers' attention, and all Halle could concentrate on was the burnt-red hand with dagger-like nails swinging back and forth.

"Anybody remember having razor blades hidden in apples?" She grinned. "We can have fun with that."

Halle closed her eyes and wished she'd never started on the quest for her roots. Suddenly, it didn't seem the least bit important who here ancestors were.

After all, would an Aborigine do anything different in this situation? She didn't know enough to answer that question.

Or did she?

The flight attendant was walking down the far aisle, carrying a box cutter in one hand, staring at each passenger in turn as she walked by.

"Who's the lucky one?" she asked as she laughed her way forward.

"You can't do this," said a passenger to Halle's left. She hadn't really noticed the woman before. She had her arms crossed and seemed to want to pick a fight. She was only in her early twenties, but her courage shone through.

It seemed to Halle that Aborigines had strong and deep character. It was one of the first thought she had when she found out she was at least partly one of them.

They wouldn't stand for this.

And neither would she.

Halle took a deep breath, holding it in to give herself courage before shifting out of her seat and standing in the aisle.

"Everybody!" she called.

She looked around to get her fellow passengers' attention.

"That woman is right." She pointed at the girl who had spoken up. "They can't do this if we don't let them!"

The pilot called from the front of the plane. "Sit down, you stupid bitch."

"I will *not* sit down."

"Looks like we have our volunteer after all."

Halle turned and looked to the majority of the passengers behind her.

"What are they going to do? Kill us all? How could they possibly explain that?"

She shrugged.

"They can't," called the girl that had spoken up earlier.

The pilot hurried down the aisle and grabbed Halle

by the arm. He squeezed tightly, and it felt like her arm was being gripped by a mountain.

The flight attendant who'd been carrying the box cutter came close and grinned. Halle could smell her rancid breath and see what looked like vomit mixed with beetles crawling around her mouth. She wanted to throw up.

"Leave her alone!"

This was a new voice, a man shuffling up the aisle. He was older, maybe in his sixties, and pudgy. The demons could swat him away without noticing, but he came to help anyway.

Then a whole group of passengers were on their feet, all moving toward Halle and the demons.

"Let her go!" somebody called.

The flight attendant glanced back and Halle took the opportunity to grab the box cutter from her hand. She tossed it under one of the middle seats.

The pilot was distracted, too, and Halle pulled her arm free.

"Leave us alone!" she yelled. She felt confidence in her voice, something she'd rarely felt before.

All the demons seemed uncertain, and they moved toward the cockpit, not knowing what to do.

As the passengers crowded closer, the demons turned and moved into the cockpit, locking the door behind them.

Halle realized she'd been holding her breath. She let it out and looked to her fellow passengers.

"Thank you all," she said.

Some of them mumbled, and they all continued to stare at the cockpit.

"What happens now?"

"It's almost midnight," said Halle. "Halloween will be over. I think we'll have our crew back."

She stared and wondered what a true Aborigine would say.

"At least I hope that's the case."

She looked at her watch as the minutes crawled close to midnight. ✖

Memories

Sometimes stories just seem to write themselves, and I look back with no real way to explain where the idea came from. It just fell out of my fingers.

"Memories" is a good example of this.

I sat down and the only conscious thought I had was this guy who woke up in the middle of the night and heard two people arguing in his home.

That's it. All I had.

But I could feel a creative urge inside me, and I just wanted to write... something! So, I did.

I was as surprised as anybody with the story that found its way onto the pages. I like when this happens, but there have also been many times where this approach just turns out crap.

This story was published in the anthology When the Clock Strikes 13, and I was very happy to send it to the editor, Steve Thompson. Steve had contacted his own favorite authors and asked them to submit to his first editing gig. I was honored and very happy with how the anthology turned out

Jimmy Conlin woke from a deep sleep and yawned. At first, he assumed it was time to wake up but when he glanced over to the clock radio and saw it was only 1:16 a.m., he felt a brief relief. Almost another five hours to go.

He was thirsty and thought about getting up to get some water, but that seemed like too much work. Instead, he rolled on his right side and closed his eyes again.

"Damn stupid woman!"

The shout shocked him. Somebody was in the house. Downstairs.

What the fuck?

Jimmy slid out of bed and grabbed the baseball bat he kept standing in the corner of the bedroom. His heart was pounding, and he held the bat with an iron grip.

In the darkness, he could see Sarah's outline as she continued to sleep. He thought about waking her but decided to find out what was going on instead.

"Just leave me alone!" cried a female voice.

Jimmy hedged his way to the bedroom door and looked out to the hallway. There were dim pot lights shining from the ceiling, so he could see that nobody was in the hall or in the study at the end of it. He walked a few steps until he could see over the bannister to the main floor below.

The light was even dimmer there.

"I'll do whatever I want to you," shouted the man. "I own you!"

The woman was sprawled on the floor, cringing with her arms held above her head for protection.

"Hey!" called Jimmy. "Leave her alone!"

For a moment, fear rushed through him. He should have just called the police instead of getting involved, but it was too late now. He walked to the top of the staircase, holding the bat in front of him with both hands.

The man and woman both ignored him.

He started to walk down the stairs while the two strangers continued to argue. The man hadn't hit the woman yet, but it seemed like it was only a matter of time.

Jimmy reached the landing halfway down the stairs and called out, "Get out of my house! I'm going to call the police!"

Again, his shouts were ignored.

He squinted to try to get a better view.

The man looked to be about Jimmy's own age, late thirties, and the woman slightly younger. They wore clothes that might have been in favor decades ago, and the colors were all faded. It was like he was seeing them through a colored filter, all washed out.

The woman looked familiar somehow, but Jimmy couldn't figure out why.

He took another couple of steps down, hefting the bat over his right shoulder. He was ready to swing. As far as he could see, the man didn't have a weapon.

The man reached down and grabbed the woman's hair. She was wearing it in a ponytail, making it easier for him. He snapped her head back.

Jimmy rushed the rest of the way but then jerked to a halt when he realized that both of the strangers were translucent. He could see right through them.

How?

"Stop!" he shouted.

They ignored him.

He took the bat and swung it half-heartedly at the man. The bat went right through him.

"Teach you, you fucking bitch!"

The man brought his fist back, and then both of them disappeared.

Jimmy was alone in his living room, and the house was dead quiet again.

He stared where the two strangers had been and then licked his lips. He knew he hadn't imagined everything. They'd been there, but now they weren't.

Jimmy couldn't move for several minutes. He wanted to somehow believe that he'd been sleepwalking, but he knew that wasn't the case. He'd been wide awake after the shouting.

That reminded him. Sarah.

He didn't see her when he glanced upstairs. She'd always slept through any noise, while he was the light sleeper in the family. For once, he was grateful. He didn't want to scare her. Not now.

The house was silent. He couldn't even hear his own breathing, and that's when he realized he'd been holding his breath. He exhaled and walked slowly to the exact place he'd seen the two strangers. He knelt down to feel the cold tile floor, as if he could somehow sense their presence.

When he stood again he asked himself, "Could I have been sleepwalking?"

Jimmy shook his head. No, he knew what he saw, and it was real.

He checked the sliding door in the kitchen, which opened to the outdoor patio. It was locked. So was the front door. Jimmy sat at the kitchen table, not knowing what to do.

Sarah.

Jimmy had a sudden vision that his wife was in trouble. He ran up the stairs and back to their bedroom. As he entered the room, he banged the door against the wall, and the noise woke Sarah.

"Jeez, what're you doing?"

"Are you okay?"

"Well, you scared the hell out of me, but other than that I'm fine. What's going on?"

He went to the far side of the bed, her side, and gave her a hug.

"Nothing."

"Jimmy? You're shaking."

"Just a nightmare. It's nothing."

The only light was from the faint red numbers of the clock radio and a bit of diffuse light from the moon hiding somewhere behind some trees.

Jimmy held her face in his hands and kissed her forehead.

"I just had a bad dream and worried. It's really nothing."

"Well, then let's get back to sleep."

Jimmy nodded and moved around to climb into his side.

"I need my sleep you know," Sarah said. Jimmy smiled, the joke half-done. He finished it for her, as he always did. "You're sleeping for two now."

Jimmy and Sarah had all but forgotten the idea of having a child. A dozen years earlier, they'd been tested after a fruitless first five years of marriage, and the results embarrassed Jimmy. His sperm count was in the lowest five percentile, and the fertility specialist told them it was very unlikely they would have a child unless they went with something like artificial insemination or adoption.

They both did a lot of soul-searching and decided their lives were good as is. If they weren't meant to have a baby, they would accept that.

Now, both edging ever closer to forty, Sarah was expecting a child.

It still seemed unbelievable, but both were ecstatic.

The only nagging problem was the phone call from Sarah's gynecologist, who wanted to see them after Sarah's routine ultrasound.

That appointment was today. They both wanted to believe it was just to confirm everything was okay, but would she call them into the office just for that?

They decided to go out to a nearby restaurant for breakfast, a tiny celebration of their new lives, while waiting.

"What was the nightmare?" asked Sarah.

Jimmy stared at her with wide eyes. "Nightmare?"

"You had a bad dream last night."

"Yeah."

"What was it?"

He shook his head, remembering the ghosts that had haunted their kitchen. "I don't remember anymore. You know how dreams are…"

Sarah nodded but kept looking at him. "Was it about the baby?"

"No, nothing like that. I think it was about some kind of monster, like a zombie." He shrugged. "Just silly stuff."

Sarah smiled and he felt butterflies in his stomach. Even after all these years, he still felt dazzled by that smile.

The doctor was walking distance from the restaurant, and as they headed there, they talked about baby names and room colors and daycare and sleep.

Doctor Stevie Thompson met them as the receptionist led them to her office. The frown on her face terrified Jimmy. He felt fear rush through him.

As they sat, Sarah spoke first. "It's bad?"

That night, Jimmy closed his eyes and pretended to sleep, but no matter how tired he was, dreamland avoided him. He could hear Sarah breathing softly, sleeping soundly. It has taken her awhile to drift off, but eventually it happened.

At 1:16 a.m., he was still awake. That's when he heard voices from downstairs.

This time, he wasn't as surprised as the night before. The low, grating voice of the man was blunt and hateful, while the woman was full of fear.

Jimmy sat up and listened, glancing back at Sarah. He couldn't wake her after the day they'd had.

Once again he grabbed the baseball bat and made his way to the top of the stairs.

He could see the shadowy figures in the same area as they'd been the night before.

Was it really only last night? he wondered. It felt like an eternity ago.

He crept down the steps. The man was clearer tonight, not just a vague ghost like before. Tonight, he looked to be about forty, but he was an *old* forty, stress lines carved into his forehead, and anger carved everywhere else. A half-smoked cigarette hung from his lips.

The woman was short, slim, blonde, and scared. Jimmy felt sorry for her. Her head was bowed in fear. The man was holding a knife in front of him, as if he planned on killing her.

"Who are you?"

Jimmy was shocked when the man turned to face him. He'd clearly heard Jimmy call to him.

Then they both disappeared.

The room was silent and dark. Jimmy was alone.

He turned the light on and crouched at the floor, looking for ash from the stranger's cigarette, but he found nothing.

The whole thing didn't make sense. Jimmy knew that, and the weight of the day was pressing down on him. He knew he needed to find some way to sleep. The mystery of the ghostly people would have to wait until the morning.

He climbed back up the stairs, each step feeling like he was lifting a thousand pounds. Part of him wanted to just sleep on the couch, but he needed to be near Sarah.

The bed was soft, and he sighed as he laid on his back and closed his eyes.

Sleep didn't come to him, though. Instead, he thought about a science class he'd attended in high school, twenty years earlier.

A baby starts as an embryo, and before that it was a zygote, consisting of little more than twenty-three pairs of chromosomes. The mother and father each contributed half the chromosomes, and the tiny strands of life carried all the genes that would be used as a blueprint for the new child.

Twenty-three pairs.

Except for when something went wrong.

Sometimes a freak mutation caused three copies of the same chromosome to be passed to the new child instead of two. If that extra chromosome was in the wrong place, it could impact the embryo's ability to grow and build the new baby.

Jimmy and Sarah's new baby had an extra chromosome, number thirteen. The resulting disease was called Trisomy 13.

The baby would likely die before birth, and if it

somehow survived, he or she would almost certainly die soon after. It was rare for a Trisomy 13 baby to live to their first birthday, let alone to adulthood.

Rare but not impossible.

When the gynecologist had told them the news earlier that day, their hearts sank. It didn't seem fair after all these years to have a baby miraculously given to them and then stolen away.

He imagined Sarah at work or walking to the store when she was further along. Everyone would be congratulating her on her pregnancy and being so happy for them both. How could she face that knowing one day her baby would die in her womb?

Jimmy knew he wouldn't want Sarah to go through that, but he hadn't yet voiced his opinion. As they walked to their car, he was sure that Sarah felt the same. It would be wrong to try to bring the baby to term. When they'd gotten home, they both went to separate parts of the house until bedtime.

Now Jimmy wanted to find the sleep that had eluded him. At one point, he glanced at the alarm clock: 4:42. Most of the night was gone, and he felt even more frustrated.

He closed his eyes and tried one more time to fall asleep.

Later, although it seemed impossible, Jimmy did manage to pry his eyes open. Sunshine flooded his bedroom. Sarah wasn't in bed with him. He jerked his head to see that it was after nine o'clock.

For a moment, he panicked but then realized it was

Saturday. No work.

His thoughts flickered between his unborn baby and the ghosts he'd seen. He couldn't seem to concentrate on one of them, as if somehow they were tied together in his mind. That made no sense.

He gathered his wits and got out of bed to have a shower. As he turned the water on, his mind went back to a similar scene many years earlier: his brother, Jay, turning on the shower in their childhood home.

"Beat you," Jay had said.

Jimmy had been on his way to the shower after a little league ball game. Jay's smirk showed that he was only butting in to bug him. Jimmy called him an asshole and then went to sit out in the back yard. His grandfather was there, smoking a cigar. A glass of scotch sat untouched on the small table beside him.

That's when Grampy told him what he called the family secret.

"Something wrong, Jimmy?"

Grampy's voice was frail, brittle, and it seemed to portend his death, which wasn't all that far in the future.

"Just Jay being Jay."

"Yeah. I had a brother once, too."

Jimmy knew that. Grampy loved to talk about his childhood. Hell, he loved to talk about *himself* no matter what the context.

Today, though, he was quieter. He picked his drink up and swirled it, staring at it as if it hypnotized him.

"You okay, Grampy?"

The old man blinked and smiled as he shook his head. "Just—"

Whatever he was just, Jimmy would never find out. Grampy stopped and looked to the sky, making Jimmy look up in case a flock of birds was about to attack.

"The family has a curse, you know."

Jimmy wondered if his grandfather had finally fallen over the edge into senile-land.

"What do you mean?"

"It happened to me, and it happened to my father. He told me it was a family curse, so I think it must have happened to his ancestors too."

"What are you talking about?"

"It doesn't happen often. Only in times of stress or a big change, which is a kind of stress, I suppose."

"Okay?"

Jimmy stared and wondered if Jay was finished his shower yet.

"We get to see the past. Or maybe the past comes ahead to the future toward us. However you want to say it."

"We get to see the past? How?"

"Looks like visions or ghosts. But it's real. Like a television that looks right into the past."

Jimmy had no clue what the old man was talking about. It was ridiculous. He just nodded and turned to face the yard. A chilly breeze kissed his face and he decided to go see if Jay was done yet.

"See you, Grampy."

That conversation happened almost three decades

earlier, and Jimmy had totally forgotten about it until now.

He stared at the hot water cascading in the shower stall.

How'd I forget that? he wondered. *Easy, because it was just the ramblings of a senile old man.*

But was it?

Jimmy tried to remember if his grandfather ever mentioned seeing the past any other time, but nothing came to him. And his father never mentioned it, either.

Maybe it never happened to him.

Of course, he remembered little about his father. He abandoned the family before Jimmy was ten years old. His mom never talked about why he left. Jimmy's recollections of his father were vague and unimportant.

Sarah wasn't in the kitchen. She'd left him a note on the counter.

> *Gone to do some thinking.*
> *I'll be back before lunch.*

Jimmy read the note over and over. He knew how the Trisomy 13 diagnosis had devastated his wife. She'd always wanted a child but had long ago given up on having that dream come true. As had he.

He made a cup of coffee and went to the living room to drink it. Without thinking, he turned the radio on to fill the room with music, so it wouldn't be just full of bad memories and equally bad futures. By the time he finished his cup, his cheeks were stained with tears.

An hour later, he heard a ding on his iPhone. He grabbed it to find a text from Sarah.

I don't know what to do.

The words bit into him as much as his teeth bit his lower lip. He knew the pattern. It had happened twice before in their marriage, when they had gone through rough times. Instead of being able to talk directly to each other and share their feelings, they'd text. He tried to think of how to help her and finally typed:

We can do this, babe. We've got each other.

This is different. Our baby is going to die inside me.

Jimmy closed his eyes and wished Sarah was with him. There was nothing he could say that would help, but if she had been there, he could hug her. At least they would be on the same side.
Wouldn't they?

Please come home.

Sarah didn't answer. That was also part of the pattern. He knew better that to badger her with more texts, pleading with her to come back. She would come home when she was in better spirits.
The other two times she went off like this, she returned later that day. He could only hope that she made the same choice this time.

Jimmy Conlin did not believe in ghosts. He did not believe in ESP, reincarnation, vampires, telekinesis, past lives, and a million other pieces of nonsense that most of his Facebook friends seemed to think were perfectly reasonable ideas.

He certainly did not believe in time travel or a time portal or whatever the hell his deranged grandfather had been trying to tell him about all those years ago. That was a non-starter.

Jimmy had a philosophical backbone constructed of pure scientific belief and mathematical principles. There was no evidence of any type of process that projected images into the future.

It just couldn't be true.

The fact that he couldn't personally explain the ghostly phenomenon he'd experienced the past two nights did not mean they had to be of some supernatural origin. It just meant he didn't know what it was.

He spent a couple of hours on the Internet, googling to see what possible rational explanations could explain what he'd seen. After eliminating all the nonsensical ideas, he ended up with only two remaining possibilities. First, he had been sleepwalking. Second, he was crazy.

Neither option appealed to him very much, and he slammed the keyboard tray and left the computer, full of disgust.

Before he knew it, he realized the sun was setting. He shook his head and checked the time. After seven o'clock.

Sarah.

He stared at the front door, willing it to open and for her to walk through, but of course nothing happened.

Jimmy felt a million pounds of stress pushing him down. It didn't help that he had had such a small amount of sleep the night before.

Still no text from Sarah. He wanted to throw his phone and smash it, but that was now the only lifeline he had to her.

She was almost certainly at her mother's house. That had always been her safe place, and Jimmy never had a reason to object to that. Her mom listened but never judged, and she make sure Sarah was safe.

That was what mattered most.

He texted her.

I miss you.

"I love you," he whispered.

Jimmy lay down on the couch, hoping just to rest a few minutes.

He woke up six hours later to screams coming from only a few feet behind the couch.

This time the man and woman weren't the slightest bit ghostly. They were solid and real.

He was mad as shit.

It took a moment for Jimmy to react, and the first thing he thought of was, *I'm not sleepwalking and I'm not fucking crazy.*

"Please don't!"

The man was on top of the woman, pressing her to the floor. She was mostly naked, with only the shredded remains of a pink nightgown covering bits of her body. The man slapped her hard.

"You fucking bitch! You've been asking for this all week!"

He was pulling his pants down with one hand while holding both her hands above her head.

Jimmy didn't think. He just reacted. The kitchen was close, so he ran there and grabbed a knife and jumped into the middle of the fight, smashing into the man, pushing him off the woman.

"Fuck are you?"

"Leave her alone!"

Jimmy barely noticed that they were no longer in his home. They were in a barn. He smelled hay and manure, and the lighting was dimmer than it was before he jumped into the fight.

The man had a manic expression on his face. His pants were undone, but that didn't stop him from jumping toward Jimmy and screaming at him.

Jimmy wanted to turn his back, but he froze, and it was purely some kind of instinct for survival that caused him to stab with the knife. It slid into the man's gut easily, and Jimmy lifted it up, slicing the stranger's body like he would gut a trout.

The man's face was a grimace, and he tried to keep on going, but he knew he was a walking dead man. He reached his hands to grab Jimmy's neck, but he had no strength left, and he slowly fell to the ground.

The woman pulled the shreds of her clothes and crawled over to the dead body.

"Tom?" Her voice was soft and worried.

Jimmy stared at her.

She turned to look at him, and as she stood up and moved closer to him, he recognized her. It was his mother.

Not possible.

Up to now, he'd never seen the woman's face closely. His mother had died a very long time ago, withered away in a hospice, her body ravaged with cancer.

She couldn't be here.

"You killed my husband!"

"Your...?"

He stared back at the dead body. He'd barely known his father and certainly didn't recognize him now.

"That's not possible," he said.

"You killed my husband!" she shouted a second time.

Jimmy backed away. "He was going to hurt you."

She went back to the dead body, crying. "But I loved him."

Jimmy felt a dizziness crawl over him. His mother and father seemed to swim in the air and he felt his face crack as he hit the ground.

He awoke on the floor of his kitchen. His face was scraped.

Not sleepwalking. Not crazy.

He cleaned himself up in the bathroom and tried to convince himself that maybe he *was* crazy.

But he knew better.

That was his mother. Marcy Conlin was a beautiful woman who had been his sole parent most of his life. She'd had a hard life with little money, two jobs, and two sons who were constantly fighting with each other.

He stared at himself in the mirror. The cuts on his face weren't deep.

"Mom..."

He only had one framed photo of his mother. It was a picture taken on the day he graduated high school. The photo was hanging in the spare bedroom, so he climbed the stairs and turned left to the bedroom that was ear-marked for their little baby.

On the wall hung the photo. She had a wide smile, which he never remembered her having any other time, and one of her arms was around his shoulder. Jimmy's younger self smiled just as widely, happy to have finished high school at last.

He stared at the photo, trying to convince himself that what he was seeing was wrong. It was still the middle of the night, and things always seemed strange when looked at in the wee hours. Everything was less spooky in daylight.

The picture was of Jimmy, his mother, and his brother Jay.

It always was. He remembered because Jay couldn't bring himself to join the other two in smiling. He had frowned for the picture, and every time Jimmy had looked at it, it was that frown that he noticed every fucking time.

Now, Jay was not in the picture.

He and his mother were alone.

"What the hell?"

He remembered Jay. He remembered all the arguments and sometimes the physical battles. He remembered walking in on Jay in the bathroom when Jay was thirteen and holding his penis in his hand, stroking it when Jimmy walked in.

He remembered the day they both acted as pall-bearers for Mom.

Now, though, he *also* remembered that he was an only child, that his father was murdered by some man who broke into the barn at the back of the property and sliced his father open right in front of Mom.

Jimmy's mother was never the same. She seemed to give up on life, even to the point of ignoring her own son.

There had been no Jay, and the memories of him were starting to fade.

Jimmy backed away from the photo and hurried to the master bedroom.

Sarah was sleeping in their bed.

Thank god.

He couldn't help it. He sat beside her and gently woke her.

"Babe?"

Her eyes blinked a couple of times and she stretched and then reached over to touch his arm.

She nodded and licked her lips.

"I'm glad you came home," he said. "I really missed you."

She sat up and they hugged.

"I'm glad I'm home, too."

He kissed her gently and held her to his chest.

"Do you remember Jay?" he asked.

She pulled back and looked puzzled. "Jay who?"

He wanted to tell her all about his brother before he lost touch with the remaining strands of their shared life, but he knew that would be pointless.

"It doesn't matter."

"Jimmy, we have to talk."

She looked down at her belly.

He nodded. "I know."

"I just don't know if I can do it."

He wasn't sure if she meant she couldn't go through with the pregnancy or couldn't go through with terminating it.

Jimmy put his hands on her cheeks.

"You know, life really is precious. Sometimes it can be taken from us easier than we imagine."

He had no idea he had planned on saying that, but the ghostly memories of Jay urged him on. A life erased and soon to be forgotten. That couldn't happen again.

Jimmy thought of his brother and the totally unimportant arguments they'd always had. They were gone now and never existed. That was completely impossible.

Yet, he knew it was true.

"We can deal with whatever happens. We need to give our child a chance. Maybe we'll have the one in a million."

Sarah's face crunched up as she collapsed into his chest. She cried, and then he cried, and then they fell into bed together. ✕

The Rules

I don't watch a lot of horror movies. Well, I don't watch a lot of movies of any type. There's just not enough time in the day to do everything I really want to do. There's little time to squeeze in movies.

Having said that, I've always loved the Saw franchise, especially the first two movies.

I think I must have been subconsciously thinking about those movies when I started writing "The Rules." It wasn't anything I was aware of at the time, but that's how the subconscious works.

In my conscious mind, I started with the rules themselves. They came from a dream, and although I lost all the context of the rules, I remembered the rules themselves, and a plot came to me which I thought would be very cool.

The only part I didn't really have a clue about was the resolution / ending. How was this all going to play out? I just started typing, trusting that the ending would come to me before I needed it, and it did.

I woke feeling dizzy, my head in a fog, having no clue where I was. My brain felt like it was leaking, unable to comprehend anything.

"What?" I asked.

A jackhammer was pounding inside my skull. I gasped for a long breath, as if I hadn't had any air for a month.

"Where...?"

It was silly to ask questions. I blinked and felt a drop of sweat fall from my forehead.

My mouth was parched. I licked my lips, but it didn't help.

There was no way to lift my arms, but at that point, I didn't understand why. I was sitting, and I wondered if I'd been unconscious for so long I had no strength in my arms.

My vision was swirling around, and images jumped at random.

When I was a freshman at university, I'd once gotten so drunk at a frat party that I couldn't stand, couldn't focus, couldn't do a damned thing except throw up.

This felt a lot like that, but I hadn't touched a drop of alcohol in two decades. Not since I met Marcy.

Marcy!

Was she okay?

I fought to keep my eyes focused. Gradually, the world stopped spinning, or at least slowed enough to let me gain some idea of what was going on.

I was indeed sitting. It was a hard wooden chair, solid and uncomfortable. There was no cushion or anything else.

My arms were tied to the chair with metal bands. I flexed my legs and could feel they were secured too, probably with the same kind of metal restraints.

I wasn't going anywhere.

Rocking didn't make a damned bit of difference. The chair could have been made of solid rock for all the give it had.

The floor was polished stone. At least that's what it looked like. I couldn't tell for sure, but the shine and pattern made me think of a granite countertop in some fancy kitchen.

Looking up and around, I could see that on all four sides of me were metal walls. And the ceiling. I was a captive in a steel box. I didn't feel claustrophobic, as the box was pretty big, maybe six feet in every direction. A single white light shone down from the ceiling, illuminating my cage.

"Hello?"

I knew where I was. Meaning that I also knew it was hopeless to expect any answers. That wasn't how they worked.

Once again, I wondered about Marcy. Chances were

very high she was in a cage exactly like mine, either to my left or my right.

How the fuck did this happen?

I tried to think back, but it was like looking through the wrong end of a telescope. Everything was hazy. The last thing I remembered for sure was being in my cubicle at work. I remember approving a travel expense for somebody in the company. It was an overnight trip to Dallas. Trips to Dallas were common enough, since that was where our advertising division was. I worked at the head office in Chicago, and that stamp of approval was the last task I did before shutting my computer down. I remember glancing at my watch and seeing it was 5:08. Marcy was expecting me at our favorite restaurant at 5:30 for dinner. It was our eighteenth wedding anniversary.

After that, things aren't clear. I must have taken the elevator to the parking garage, and I would have walked to my Subaru, but I'm not sure if I have actual memories of that or if the repetition of a decade working at the bank just made it seem like I *must* have done that.

I don't remember leaving the parking lot.

And Marcy? They must have gotten her as she left her office, too.

But... Oh, god, no.

I froze as I realized that Alex must also have been taken.

"No!" I screamed, knowing it would do absolutely no good. "Not Alex! Don't make her do this!"

My words seemed to just bounce off the metal walls of my cage. I knew nobody would care. If they could hear me at all, they'd probably just be laughing.

Alex.

Last week our little girl turned sixteen. Hard to imagine, but it's true. When she was born, she changed everything about our lives. Marcy adores her, and that has never changed. I love Alex just as much as Marcy does, but sometimes a father shows things just a bit differently. I built her a toy doll house, I drove her to her ballet lessons, I helped her with her math homework, and I watched her leave on her first date when she was fourteen, stricken with both fear and happiness.

She was the best part of my life.

Now she was stuck in the middle.

I yelled one more futile time, but all that did was make my head hurt more. They must have used some kind of drug to knock me out, and maybe the imaginary hammer that smashed onto the top of my skull was a residual effect of that.

I wished I could see Marcy, just one more time. The way the show worked, though, I knew I'd never see her again. My heart sank as that realization hit me. I wanted to hold her, to reassure her that I would save her, that this was all a bad dream, and that we'd both wake up very soon and be back to being our loving family again.

All that was bullshit, and Marcy would know it as much as I did.

I closed my eyes and sat calmly. Somehow, I fell asleep.

When I woke again, the front section of my cage was gone.

The metal walls were still on both sides of me and behind. Only the front was open.

I felt cool air on my face, and I knew that the front wall had only just then been taken away, waking me.

"Marcy!"

I only called out the one time, and then paused to listen. No response.

The room in front of me was darkened, but it felt like an old warehouse or storage facility. I wanted to make a mental map of the place, but there were so few items I could identify. In the distance was a series of shelves that seemed to reach pretty high, but I couldn't even begin to estimate how high because the light didn't reach the ceiling. There were objects on the shelves. Some books, but the other things were just random shapes.

In front of me was exactly what I expected.

There was a podium made of wood—at least that's what the speculation on the Internet says. The authorities have never commented one way or the other. I don't think they have a clue. The podium was only about six inches high and about ten feet square. It was dark and looked like it'd been crafted by a professional.

On the podium was something like the box that a person might stand behind when giving a speech. I think it's called a lectern? Anyhow, it wasn't exactly that. The shape wasn't quite right. Sitting on that was the weapon.

I stared at it, even though I've seen it a hundred

times before, the same as everyone else. Somehow it's different when it's pointed at you.

From my perspective, all I focused on was the long barrel aimed at me. It wasn't a rifle, because instead of bullets it shot a laser beam that spread out horizontally and could slice through my neck. My head would topple off like it'd never been attached.

That was half of the possibility, because there was a second barrel that sprouted from the weapon controls. That second barrel was pointed at the second cage immediately to my left. I couldn't see it, but I knew it was there. And inside that second cage was the love of my life, Marcy.

"Marcy!"

Still no answer. Maybe she was still unconscious.

"Hello? Is anybody there?"

My voice echoed back from the warehouse. Nobody replied.

Suddenly I heard banging on the back of my cage. I imagined somebody with a baseball bat smashing the metal rear wall.

Shit.

This whole thing was *so* fucked up.

My mouth was dry. I wished for water, but that was ridiculous. The people running the show weren't interested in my comfort.

I don't know how long I sat there in the semi-darkness. An hour? Two? More? It felt like more. My butt was hurting from sitting on the wooden chair, my wrists were on fire from the tight binding.

The worst thing was waiting for the next step. I just wanted them to get it over with.

Finally, they did.

"Mom? Dad?"

I must have dozed off again, because I hadn't noticed Alex step onto the podium and stand behind the weapon.

Even more surprising, I hadn't felt them put tape on my mouth. I tried to call to Alex, but I couldn't make a sound.

Like everyone else, I've seen the recordings of all the other times this scenario had played out. They were all easily available on the Internet. *The Rules* was a bigger draw than *Survivor*.

Nobody had shown any success in stopping these animals. As far as I know, nobody even has the vaguest idea of who they are. The FBI keeps saying they're dedicated to the case, but most people I know think they're just chasing their tails. Whoever was doing this was too smart to get caught.

Alex looked terrified. I could only see her from the chest up. She cried out for us, and I tried in vain to get out of the damned chair I was stuck in, so I could go to her.

I wanted to fucking kill the people who did this. Who the hell tears a family apart like this, apparently for no motive other than that they could.

"Rule number *one*."

I knew the rules. Somehow, though, I forced myself to listen as the speakers blasted the words. They weren't clear, as if somebody was using a scrambler of some kind. When it was on the Internet, the voices were removed and the rules were listed as captions on the bottom of the screen.

Alex had been crying, but she lifted her head to the voice. She had hope in her eyes, and it occurred to me that she may never have seen an episode of *The Rules* on the Internet. Marcy and I had never allowed her to see it.

Oh, god, she has no idea.

Now that she was paying attention, the loudspeaker repeated, "Rule number one: Alex, if you disobey any of the rules, your mother will be immediately killed, your father will be immediately killed, and *you* will be immediately killed. Do you understand?"

Alex stared up toward the ceiling as if hunting in vain for whoever was talking.

Please say you understand, sweetie.

The voice said, "Alex?"

She still didn't reply.

"Alexandra Stacey Coldwater, please listen carefully. This webcast has aired sixteen times. There were another eighty-two episodes that did not air because the star did not fulfill his or her duties. All family members were killed immediately.

"So, I will ask you one last time. Do you understand rule number one?"

Tears were streaming down her face, but she nodded.

"I understand."

I could barely hear her words, but that was okay. She said them.

Like everyone else, I knew about the sixteen episodes mentioned. They were all over the map, from

Alaska to Florida, with two in Canada, and even one in Mexico. All thirteen American cases were in different states.

Make that fourteen.

"Rule number two: Once the clock starts, you have five minutes to make a choice. If you do not make a choice and act on that choice, your mother will be immediately killed, your father will be immediately killed, and *you* will be immediately killed. Do you understand?"

"Yes, damn you."

"Rule number three: you cannot talk to your parents at all. Do you understand?"

"Yes."

"Rule number four: There is a dial in front of you that points either left or right. It is currently in the middle position, pointing at neither. You must turn it. If you turn it left, a laser will be directed at your father. If you turn it right, a laser will be directed at your mother. Do you understand?"

"Yes."

"Rule number five: After you turn the dial, you must push the red button in front of you. That will activate the laser. Do you understand?"

She nodded, and I barely heard her whispered, "Yes."

"Rule number six. After you have pushed the button, you and your surviving parent will be returned home unharmed. Do you understand?"

"Yes."

"Your five minutes start now."

I could see the glow of the countdown clock above

the top of the cages holding Marcy and me, but I couldn't see the actual time. I would have no idea when time ran out. Of course, Alex had to make her choice before then, or we were all dead.

She was too smart to allow that to happen.

I think that's when reality hit me.

I was going to die.

Alex only had two options: kill her mother or kill me. She loved her mother with every cell of her body. She adored her.

That doesn't mean she didn't love me. Of course she did, but the bond between a mother and a daughter is tighter than any other relationship could ever be. She grew from her mother's body, and I believe part of Marcy's soul sliced off to become Alex when she was conceived. No matter how strong a bond I had with my daughter, there was no real competition. No decision to be made.

Alex was going to kill me.

At the lectern, Alex stared at me. Then she blinked, and I saw her eyes shift to her mom. Then back to me.

She was trying to hold in her tears, but some spilled down her cheeks.

I watched as she glanced at the bright countdown clock above our heads.

And I thought I heard her whisper, "I'm sorry."

She adjusted the dial, locking in her decision, closed her eyes, and pushed the red button.

TWENTY YEARS EARLIER.

She was in a coffee shop ordering some complicated weird-ass drink. A latte with some kind of fancy ingredients and skim milk, I think. I never really understood the attraction. For me, plain black coffee was all I wanted.

I was in line behind her, watching her glance up to the sky as she recited her order. I think I fell in love with her that very second.

Sounds silly, right? But sometimes even clichés can come true.

When I ordered my plain old coffee and it arrived sooner than her fancy contraption, I probably should have just wandered off, but I wasn't able to do that. I stood beside her, trying to gain enough courage to say hello to her. The words just wouldn't come. She finally laughed and let me off the hook.

"Hi, I'm Marcy. I think you're trying to talk to me?" Her laugh released all the tension I'd felt, and I found myself smiling and giggling like a school girl.

"I'm Peter. I just… well, noticed you."

"Don't be so nervous. I'm not going to hit you or anything."

I must have looked a bit concerned about hitting even being a possibility. She laughed some more and said, "Come on, let's go sit down."

So began the best part of my life. I don't need to spell out every date, every lovemaking session, every time I went to sleep thanking whatever gods there might be for bringing me to my amazing dream girl.

We were leading the lives that legends are made of,

and somehow (even though I would have sworn it wasn't possible), our love grew even deeper when Marcy became pregnant with Alex. Our world grew, and our love expanded to fit.

Alex grew up with the very best of Marcy's qualities: long blonde hair, a quick smile and laughing eyes, and even the same taste in clothes. She was a mini-Marcy.

Alex and Marcy went shopping together, cooked together, watched romantic comedies on TV together. They were joined at the hip, and I loved seeing that every day.

Now Alex is sixteen and forced to kill me.

I imagined more than saw her finger pressing the button. I wanted to scream, but the tape across my mouth just made it a muffle.

The laser beam was light blue. It was a long, thin ribbon that punctuated the air, joining Alex to her mother.

I *saw* it.

Meaning: I was still alive.

I heard a thump, and I knew Marcy's head had just bounced to the floor.

"No!" I screamed but of course nobody heard me.

There was no way to pull myself free from the chair, even though my body was pulling as hard as I fucking well could. Later, I wondered how I avoided a heart attack or aneurysm when my beautiful wife was decapitated.

More screaming and crying and attempts to escape all came to nothing.

At the base of my cage, near the front, I could see a red stream trickle into my field of view.

The thought was unbearable. I don't know if I passed out at that point or if they gassed me. Either way, I was dead to the world for a long time.

I woke up in the hospital, and like all the other victims before me, I had no real clue to help find the animals who set this murderous scheme in motion.

Our segment of *The Rules* showed up on the Internet four days after our release.

It took me six months to get over losing Marcy. It was the worst half year of my life, by far. I woke up every morning racked with sorrow and spent most of the day just staring at the walls like a zombie.

The FBI agents stopped by every once in a while, sometimes to ask me or Alex questions, sometimes to tell us about a new family that had had their lives ruined, sometimes just to give me a pat on the back and see if I was doing okay.

I was never going to do okay again.

Sometimes when you lose the thing that is most important in your life, you just can't think about carrying on. Somehow, though, I fought the urge to slit my wrists or blast my brains out with my handgun. That urge did call to me, and at times it felt overpowering, but it always passed.

Beer was my friend.

I'm not proud of that, but if I drank enough Heineken or Stella Artois, I'd eventually get drunk and pass out. Without that, I'd be staring at the ceiling every night.

Six months. Longer than I like admitting, but my head did finally clear. I was able to get through the day without crying and at night, I'd weaned myself down to just one or two beers. It was just a habit now, no longer something I needed to get to sleep.

Through it all, one question haunted me, and up to then I hadn't had the courage to ask Alex.

Why in hell had she chosen for her mother to die instead of me?

Survivor guilt was as big an emotion to me as the loss itself. Why would she save me? It made no sense whatsoever. The only thing I could come up with was that there was some deep-seated disagreement between Alex and Marcy, and this was the time Alex chose to pay attention to it.

I'd never heard a whiff of such a disagreement, though. Was that really possible?

What else could it be?

I was afraid to ask her.

In fact, I was afraid to talk to her at all for that first six months. It's just as well that she stayed with Marcy's sister much of that time. I wasn't in any space to be able to deal with her loss in addition to mine.

Whenever I thought of Alex, what I remembered was her looking at Marcy and pushing the damned button. She took the love of my life from me, and I hated her for it.

I didn't work for that six months. It barely occurred to me, and at some point I was fired from my job at the bank, but I didn't give a flying fuck. Marcy and I had both taken out small insurance policies years earlier. I actually forgot about it, but with our kidnapping being the hot news of the day, the insurance company contacted me and pushed the money into my hands. I'm sure the last thing they wanted was to be seen holding up paying the policy. It wasn't a lot, but it got me through the dark times.

On the six-month anniversary of Marcy's death, I went to visit her at her grave.

Alex happened to visit at the same time. I looked at her face and could see the pain and sorrow had aged her. Her skin was tight and her beautiful blonde hair was ratty and frizzled.

She wasn't my little girl anymore.

Part of me wanted to hug her, to tell her that everything was going to be all right, that we still had each other.

Instead my mind focused on the disgusting thing she'd done. At that moment, I truly hated myself as much as I hated her. I knew that she could only save one of us. That was the rule. I *knew* that. It just didn't matter.

We both looked at the tombstone in silence. I tried to focus on only the good times.

When I turned to leave, Alex did as well, walking beside me back to the cars.

I couldn't help myself.

"Why did you kill her?" I knew she could hear the rage in my voice, but I couldn't control it.

She stopped walking and stared at me.

"Why?" I asked again. "You should have chosen me."

The old Alex would have cried at my harsh voice. No longer. This was not the loving and sensitive child we'd raised.

She stared defiantly at me and said, "If I had chosen you, Mom couldn't have survived. She adored you, more than you'll ever know. If I'd saved her, she would have been shattered into a million pieces. I would have lost both of you. There is no doubt in my mind about that."

She rubbed her cheeks and added, "I saved you so that I would still have one parent."

I stared at her, not really understanding. I wanted to accuse her of lying, but I knew she was telling the truth. I didn't care. It wasn't a good enough reason.

"So, how did that work out for you?"

My car was only ten feet away. I could have hugged Alex, but instead I didn't say a word. I just went to my car and drove off.

I didn't sleep that night. I had just built up a huge wall between my only child and myself. All because she'd chosen to save my life.

Part of me knew it was ridiculous to hold her responsible. It was the criminals who kidnapped us that caused the problem, not Alex. I even wrote that down on twenty different sheets of paper and stuck them all over the house: It wasn't Alex.

But my heart refused to believe.

Two months passed, and I didn't hear anything more from Alex. I knew she was living with her aunt, so I could have gotten in touch any time I wanted, but I chose not to.

Then, one morning, I woke with a cloudy fog in my

head.

Oh, my god, no.

I tried to force my eyes open, but they weren't co-operating. My head was bobbing from whatever gas they'd used on me. I felt the familiar pounding in my head.

"Not again," I mumbled.

When I finally did come to, I saw some familiar surroundings. There were two crates in front of me. One was empty, though, which didn't make any sense to me.

In the second crate, Alex sat, bound to a wooden chair, tape covering her mouth.

I was chained to the lectern.

It made no sense. They always had two targets to choose from.

"Alex?"

She struggled, but of course she could do nothing to escape or even make a sound. I couldn't get anywhere, either, so I just waited.

Instead of a double-barrel weapon pointing at the two crates, one barrel was pointed at Alex. The other was curved back and pointing at me.

Soon, the instructions came.

"Rule number one: Peter, if you disobey any of the rules, your daughter will be immediately killed and *you* will be immediately killed. Do you understand?"

I nodded.

"Please answer verbally."

"Yes."

How could this be happening? The only guess I had was that they were getting bored of the same old same old and wanted to change up the game. Maybe ratings were down.

"Rule number two: Once the clock starts, you have five minutes to make a choice. If you do not make a choice and act on that choice, your daughter will be immediately killed and *you* will be immediately killed. Do you understand?"

Tears fell down my cheeks.

"Yes."

"Rule number three: you cannot talk to your daughter at all. Do you understand?"

"Yes."

"Rule number four: There is a dial in front of you that points either forward or backward. It is currently in the middle, pointing at neither. You must turn it. If you turn it forward, a laser will be directed at your daughter. If you turn it backward, a laser will be directed at you. Do you understand?"

"Yes."

"Rule number five: Once you turn the dial, you must push the red button in front of you. That will activate the laser. Do you understand?"

"Yes."

"Rule number six. After you have pushed the button, whoever survives will be returned home unharmed. Do you understand?"

"Yes."

"Your five minutes start now."

Above the cages, a bright red digital timer flashed on and started to count down.

5:00.

Of course I would set the laser to myself.

I thought back to when Alex was a little six-year-old, where everything in the world was shiny and new. I remember her always asking how the world worked. Why are there rainbows sometimes? Why do fingernails grow? When I get older will mommy still be my mommy or will she be grandma?"

Nothing made me happier than watching her grow, even through the occasional temper tantrum. She was my girl, for sure.

And her mother's.

I remembered building her a tree house and teaching her to ride a bicycle and to ice skate. I held her hand while she had stitches put in after cutting herself one time. She was so brave, smiling at me and trying so hard not to cry.

Of course there was no choice. I loved Alex, and I could never hurt her.

When she grew older, she was a girl guide, and I helped her sell her cookies. I watched her give a speech about her dog at an assembly at school, and I admired her bravery.

And I remember her killing my soul mate in cold blood.

My emotions flipped, and I could once again feel the anger boiling through my body. She'd taken my love, my best friend, my lover, and she'd slaughtered her. I was unable to ever forgive her for that.

0:38.

I hadn't noticed the clock running down so quickly. I had to decide or we'd both die.

Maybe that was the best choice... no choice at all.

0:31.

She murdered Marcy.

She's my little girl.

I hesitated but then found my hand on the dial, and I turned it.

0:15.

God forgive me.

I pushed the red button.

And shortly after that I was gassed again.

This time, when I woke up, I was in my own home, sprawled on the floor. As with the other times, my head was spinning and a headache shot through my skull. The house was dark, and I had no idea what day it was, let alone what time. Night.

There was a note.

> Do not mention any part of this round of *The Rules* to anybody. If you do, both you and your daughter will be killed instantly.

Alex will be killed? Did the note mean she was still alive? She should have been dead. I pushed the damned button.

I grabbed the counter and pulled myself to my feet. When I walked through the house, I didn't see her anywhere. When I finished searching the house I stopped in the master bathroom and looked at my face in the mirror. I'd aged a million years over this fucking thing. I wanted Marcy back, but I knew that was not possible.

All I had was Alex, and I had just tried to murder her.

I was tempted to phone the police, but what could I say? We were kidnapped, and I thought I had killed Alex, but maybe she was still alive somewhere?

What a mess.

I went to my bed, sprawled out as I did when Marcy shared the space beside me, and I fell asleep almost instantly.

It was three days before I found Alex.

She came home, probably not expecting me to be there. Or maybe she just didn't care. She hesitated when she came in and saw me, but it was only for a few seconds. Then she stormed past me and went to her room.

As she rushed past me, I could smell the perfume she'd worn since she was twelve. She was a petite girl, barely reaching my shoulder, and as she passed, I felt an unexpected feeling. I wanted to grab her and hold her to me.

Of course I didn't.

She knew what had happened.

When she'd gathered a few things, she stomped back to the living room and was about to leave.

"Alex?"

I thought she'd ignore me, but she stopped in her tracks, her back to me.

"Please," I said. "I just want to—" What did I want to do? I didn't know how to finish the sentence. Finally I blurted out, "I'm so sorry."

I collapsed onto the couch and started crying. I had no idea what to do with myself and certainly no idea what I wanted *her* to do.

"Dad?"

I struggled to lift my head. She looked at me with those beautiful eyes she'd inherited from Marcy. I blinked back the tears and wiped my face with my hands.

"I didn't know what you were going to choose," she said. "But then, when you pushed the button, I saw that light blue ray coming from that gun and hitting my neck. If it was a real laser, you would have killed me. We both thought it was real, like the one that killed Mom, but it wasn't. I think they just wanted me to know that you were ready to kill me."

"I didn't know what I was doing."

She thought about that for a moment, and I wanted to rush over and hug her. I wanted to tell her how I was wrong to have blamed her and that we could work things out. We just needed to *want* to make things right. We were family.

She smiled and said, "I hope they take us again. I want it to be my decision this time, so I can kill *you*."

My smile fell away from my face.

"I never want to see you again."

She turned and left.

I stayed on the couch for an hour. It was the longest hour of my life. I'd lost both my girls, and it was sinking in that nothing would ever change that.

I had a gun in the bedroom. It'd been there ever since we first moved into the house. Like many people, I wanted to protect my family, and that was one tool I thought I might one day use to do that.

Protecting my family was no longer an option. But I

could remove some of the pain.

I felt old and alone.

I put the cold steel barrel of the gun in my mouth and counted down from five.)(

Anniversary

One day in the summer of 2019, John J. Questore emailed me to ask if I'd be interested in contributing a story to a charity anthology he was editing called Dark Tides.

Unfortunately, the theme of the book would be oceans and other bodies of water, and I had nothing already written that met the theme, nor did I have any ideas. I replied to John that I had to reluctantly decline.

Later that day, I visited my wonderful sister, Susan Van Aarsen, and her husband, John.

Susan indirectly gave me the idea for a new story, and it was set on a beach.

As soon as I got home, I wrote John Questore telling him to forget my decline and that I would be writing a new story for him.

"Anniversary" ended up being one of the most emotional stories I've ever written. I wrote it over a few hours, barely taking time for a breath.

You see, I wrote the story about my sister and brother-in-law. John was dying, and Susan was recovering from a knee replacement. (In the story, I aged them 20 years but kept their love story.)

I kept the story a secret because I wanted to surprise Susan and John with the published copy. I never had the chance.

Dark Tides was published on October 1, 2019. John died of cancer a day later. Susan died of a broken heart two days after John.

"Anniversary" means so much more to me now, because it's the story of their love that I never shared with them.

IT WAS SIXTY YEARS ago to the day when they first met.

Jimmy Lamars didn't need any help remembering, because it was not only the anniversary of the day they met, a year later they married on the same day. August 1st.

To add to that, August 1st was also his birthday.

He'd wandered down to the beach that day when he turned twenty-three, expecting nothing but an afternoon of reflection and peace.

Jimmy had just changed jobs, and the new one wasn't really working out for him. They expected him to work long hours and to be available on weekends.

He wasn't too into that, because he was finding he had almost no time to himself.

Who wanted to be locked into a career that left him no free time to enjoy his life?

He was twenty-three for Christ's sake. His life was just beginning, and he knew it.

"Not me," he said as he took his sandals off and walked slowly out to the water. The beach sand was squishy between his toes, and he loved the feel of the blistering sun beating down on him.

It was a hot day, maybe the hottest of that summer.

Hibbon's Cove was off the beaten path. He had driven fifty miles from Bangor to reach the secluded area just south of Bay Harbor. He'd found the place by accident two summers earlier while wandering along the Maine coastline.

Jimmy never told a soul about Hibbon's Cove. He'd been there a half dozen times since then, to walk in the refreshing water, watch the tides come in and out, and to just be alone with his thoughts. It was the perfect place to go when he needed to make a big decision.

He was already a heavy man, more than two hundred twenty pounds, and when he was walking his beach alone, he never had to worry about anybody laughing at him.

It was his own private paradise. Until that day.

Gail Sommers had also tripped across Hibbon's Cove by herself. Well, in her case, it was her and two girlfriends who had found the quiet little beach together. She was twenty-one and her two besties were both leaving Bangor to move to New York City.

They'd only given her two weeks notice that they were going to the Big Apple to find themselves. Whatever that meant.

They hadn't asked her to join them, which hurt, but she also knew she wouldn't have gone. Maine was where she'd been born and where she would probably live her entire life.

"I'm going to miss you guys so much," she said as they walked the lonely beach. Trish and Amber smiled and nodded. It was during that walk that Gail realized that although they were her besties, she wasn't theirs.

Secretly she couldn't help thinking it was the same as always.

According to her daddy, Gail was big-boned. That sounded like something she was born with, so it wasn't her fault she was bigger than the Barbie dolls walking with her. They were twigs compared to her, and when they didn't invite her to go to New York with her, she knew it was because they didn't see her in the same league as them.

Walking on the deserted beach and understanding that fact made Gail horribly sad.

Ten days later, Trish and Amber left with a small trailer dragging along behind Trish's car (the one her own daddy had given her for her 18th birthday), and they hit the road.

They never answered her phone calls or letters. This was before emails and texting, but she later knew they would have ignored those too.

Hibbon's Cove should have been a sad place for her, but it wasn't. It was a place of transition for her, moving from being a dumb girl who had no clue to a woman who was starting to understand how the world worked.

From that day, Gail thought of the Cove as a place she could just be herself, without worrying about what anyone else thought about her.

On August 1st, *that* August 1st sixty years ago, Jimmy and Gail both walked on the sand at Hibbon's Cove, each expecting to find nobody else to share the beach with, and so each was shocked to see another person there.

Jimmy saw Gail first, and his initial reaction was to want to cover his belly, but he had left his T-shirt in the car. He had nothing to hide behind, and his belly fat spilled out over his bathing suit like always.

He wanted to just turn around and leave, but he could tell that Gail saw him. If he left now, he'd look like—what?—like a freak? A coward? He didn't even know, and he didn't have much time to think about it.

The girl was walking toward him.

He looked at her and tried to smile. He felt trapped, mentally as well as physically, since his feet were being sucked into the wet sand as waves spilled over his toes. It felt like quicksand, and for a moment he was afraid he'd be sucked right down, but of course no such thing happened.

After hesitating, he started to walk toward her. She was smiling at him.

When they got closer to each other, she said, "I thought I was the only person who knew about this place." She laughed.

He felt a wave of relief wash over him. Something about that laugh just set his mind at ease.

"And I thought that, too."

They stared at each other, as if they were the only two humans left in a dead world.

Jimmy didn't know what to say. He just wanted to see that smile again.

Gail had smiled because she was afraid. It was an odd habit she knew she had, but there was nothing she could do about it. She smiled in lots of other circumstances, too, but this time it was due to fear.

Who was this strange man who was encroaching on *her* beach?

"I'm Gail," she finally said.

"I'm Jimmy."

He didn't know if he should offer to shake hands. That might be weird.

Gail was calming down. She liked the sound of his voice. It wasn't scary. In fact, he seemed as nervous as she was.

It took them ten minutes before they both shook their jitters and were able to be comfortable.

Neither one knew that this was the start of a lifetime together.

Now, Jimmy was turning eighty-three on this August 1st.

Gail was eighty-one, going to turn eighty-two on December 14th.

They'd woken that morning, full of the normal pains and problems they woke up with every day. Growing old is not for the meek, especially when serious health problems come along for the ride.

Jimmy was taking a chemo-break. It'd been two years since the cancer first showed up in his bowel. At times he considered himself lucky to have lasted until then without any serious problems, but once that bit of cancer showed up, everything changed.

Hastily arranged surgery removed part of his bowel, along with his prostrate and his bladder. Those organs were collateral damage since they couldn't get the bowel cancer out without taking those, too.

Since then he wore a couple of bags stuck to his body all the time, taking care of his piss and shit.

Maybe that would have been okay if that was all there was to it, but oh no, the cancer had other ideas. After some initially promising check-ups, the cancer showed up again. This time in his liver and a spot on one of his lungs.

Jimmy was subjected to radiotherapy and lots of chemo sessions. Lots.

Sometimes the chemo made him nauseated, and he wouldn't eat for days on end, even when pushed to it by Gail.

The last rounds, though, were different chemicals, and these ones made him want to eat non-stop.

Weird.

He'd ballooned back up to two hundred seventy-five pounds, and he supposed he would die one day soon, way too big for a standard casket.

Have to make those arrangements before it's too late, he'd often think to himself. But he hadn't ever followed through on that. He didn't want to leave the funeral details to Gail, but it felt like if he went to chat to the local undertaker, he'd be giving up.

Gail's health problems weren't life-threatening, but they were equally debilitating.

She'd had her right knee replaced ten years earlier, and now she'd had to have the left one replaced. She could barely walk, even with crutches, but at least she knew that was temporary. After a few months, she be waddling along the same as she always had.

Gail never commented about Jimmy being so overweight. After all, from the day they'd met, she'd never been slim, and now although she knew she tipped the scale at 204, she wouldn't ever mention that to him.

Jimmy loved Gail with all his heart.

Gail loved Jimmy just as much.

Sixty years together didn't seem nearly enough, but both knew they'd be lucky to celebrate 61.

That morning, Jimmy creaked to life when the dawn sunshine reached down from their bedroom window. He'd been dreaming about that long-lost day when they first met.

It hurt to move at all, and it took a lot of energy just to roll over to face Gail. He was breathing hard and took a moment to catch his breath.

Gail smiled. She knew the effort it took him. It was almost as bad for her.

"We should go to Hibbon's Cove," he said.

She frowned and said, "What are you talking about? It's been years."

Jimmy nodded. "I think it's been twenty years since we were there."

He wondered how that was possible. It was their special place, but somehow, they seemed to have forgotten all about it.

Twenty years? Really?

Yes, maybe twenty-one or twenty-two. He wasn't

sure.

"It'd be awfully hard on us," Gail said.

Jimmy shrugged. "Easier today than next year." He paused and added, "I think we deserve to see it one last time."

Gail nodded, knowing she would do anything for the man she loved.

"Should we pack a lunch?"

"Yes. Tuna sandwiches and Coke."

She smiled. That was the same lunch they'd taken almost every time they'd gone to visit the Cove when they were young.

She remembered them running out to meet the tide, catching the waves that crashed over their bodies, laughing as the powerful water pulled them every which way, and grabbing each other's hands to help them stay stable.

Jimmy leaned over and gave his wife a long kiss. He didn't care how much it hurt.

Jimmy had given up his driver's licence a year earlier, and Gail couldn't really drive with her new knee still in training mode, so they called an Uber to take them to Hibbon's Cove.

It took them more than a few minutes just to get themselves out of the car. The Uber driver had to help pull each of them out in turn, and he asked, "Are you sure you folks will be okay? You don't look too..."

Stable? Healthy? Alive?

Jimmy didn't know how he had planned to finish that sentence, but he supposed any of those words would fit.

"It's okay," he said. "We come here all the time."

"Okay, well, you can request me when you want to go back home if you want."

Jimmy nodded and didn't look back as he and Gail shuffled down the skinny little path that led through some trees and eventually down to the Cove.

"Think anyone else has found our little paradise yet?" he asked Gail.

She smiled and looked at him. He still loved that smile.

There was nobody else on the beach, which is what they expected. They set the bag of sandwiches and cans of Coke down and looked out to the water.

It was as beautiful a day as either could remember. The sky was pure blue, a deep blue that somehow seemed to reflect the deep color of the water below.

The beach was empty of people, empty of garbage, empty of all signs of humanity.

Jimmy liked that.

They looked out to the water. It was low tide, so the ocean seemed a very long way from them.

He hesitated, not sure he could walk that far. He didn't have to look at Gail to know she was thinking the same thing. She had brought a single crutch to use on her left side, but it was as hard for her to walk as it was for him.

It wasn't just his cancer or her knee. Their bodies were old, and they just couldn't support their heavy weights like they used to.

Fuck it, he thought. He looked at Gail and smiled.

"We'll never come back. This is our only chance. We

can't miss this last chance."

Gail didn't answer for a moment, and he was afraid she was going to say no.

Finally, she nodded and said, "It's our life."

The first steps were easy enough. The sand was mostly dry, and they didn't really sink in. Jimmy's feet seemed to have some kind of memory, as if they were young and happy to be in the sand.

Twenty years? Really?

Gail used her crutch but was struggling to move. He wanted to take her hand and help, but with him being a bit unstable himself, he was afraid he'd make both of them fall.

They moved slowly, occasionally glancing at each other and smiling support.

The sun bounced off Gail's hair, and it almost brought tears to Jimmy's eyes. She was beautiful.

He had dropped his shirt, so he was wearing only shorts. He no longer owned an actual bathing suit. Gail was wearing an old dress she didn't care about. It was bright yellow, perfectly matching the sun.

The sun itself was beaming down and was hotter than Jimmy could ever remember. Was it always this hot? He was sweating, rivulets of water flushing down the rolls of his upper body.

He didn't see any sweat falling from Gail. *Figures*, he thought.

Gail didn't notice any of that. All she could think of was trying desperately to put one foot in front of the other without falling. She didn't want to look like a fool in front of Jimmy. She'd done that quite enough times in her life, thank you very much.

She never would have tried this without his encouragement. She wanted to look back, to see how far they'd walked out, but she was afraid that if she did, she'd lose her nerve.

She had to be strong for Jimmy.

Jimmy was breathing hard. He was already worn out, and they'd only covered about half the distance to the water.

"Wish it wasn't low tide," he said softly.

"We would have come no matter what," Gail said.

He grunted.

She added, "Back in the day, we'd have run out to the water in seconds. At least this way we get to enjoy the walk."

Jimmy burst out laughing in spite of himself. "Yes," he said, "It's a beautiful walk."

And it was.

His one and only love was walking with him on an amazing afternoon. How could he complain about that?

"It would have been nice to have a cool breeze," he said.

"Sure would."

Jimmy wondered how long they'd been walking, but he wasn't wearing his watch. It wasn't waterproof and he was firm in his belief that he'd be out sitting in the water very soon.

Another ten minutes passed, and they reached the water.

It started with little pools that had held the last of the retreating water. Jimmy wondered if that meant the tide was still going out or if it was coming in now.

He hated that his memory was failing. Even ten years ago he would have known how the damned tides worked. Now it was just a big puzzle.

"Oh, it's cold!" said Gail.

"It always feels that way," Jimmy answered. "But, you're right, I'd forgotten that, too."

"It's nice on my toes."

He nodded. "Let's keep going."

They walked more, and Jimmy tried to convince himself it was getting easier. His feet were all wet now, water up to his ankles. The cool water was soothing the pain in his feet, but it wasn't helping the pain in the rest of his body.

He felt weak, and he gritted his teeth to try to gain control of himself. He would *not* fall down in front of Gail.

"Should we stop here?" she asked.

"Just a little farther," he whispered. He wanted to stop there, too, but it would be like they were little two-year-olds splashing in the water on their first trip to the beach.

He was a man, not a baby.

He walked another step and Gail followed.

"Just up to our knees," he promised.

She didn't answer, and he wasn't sure if she was okay with that decision or not, but he really needed them to go a little farther. Just a bit. Far enough that he would leave the toddler area behind him.

"Remember we'd come out here with our Frisbee and stand fifty feet apart throwing it to each other? Other times we'd toss a football," said Jimmy.

"We'll not be doing that today, my dear."

"Oh, I know. It's just the good memories flooding me."

"Me too."

"Sometimes we'd go a bit deeper and you'd stand on my shoulders, looking like the Statue of Liberty. I'd crouch down and then push you up as high as I could, and you'd do a freedom dive into the water."

She smiled, and this time she reached out and took his hand.

"I remember," she said.

They stood still and looked out together. The water wasn't up to his knees, but they'd gone as far as he could manage. He was exhausted.

He turned to her and smiled. A tear fell down his cheek.

"Jimmy? What's wrong?"

He was choked up with emotion and couldn't answer her. He just shook his head. Then he sniffed and tried to get control of himself. He made a downward motion with his hands and both of them took some very cautious movements to lower themselves to sit on the sand.

Jimmy was almost out of breath. He tried to take a deep long breath, but it was hard. *That* was the effect of the chemo, he was sure.

He looked back to shore. From the perspective of sitting there, the shore looked forever away.

"Are you okay?" Gail's voice sounded concerned.

"I'm fine. I just needed to catch my breath. "How are you doing?"

"Well, I don't know how I'm going to get back up, but right now I feel fine!" She laughed. She'd used her crutch to get herself down to the sandy ground. Now she set it on the other side from her. She kept a hand on it so it wouldn't float away.

Jimmy watched the waves lap at them. When they slapped his belly, it sounded like a tiny cheering section.

Clap, clap, clap.

He tried to shimmy himself a little bit closer to Gail, but he couldn't manage it. The sand was sucking his body down, and his eighty-three-year-old muscles didn't have the strength to argue.

Gail said, "I think we were sitting right around here when you asked me to marry you."

Jimmy opened his mouth in surprise. He'd forgotten proposing to her here, but that was right! That's exactly right!

"You're as beautiful now as you were then."

She smiled and then looked out to the water.

"I think the tide is coming in."

Jimmy glanced over and saw waves that looked a little bit bigger than he'd expected. They continued to slap at his belly.

"I think you're right. Might make it easier to walk back."

"I'll take all the help I can get!"

If I can't move my whole body over... he thought. He lay down and supported himself on his right elbow. Then he could reach her with his outstretched left arm. He just wanted to touch her.

"Sixty years," he said.

She was lost in thought and didn't reply.

They sat for thirty minutes, each swimming in their

own memories of the many wonderful times they'd spent in this same water. They'd make comments occasionally, but all they really needed was to touch hands.

Gail was also lying down now, trying to regain some of the strength she'd lost by walking out this far. Her knee throbbed and screamed to her brain to not be so fucking stupid, but she ignored that, preferring only to think of wonderful memories with her husband.

"Do you think we should go back?" asked Gail.

Jimmy really didn't want to, but he knew she was right. They'd done what they came for, and the memories of this day would have to satisfy them in the future.

That's not such a bad thing, he thought.

He was still lying down, and he pulled his legs toward himself.

They hurt and didn't want to move. The tide was indeed coming in, and he was surprised that his legs were totally covered. How did that happen?

He took a different strategy and leaned over to his right, bringing his left arm around as if he was going to do a push-up.

As if.

That didn't work, either. He didn't have the strength to push himself up.

Not even close.

"Sweetie, I think I'm going to need you to help me up."

Jimmy was embarrassed at having to ask for help.

Getting old really sucks.

He kept trying to move his body around to get some traction, but nothing seemed to work. He was stuck lying in the water and had no way to help himself.

"Good thing I've got you here," he said.

He glanced over at Gail, but she was struggling, too. That's when he noticed her crutch had somehow gotten loose and was floating independently toward shore.

He'd have to help her walk, once they got up.

That's okay. I'm still her knight in shining armor. I can do that.

Now, Gail was struggling with her own breathing. She'd pushed and pushed but she was too frail to get her own body lifted off the sandy bottom.

Stupid fat woman.

She never called herself fat out loud, but she'd used that term her whole life in her deepest, most private thoughts. Now, she was glad the word hadn't slipped out. She felt totally useless. What kind of a woman can't even stand up?

She was out of breath and hadn't moved an inch.

In frustration, she looked over at Jimmy. He was squirming around, having as much trouble as she was.

She needed his help, but he needed hers.

"This is ridiculous," she said.

The water lapped on her belly, and she wanted to yell at the damned ocean. It was like the tide was laughing at her.

How the hell could we both be stuck out here?

More importantly, how can we get back to shore?

Gail tried to turn herself over, to try to crawl, but she couldn't make the transition. She had no muscle power to push her body over. It was like trying to use a pitchfork to turn over Mount Everest.

"Jimmy, what are we going to do?"

Jimmy had no answer for her. He kept squirming as much as she was, but he wasn't having any more luck than her.

Finally, he stopped. He was overcome with the effort and saw black spots in front of his eyes. He knew he was about to faint, but he couldn't allow that. The water was only a foot or so deep, but it was enough for him to drown.

He pressed his eyes closed, as if that would somehow stop him from blacking out, and maybe it worked. He kept conscious. Barely. In a corner of his mind, he heard Gail calling to him, but he couldn't make out any of her words.

Jimmy wanted to just turn back the clock and not have this crazy idea of going out into the water.

What was he thinking?

Water splashed onto his face, and he flashed his eyes open.

"The water," he mumbled.

"What?"

He took as deep a breath as he could. "Water is rising. Fast."

Gail noticed for the first time. The water level had been rising so slowly, it hadn't registered, but she could see it was higher now. *Much* higher.

"Oh, god…"

"Don't panic," said Jimmy.

"But, what can we do?"

"I... I don't know."

Gail tried to look back toward shore, to see how far away her crutch was, but she couldn't see it. Water was lapping in her face, too.

"Jimmy, I'm afraid."

He didn't hear her. A larger wave had splashed onto his face, and he'd started choking from the water he'd swallowed.

With the tide coming in, his body wasn't as pinned to the sandy bottom, but it didn't seem to matter. He still couldn't find the energy to move his body around or to sit up. He was paralyzed, with no energy reserves. The cancer treatments had sucked all the life from him, and now it was leaving him for dead

The next wave came quickly and then the next.

Gail couldn't really see much, because she was battling her own fight. It seemed like the waves had just started a battle that only they could win.

Her knee was killing her, but she knew it was old age that had sapped all her strength.

After another dozen waves splashed over her harder and harder, she knew she wouldn't last long.

All she wanted was to hold Jimmy's hand one more time.

She reached out, but she wasn't sure if she was touching him or if it was just her imagination.

The waves kept rolling over the two lifelong lovers, and eventually they both stopped fighting.

It was three days later when Allan and Theresa Gilson

walked through the pathway to find their way down to Hibbon's Cove. It was their own private beach. As far as they knew, nobody else ever came here.

This was their third wedding anniversary. They'd made a habit of coming to the beach each August 4th, and they hoped it would be that way their entire lives.

After all, this was where they had met, five years earlier.

They laughed and ran down to the beach. As they got close, they flipped off their sandals and kissed, a long loving kiss that would start their little anniversary off on the right foot.

As they broke the kiss, Theresa pointed out a bag that was sitting on the sand. They went to look and found there was some sandwiches and a couple of cans of Coke.

"That's odd," Allan said.

"I guess somebody else knows about this place after all."

"I guess."

They looked around. It was Theresa who saw them.

"Over there."

They ran two hundred feet down the beach and out toward the water. As they got close they could see the two bodies. A man and a woman, partly eaten by birds and crabs.

Some of their bodies were under sand, and great patches of skin were peeled off.

Their faces were horrible. Grotesque. Barely recognizable as human. Theresa and Allan couldn't help tears falling from their eyes when they saw that the corpses were holding hands. X

By Insanity
or Reason

You may know Lisa Morton as the past president of the Horror Writers Association. Or as the world's premier expert on Halloween. Or as a wonderful novelist and short story writer. Or as a screen writer.

I know her as a very dear friend.

We'd chatted for years about writing a story together one day, something that would merge our respective writing strengths and produce something neither of us could produce alone.

Eventually, we got serious. I suggested an overall structure and Lisa immediately created an outline we could both follow. We took turns writing chapters (and in case you're curious, she wrote Crystal's chapters while I wrote Richard's.)

The writing was a blast! I think we both had more fun writing this than anything else for years.

The story was published originally as a standalone novella by Bad Moon Press, and it remains one of the stories that gives me the fondest memories.

CHAPTER 1: CRYSTAL

I DID SOMETHING very, very bad.

I think that's what they want me to say. Dr. Reeves and the rest. They think I don't understand what I did. Or that I haven't "owned" it, as Dr. Reeves likes to say. Sometimes I wonder if she got her degree from a self-help book. Most of the time she's not so bad, though.

I *do* know what I did. The problem is... I don't think it's—

There goes Sarie screaming again. I thought we'd have a nice quiet dayroom today, but something's set her off. She thinks her children are burning. Again. It's always that.

One of the nurses here told me Sarie never had children. She's sixty-three and has been in here since she was twenty-four.

She's really bad today. Nurse Danetha and Nurse Anna can't hold her still long enough to wrap her or shoot her, so they're calling for Ben, the big men's ward intern. Ben scares me. He weighs at least 300 pounds, has a badly broken nose, and an ugly tattoo under the gray fur on his right upper arm. Somebody —I forget who—told me once that he was in the Navy but got kicked out. Dishonorable discharge. I believe that.

He comes into our dayroom like a bull fresh out of the gate at a rodeo. He grabs Sarie from behind, and she just folds. She's got that much sense left, at least. He drags her out of the room as the nurses trail behind, cursing and muttering.

When they're all gone, the dayroom goes back to being uneventful. It's not really accurate to call it "quiet," ever, because there's always the television blaring from the ceiling, and there's usually Maggie, humming the same five notes in a tuneless disorder, over and over. Maggie's humming blends with the television's drone and rises to join with the buzz of the greenish fluorescents high overhead. I wonder if the sound goes farther up to meld with something else, wind or the whispers of stars. Or God.

Something from the television makes me tune out Maggie and the lights and God and I listen. It's set to a game show, and the category is flowers.

I used to love flowers. I think I had a garden, where I grew... what? Was it... begonias? No, that's not right. Pansies? Violets? Violence—

I can't remember. I can't remember what I grew.

I asked Dr. Reeves about that last week. She said it was a side effect of one of the medications.

But I don't want to forget. I had... or I think I had... a good life. I want to remember, but here, in this lost place, it's slipping away more and more every day... lost...

What I did wasn't wrong.

I'm going to tell that to Dr. Reeves at our next session. Wait... I think I've said that already, but ...

How long have I been here?

I don't think it's been long. For one thing, I'm still much younger than most of the other women. They have gray hair and sagging skin and dull eyes. I have dark brown hair and good skin and...

Suddenly I want to cry. I'm not even sure why, except that some part of me is screaming that my eyes aren't dull *yet* and I want to go home and I want see my—

"See what?"

I look up, surprised, and realize I'm not sure how long I've been sitting here in Dr. Reeves's office. Her face is even younger than mine, her expression still kind and curious.

That'll change after she's been here a while longer.

But for now she's peering at me closely, and I know something is expected of me. "See my children."

"Crystal, you know that's not possible."

I think about that for a moment, and then I'm thankful for the pills she gives me, the pills that dull some of the pain. "Oh. Of course."

Dr. Reeves watches me a few more seconds, then takes a deep breath and writes something on her pad. "We're going to try adjusting some of your medications. You seem to be having a lot of trouble focusing."

"Okay." I hope that's the right answer. I never know with her.

She looks up again. "Is there anything else you'd like to talk about today?"

I shrug, try to think back. "Flowers..."

"Flowers?"

"I grew them. I loved flowers."

"I think we all love flowers. Did you have a nice garden?"

I nod. "With a fountain, and I remember that he loved..."

I realize I'm not sure who "he" was.

I try to remember. Dr. Reeves prods. "Tell me about him."

And then out of the word "he," images come, flinging themselves at me. A man, tall, a slight paunch, with a heavy five-o'-clock shadow and the beginnings of silver at the temples.

And I've got a knife and I'm driving it into him, over and over. Maybe this isn't a real memory, but... no, it is. I remember the strange metallic scent of the blood, and how warm and sticky it was when some got on me, and there was a *lot* on me—

"I killed him," I say.

Dr. Reeves smiles now. It might be the first time I've ever seen her smile. It bothers me. "Very good. We're making some real progress now."

"I killed him," I say again, then add, "and I don't think I did anything bad."

The smile vanishes.

And I realize that was not what Dr. Reeves wanted to hear.

CHAPTER 2: RICHARD

(one month earlier)

THE BAR IS TWO blocks from home, one block north and one east on Fairway Road. I haven't been here in years, and it's not a fuck bit different now than it was last time.

Same fat, bald bartender even.

I sit and light a cigarette and wait for fatso to notice me.

"Beer. Draught."

He frowns and walks to me. "We have four kinds. Heineken, Bud—"

"Yeah, Bud. I'll take two."

As he walks back, I yell out, "Hey, fuck that noise. Make it Heineken tonight."

He shrugs and I laugh and I enjoy that sweet tobacco taste.

The bar is full of smoke and it stinks. There's nothing good to say about it except it has beer. And it's walking distance. And sometimes, hard-up skanks come in looking for a bit of fun.

It's celebration time.

Fatso drops off two pints of beer. "Run a tab," I tell him.

Yup... celebration time.

I drink a long slug. It's cold and feels like liquid gold.

There's a television hanging above the bar. Wolf Blitzer is talking about some political crap. Another election. Whatever.

It's 3:00 in the afternoon and I just walked off my job. Told Markie to go stuff himself. I'm sure I'll see a pink slip in the mail. Like I care. I've had it with grunt work manufacturing. Time to do something fun.

"Is this chair taken?"

She's prettier than I'd hoped for. About my age, thirty or so, shoulder-length straight red hair, a nice smile. Killer body.

"Help yourself."

I move my second beer over to her.

"Oh, I don't know if I—"

"Go ahead. Neither of us needs to pretend."

She hesitates but then smiles and takes the beer. *That was easy*, I think.

"Do you live around here?" She checks out the Nike swish on my fake T-shirt and seems to like it.

"Yeah. You?"

"Yes, I live nearby. What do you do for a living?"

"Retired."

"Really?" Her eyes open wide and I can see that she really *is* a pretty girl.

"As of today. I'm celebrating."

"You look so young to retire. What will you do?"

Stupid girl. "Charity work. I fund a foundation that does cancer research. I'll probably write a book now that I have the time. Travel. See the world. Maybe give the occasional lecture, just to keep in practice."

"Wow."

"Retiring is nice. But that's not why I'm celebrating."

"Why are you celebrating then?"

I lean over to her and whisper into her ear. "It's a secret."

Stupid-girl takes a drink and licks her lips. I imagine licking them for her.

"I won't tell anyone."

"I'm not sure I could really say..."

"It sounds like a big secret."

"Oh, it is. It certainly is."

I know I've got her hook, line, and pussy. She puts a hand on my thigh.

I'm not ready yet... part of the celebration is the beer. It's been a long time. I wave at fatso and he pours us two more pints.

As I slide stupid-girl's glass closer to her, I see her look down at my ring finger.

We both stare at the wedding ring. It's got three diamonds embedded in a beautiful wide band. The only thing of value I ever really owned. Well, it *looks* that way, anyhow.

I twist it off and give it to the girl. "Old times," I say. "It's yours."

I imagine her trying to figure out what she can buy with the cash this would generate, and it's so tempting to follow her when she takes it to the pawn shop.

"I'll treasure it always."

"I know you will."

We drink in silence for a few minutes. The place stinks of stale beer. Nobody can hear Wolf on CNN because there's a constant stream of 70s music playing over a loud speaker. Elton John, Queen, Paul McCartney and Wings, James Taylor... it feels like a time warp, back to a time before I was born.

I take the last slug of beer and smile. "Let's go. Your place works."

She nods and leaves an inch of beer. I drop a twenty and a ten on the counter and walk stupid-girl out the door.

Her place is a basement apartment a block away. The bar would be her local hangout, so I wouldn't be back there again. No need to see her a second time.

When we get to her place, I don't waste any time. I tear all her clothes off and she rips into mine. We kiss as we do that, and I can taste raspberry lipstick.

I take off her bra and panties and throw her on top of her bed and then pounce on her. I kiss her breasts and feel her pussy to be sure she's wet and then I just move between her legs and fuck her. I fuck her hard, pounding into her. I couldn't give a shit about her pleasure; we both know this isn't about her. Even so, I can see she actually is enjoying it, and fuck if she doesn't come before me. I don't care, just keep pushing harder and harder until I come, too.

I push deep inside her when I come. "Oh, fuck, that feels good."

I roll off her and catch my breath. I want a cigarette but that can wait a minute.

She rubs my arm. "You liked that, huh?"

"You were great, babe. What's your name?"

"Mary."

"Hi, Mary. Nice to meet you. I'm Richard."

"You look like a Richard."

Fuck? I *look* like a Richard? Jesus, what a twat.

"Can you tell me now? What are you celebrating?"

The apartment has some weird smell like some kind of flowers. That's the last thing I need. Time to get moving.

"Sure. I was celebrating freedom. Not freedom 'cause of retirement, 'cause that was just a lie to get you into bed. Really, though, freedom. Real, honest freedom. Freedom from being pursued by people who want to do me harm."

I stare at her, her smile long gone. I laugh and get dressed and leave stupid-girl to her plastic ring.

Chapter 3: Crystal

(five hours earlier)

It's 10:32 A.M. now, and the jury's still out.

(God, that's such a clichéd phrase. It's strange when you realize it's true, it's what is really happening right now.)

It's the second day they've been out. My attorney says that's good.

I don't understand that. How can it be good?

Oh, I think I see. If they were going to find me guilty (a death sentence?), they would probably have done it quickly.

This might sound ridiculous, but... I don't want to die. Even after everything that's happened, after... well, you know. A lot of people would want to die after something like that. They might kill themselves, or just let themselves wither away. Of course some people argue that what I did was a form of suicide, but that was never my intention.

At least I don't think it was.

I just wanted that bastard dead. And then it

happened. He was dead. And I wanted to go on living. I still do.

I want to live now so that I can celebrate the fact that he's dead. That I killed him, and he's gone. If I have a year, ten years, forty... every day will be a celebration from now on. The more the better.

I'm still a little surprised that I'm here at all, frankly. I mean that I'm here on trial for what I did. Isn't it obvious that it was the right thing? That the man was a monster, and I stopped him? I should be rewarded, not put through this. What I did...

It was murder, wasn't it?

But it was a *good* murder.

It was the only time in my entire life that I ever felt powerful and in control. Before that... well, I've always been the good one, the over-functioner, Miss Non-Assertive. I'm just a girl who can't say no. Need a maid? Me. Can I get you another cup of coffee? Right away. A doormat? Here I am. Excuse me, sir, scrape again—you missed a clump on that foot. I went from taking care of two brothers to taking care of one husband, all at the tender age of 19. I never had time for myself. Who knows what I could have done? I might have run my own nursery. Maybe even been a... what do they call an expert on plants? ... a botanist.

All right, maybe I was never that smart, but the nursery... I could have run a nursery.

I'll never know now. The jury won't be delivering a "not guilty" verdict. We never tried for that.

I don't even know, really, if he was a good or bad husband. In the beginning, I mean. He was the only man I'd ever dated, let alone slept with. The sex was nothing great to me, but my girlfriend Joanna told me it was that way with her husband, too. In other respects he was no crueler or more distant or dismissive than my brothers or my father had ever been. I guess he was about average.

In the beginning.

Oh, the jury's coming back now. As they file into the jury box, I look at them to see if I can guess how they've decided.

None of them look at me. That's probably not good.

My attorney, Aaron, grabs my wrist. Maybe he means it to be calming, but it's not. He seems agitated; he's gripping too tight. He's obviously more anxious about this than I am.

I suppose that makes sense. After all, he's got a reputation resting on the outcome. I've only got a life.

But I did say it was a life I wanted to keep, didn't I?

The judge is saying something. I'm not really paying attention to that part. The jury foreman stands up. It's a middle-aged woman, wearing a prim business suit, her hair neatly cut and styled. She looks successful; the suit is nicely tailored, and I think the single gold chain around her throat is probably real.

She could have been me.

She has a piece of paper in her hand, and she starts reading from it. There are a few preliminary words I don't really hear. I'm only waiting for the important ones. And then she says them:

"...by reason of insanity."

Next to me, Aaron lets out a breath and turns to smile at me. He releases my wrist and claps a hand to my shoulder. He's obviously relieved and pleased.

I know it's supposed to be good. It means I won't be facing the death penalty or life in prison, that I'll be in a well-staffed care facility with medications and doctors. But...

It still startles me, to hear it spoken out loud like that. For a second I want to stand up and shout at little Miss Executive: "I'm not insane, not now and not then! How idiotic are you to even think that?"

But I don't. Instead I concentrate on sitting still.

There's activity in the courtroom now. Murmurs behind me, the judge saying something in front of me... but it's taking all of my energy to just stay seated and calm.

Then I look down and see something that rivets me:

My ring. The wide band with the three diamonds.

I remember the day he slipped it onto my finger. Our wedding. I stood there in my white dress, in front of 200 relatives and friends, and I thought, This is the happiest day of my life.

But even then I knew the truth: It wasn't. I didn't feel anything. I thought only that it was a lovely ring, and must have cost him a fortune.

I wonder briefly if the ring will be taken from me when I arrive at the hospital. My new home.

Probably forever.

I realize I don't want it any more anyway. So I take it off. I have to struggle a bit; after all, I haven't removed it from that finger in 17 years. But it finally slides off, leaving a little circle of differently-colored skin around my finger.

I hand it to Aaron.

He looks down, mystified. "What's this?" he says.

"A gift," I tell him. Then, because it's funny to me, I add:

"From my husband."

Aaron doesn't laugh.

CHAPTER 4: RICHARD

(one week earlier)

SHE WAS ON THE news again tonight, or at least her scummy lawyer was. Guy just looks like a weasel, graying moustache above a twitching lip. Says he believes justice will be served and his client will be found not guilty.

Is he watching the same fucking trial? Didn't he hear what I testified to?

The reporters yell questions at him but he just waves and wanders off, enhancing his own reputation while probably not caring about her.

I go back to my little job. The scissors slide smoothly as I pick up a pair of women's panties and cut them into small pieces of fabric. Pink. Fluffy.

Pfft.

I take a drink of beer and an anxious feeling runs through me.

What if the bastard actually does get her off?

Where does that leave me?

I pick up the last pair of panties. Blue frills. I

suppose she thought she was sexy in these. I snip one edge and imagine the scissors cutting her whole thigh apart, the blood spurting out everywhere, she crying out in pain as her life gushes out from her.

Snip. Her other thigh. She's the legless wonder now, sliding around in a pool of her own blood. I laugh at the thought. Bitch deserves it.

I finish chopping up the panties and throw the pieces into the fireplace to join all the rest. I'd done her bras earlier.

I want nothing of hers in my home.

She's dead to me.

Just like—

Just fucking like the children.

For a moment, I can't help feeling sentimental. The funeral was exactly six months ago today.

It's a lot quieter in the house, of course. No talking, no music.

And thank God, no flowers. I threw them all out. I'll never understand why people waste money on flowers when somebody dies. It's not like the greenhouse wasn't full of the damned things. I let them all rot. Call it my tribute.

The weasel lawyer thought I'd help by taking the stand. Fine with me. I think he got a big surprise when he asked me the first question.

"Mr. Armstrong, can you describe the demeanor of the defendant on the day after the murder?"

He knew I'd say she was troubled and very repentant and sorry and all that rot. After all, that's what I told him I'd say.

"Well..."

I stared at her, my rehearsed words slipping out slowly, reluctantly.

"She said she was happy she'd done it. That he deserved to die."

Weasel stared at me as if I was talking Chinese. "Mr. Armstrong?" He looked back at his client and then to the jury, as if they could tell him what the hell had just happened.

"You honor, I'd like a short recess, please."

"Denied. We just started. Carry on."

And carry on, we did. Weasel didn't have any other questions, but the prosecution sure did.

Crystal sat there and stared with that freaky blank expression on her face. It was the same look she's had since the trial began.

I take another sip of beer and turn the TV to another channel, hoping to find more coverage of the trial, but no such luck.

No biggie.

I pour lighter fluid on all the bits of fabric that touched her bare skin and then toss a match to poof the bits into a small bonfire in her memory.

Good riddance.

The phone rings and I just let it go to voice mail. Maybe it's Weasel, wanting to know what the fuck I was thinking of.

Maybe it's even Crystal, since she can still phone me. I doubt it, though. She was still just staring straight ahead into space when I finished testifying. It's like she didn't even know I was there.

I finish my beer and pop another one.

The fire burns down and I scrape ashes into a pan

and carefully walk them out to the greenhouse. The dead stalks of her prize roses stink from rot. I sprinkle the ashes at the roots.

Yesterday I took most of her other personal items to the dump: her toothbrush; her blue jeans; her nail polish; her pillow; even the vibrator she didn't think I knew about that was hidden beneath her T-shirts. All so much trash. She won't need them anymore.

The house is starting to feel like it belongs to me alone, and that's exactly how I like it.

No more pretending to give a shit about her. No more having to find excuses to avoid dinner with her. No more endless reruns of CSI always blaring away in the living room.

And no more fucking kids crying.

Feels like freedom to me.

Now as long as that prosecutor does his job and keeps the bitch locked up forever.

CHAPTER 5: CRYSTAL

(four months earlier)

TODAY WAS A PRE-TRIAL hearing. I'm learning a lot of things about the law. I never followed murder cases much, the fake ones on television shows or the real ones in the news. Now I'm one of them.

My attorneys have talked a lot about "NGBI" lately—not guilty by reason of insanity—so today they talked to doctors. It was hard to follow, even though it was me they were talking about. It's strange to hear yourself talked about that way, as if you're not in the room listening. The one psychiatrist wouldn't even look at me while he talked. It was like I wasn't there. I didn't like him when we met, just the two of us alone in a room. He had beady eyes and food stains at the sides of his white beard and he asked me ridiculous questions like did I ever hear voices, or did I think people were out to get me. Other things were just obvious, like did I ever have a hard time making up my mind (who doesn't?), or did I sometimes have trouble remembering things.

I had to answer "yes" to that.

I'm just sane enough to know that there is something wrong with me. I know I wasn't always like this. I know in the past I was an organized person, that I got things done. I know my memory wasn't full of gaps. There are too many things I don't remember now; there are other things I remember but I don't know when they happened exactly. One of the doctors today talked about "TBI", and I remembered that stood for "traumatic brain injury." Several doctors had discussed that around me, so I remembered it.

But I can't remember what my children looked like. What they liked to eat. What their favorite colors were. What television shows they liked, or what they got for their last birthday, or who their favorite superhero was. I have these sort of floating images—like a little boy next to me, and we were reading a book together, a Dr. Seuss children's book—but I can't tell you how old the boy was, or where we were.

I do know the boy was my son. My son, and I can't remember all these things about him. That's why I sometimes start to cry, out of nowhere. It's not because of what I did, and it's not even because the children are gone now. It's because I can't remember them.

One doctor in the courtroom today talked about MRIs and CT scans. She used a phrase I thought was interesting, so I wrote it down—"thalamic volumes." I guess mine were smaller than usual. She said that indicated psychosis. She said the MRI results were also consistent with "post-traumatic amnesia."

Did you know that a machine can tell if you're

crazy?

But I don't think I'm crazy. I know I've had trouble remembering, and sometimes I forget to do simple things like take a shower or put on my shoes. One doctor told me these symptoms were all to be expected "with anyone who'd received a blow to the head" as "severe" as mine. That doctor said there were treatments that could help, and in time I might make a full recovery.

But that doctor wasn't in the courtroom today.

At one point they had me talk to the judge today. The judge seemed like a kind man; he had a patient look and he smiled when he talked to me. "Mrs. Armstrong, do you understand why you're here today?"

I didn't want to disappoint him. He expected an answer, so I said, "Because it's not clear yet."

He frowned, and I felt bad. I should have said something else.

"I'm sorry...?"

I thought for a minute, then said, "Because it's not clear that the man I killed deserved to die."

Suddenly my attorney jumped up, and so did the other attorney, and the hearing ended not long after that.

I guess that means we're going to trial. My attorneys said they'll have a date soon. In the meantime, I'll be here in the county jail. It's pretty awful. They let me have this pad of paper because my doctors say it's good for me to write things down, and it *is* good—it helps me think things through a little better. But I don't like the other women here. A lot of them are here because of drugs, or prostitution. They have tattoos and missing teeth. They push each other and curse and are what my father would have called "low class."

My attorneys say the institution will be better.

If the trial ends with a verdict of NGBI, that is.

CHAPTER 6: RICHARD

(three months earlier)

I KNOW I REALLY shouldn't be here, but I can't stay away. Why? What am I feeling? Gruesome curiosity? Guilt? Sadness? Fuck if I know, but here I am.

The casket is at the front of the church, and some woman in purple robes plays crappy hymns on an organ nearby. I join the line to view the body. There's not that many people in the church, but it looks like a widow in the front row with a couple girls maybe eight or ten years old.

Jack, I never even knew you were married.

I don't dwell on the family. Last thing I want is anyone asking who I am.

We shuffle along, sad faces all, and...

There you are.

I've seen dead people before. Mom died God knows how many years ago, then Dad. Cancer ate them both up. But, I've never been personally responsible for anyone's death. It feels weird looking at him.

Jack's face is more peaceful than it was when he

was alive, fake rosy cheeks, and a calm relaxing pose. Nothing to indicate the boisterous and over-the-top character I knew. They even found a suit for him. It looks new.

I look for signs of his murder, but the folks at the funeral home have done a good job. I thought I might see the top of his head caved in but it all looks normal. Of course all the blood is cleaned up, and he lucked out by still having his face intact.

I'm tempted to lift his head up, just to see what the back of his skull looks like.

The woman behind me shuffles her feet and I move on, back down the center aisle. I see people looking at me, but I don't meet their eyes.

The widow stands as I walk close to her. Shit.

"Do I know you?" she asks.

She's wearing a long black dress with a white shawl. Her face is strained and her eyes bloodshot. Other than that, though, I can see she's a hottie. Can't be over 35. Jack was closer to fifty. At least I think so. Lucky bastard.

Widow has bright green eyes and doesn't seem to be wearing any makeup. She'd be a natural beauty if she wasn't in mourning.

"I met Jack a few times," I answer. "Just some standard business dealings."

I want to add something to the effect that maybe we could talk more about the dead guy at the bar later, but even I know that's crass.

Wait till Jack's in the ground at least.

"Did he hire you to help him?"

I look around and see too many people paying

attention to our conversation, so I pretend not to hear the question.

"I'm very sorry about your loss, Mrs. Jakobi."

I shake her hand and smile before continuing down the aisle to the doors of the church and out into the sunshine. There were probably fifty people in the pews waiting for the service to start. I don't need to be there for that. I just wanted to see that he was really lying there in that casket.

I can't help wondering how I really feel about seeing Jack's dead body.

It's not guilt. I got what I needed, and the price doesn't much matter to me. That bitching widow'd probably would have fucked him into a heart attack one day anyway.

Sadness? No. He was a loose end. If he wasn't dead I'd wonder if he'd betray me the rest of my life. So, it's good he's gone.

Regret? Maybe. He did help me and he might have been useful in the future.

I drive back home and go to my computer and pull up my e-mail. Nothing there from Jack. Good. I check my Sent Items folder. Nothing there either. Can't hurt to double check. I delete him from my contacts list.

Hopefully he really did delete all our e-mails at his end, too. He always told me he did.

They weren't that incriminating, but I don't need the cops ever asking questions. "What exactly was the nature of your dealings with Mr. Jakobi?" That might be hard to answer. I make a mental note to figure out an answer, just in case.

I've already burned his business card.

And now Crystal is in jail for his murder.

The house is quiet. Dead quiet. That's nice. The bitch is out of my life. For now at least. Now, I just need to be sure she's found guilty.

Yay.

I like the quiet. I like having the house to myself. If I don't move, I can only hear the slight sound of a clock tick-tocking in the kitchen. Nothing else. There's nobody to answer to, nobody to criticize me, nobody to complain, nobody to fuck up my fun.

Suddenly I realize the emotions I've been feeling since her arrest: relief.

I think I should go out and get laid. Widow lady might not be available, but lots of other girls are.

CHAPTER 7: CRYSTAL

(three days earlier)

OH DEAR GOD the blood I scrubbed and scrubbed but there was so much of it and he was a big man and it was on my flowers on my roses on the ground soaking into the soil --

Then I stop and look at him and I am filled with exhilaration and joy. I want to dance and leap and sing. I think I'm crying, but it's from the sheer wonder of it.

Of seeing this cocksucking bastard dead.

There's a word my father would have slapped me for, if he'd ever heard me say it out loud. "Cocksucker!" I do say it out loud this time, and I then I laugh, and then I say it louder. "Motherfucking dead cocksucker!"

I stop laughing as that one word hits me: Dead.

Oh my god. He *is* dead. How did this happen?

My legs go out from under me and I fall to my knees, and the ground beneath is soft and sticky and still warm.

And I replay:

I was in the greenhouse. I'd been there a lot, it gave me comfort to care for something. Something still alive and growing under my nurturing.

Unlike... no. I can't think about it again.

But I can't stop myself. And there they are, Greg and tiny Heather, him with his Spiderman shirt and the perpetual Band-Aid on an elbow, her with her missing front teeth and that downy blonde hair and that shy, cautious look she gave anyone she didn't know. I think about them coming out here, to the greenhouse, asking if they can help, digging clumsily in a pot or misting some newly sprouted seedlings, and of course I'm crying again...

No, wait. This was earlier. That's right—I was crying *then*, too.

I was in the greenhouse crying when he came in.

Jack.

"Hello, Mrs. Armstrong."

It took me a moment to remember who he was; that'd happened a lot since I'd been hit. On that night.

Then I experienced a rush of hatred so strong I think it would have knocked me over if I'd been standing.

Hatred for *him*. Him, with his fat stomach and those stupid cheap button-down shirts he wore and the pouches beneath his eyes.

He must have seen some change in me, because I remember (why do I remember *this*?) that he stepped back. "Uh, Mrs. Armstrong, I..."

I looked at him and I knew. The knowing was sweet and felt solid.

He did it. He's the one. He's come back here to gloat.

He killed Greg and Heather.

"You bastard," I said. I got to my feet.

Jack stared at me. "Mrs. Armstrong –"

I took one, two steps towards him. "I know it was you."

His mouth made a big "O" in the middle of his ugly face. "You know...? Oh, wait, Mrs. Armstrong, that's—c'mon, let's just talk this out—"

Then my hand was swinging up and I hadn't realized there were garden shears in it my garden shears the ones with the big orange rubber handles and the sharp beak-shaped blades and while I watched they came down first into his shoulder and he made some stupid noise and put his hands up and then the blades were in the side of his neck and blood shot out like a tiny high pressure hose and his eyes were wide and he was making that sound and then he stumbled back and went down and *crash* he fell through a pane in the side of the greenhouse and his head came down on shards of glass still standing in the frame and he was shaking all over like he was being electrified and then I was beside him and the shears went into his fat stomach and I felt something rip that wasn't the fabric of that horrible shirt and then into his chest and blood was in my eyes and I shook my head to clear them and when I looked again he wasn't moving.

He was dead. I'd killed him.

And now I'm cleaning up and the smell of him is gagging me and damn it he fell into the tulips I'd just managed to get to come up and they're damaged now beyond repair.

"Asshole!" I yell at him again.

I kick his body, but only succeed in getting blood all over my nice new sneakers.

"Crystal...?"

I hear a voice behind me, coming from the house.

He reaches the greenhouse. "I thought I heard—"

Then he sees Jakobi and the blood and the shears I left beside the body, the shears with the blades that now have little bits of Jakobi stuck to them.

"Oh Jesus... "

Then he does a strange thing:

He starts to smile, then laugh.

He laughs and laughs. I want to laugh, too, but I don't know what the joke is. So I wait, feeling Jakobi's blood congealing on my skin.

"What's so funny?"

He stops laughing, looks at me, and utters in a fake, deep voice, "My god, Crystal, what have you done?!"

Then he laughs again. He's still laughing as he turns around and walks back towards the house.

He knows, I realize a few moments later. *He knows that Jakobi killed our children, and he's happy now. I've done the right thing.*

I feel better as I go back to washing blood from my arms. I wash off the shears, too; the blades are stainless steel, but I don't want to risk his blood causing any damage. They're my best shears.

A few moments later I hear a siren approaching.

I feel one stab of apprehension, then think it through:

It'll be alright when I tell them what this man did. Richard knows, too, so he'll back me up. They'll probably just question us, then let me go.

I get the last of the blood off just as two uniformed cops step up to the greenhouse.

"Ma'am, please step out into the open," one of them shouts.

"Of course," I answer.

Then I step out to meet them.

I smile.

CHAPTER 8: RICHARD

(earlier the same day)

FUCK, WHAT A SHIT-HOLE. I don't know how much longer I can stand working here. The shop floor is cramped and noisy and hot.

The only thing worse that working here is *not* working here. Being at home with Crystal. *That* would be worse. I can barely stand being at home with her for just a couple hours every night, and it's worse now that the kids are dead. She just hangs on to me, following me around the house and talking about the goddamned petunias or whatever the fuck it is she's growing.

Stinks in here.

I take a break and walk off the floor, head outside, and catch some fresh air.

"Richard."

I turn and see Jack smiling that silly grin of his.

"You're late. It's almost ten."

"Traffic. You know how it is." He shrugs, not caring about the time.

He lights a cigarette and offers me one. I take it but don't let him light it. I just want to make a point, so I throw it on the ground.

"We aren't finished yet."

"How's that? I got you the information you wanted, and now you should be handing over my fee. What's more to finish? And where's my cash? You promised it today."

"One more thing you need to do, then you get the money."

"What's that?"

I look around to be sure nobody sees us. Not that I need to worry. None of the Joes on the site could give a shit who I talk to. As long as I'm not on their case, they're happy.

"I need to know who she thinks did it."

"Well, Christ, you live with her. What does she say?"

"She's so fucked up. I don't know what she thinks. I can't have her getting a clear head and deciding she knows what happened."

Jack stares at me and takes a long drag of the cigarette.

"That's worth an extra C-note."

"Jesus, you're already charging me a thousand for a bit of poking around on the Internet."

He stares at me and I stare right back at him. His eyes blink and I know I've got him hooked. He wants to know as much as I do. The first time we met, I wished we could end up at a poker game together. He had such a sucker face.

"You know you could do the same poking around on the Internet yourself if you think it's so easy."

I shrug. He's got a thou sunk here and he's not going to risk it for one more meeting with her.

He stares at me, but I don't back down. Finally, he takes a suck on the cancer stick and lets out a long plume of smoke.

"What exactly do you want?"

"Who does she think killed the kids?" Jesus, hadn't I just told him that?

"Why would she tell me if she won't tell you?"

"Cause she knows that you know her secrets. She's scared of you. Or maybe she fuckin' respects you. I don't know. But you got her to tell you things she couldn't tell me. This is just one more."

Jack seems startled for a second and pulls out his cell phone from his pocket. He glances at the number and puts the phone back in his pocket.

"This is it, Richard. No more add-ons. We're through after this. And I want my money. Got it?"

I smile. "Sure, Jack. After this, we're done."

CHAPTER 9: CRYSTAL

(five days earlier)

"CAN I GET YOU ANYTHING ELSE?"

The voice startles me and I look up to see a young girl standing over me. She has black skin and a kind face and she's looking at me with her eyebrows raised, and a name comes to me.

"Erica."

"Yes, Mrs. Armstrong?"

Who is she? Why is she here? I search my mind, grasping at clues, shreds...

Richard hired her. Of course. To... what? Help me.

"Mrs. Armstrong...?"

"What?"

She's startled me. I try not to jump, or look too frightened. She seems nice, I don't want to disturb her.

"I'm sorry, Erica. I'm just a little... confused today..."

She gives me a look of sympathy. "That's understandable, after what happened."

What happened...

"My head hurts."

She looks at her watch. "Oh, I'm sorry, but you can't have another Darvocet until six p.m. tonight. I won't be here, but I left a note for your husband."

My husband...

Suddenly I realize the house is quiet. Too quiet.

"Are the kids home from school yet?"

Erica gapes for a moment, then something like alarm followed by sadness crosses her face. "Mrs. Armstrong, you need to try to remember—they won't be coming home from school. Anymore."

"They won't..."

I do try to remember. And there are flashes:

Heather. Sprawled. Blue. Greg. In a corner. Still moving, feebly. Police. Ambulances.

Screaming.

The screaming is me.

Now.

In the present, Erica is staring at me, her sweet face contorted in horror as she backs away. "Where are they?!" I demand from her.

She stutters out, "They're gone, Mrs. Armstrong. Gone—"

She knows what happened to my children. Before I can stop it I'm on my feet, ready to hurl myself at her and tear the answer from her, if I have to. "Goddamnit, you know what happened—!"

She bumps up against the living wall and puts her hands up. "*Think*, Mrs. Armstrong! The children are *dead*."

All I can think is, How can she say that? What kind of monster is she, to say that to a mother?! I want to slap that look off her face, make her take those terrible words back, admit that she's sick to even say such a thing—

She turns her back and runs. She's out the front door and running for her car. I start to go after her, but something makes me stop.

Oh my god. She's right—the children *are* dead. Greg... Heather...

"Crystal...?"

I look up and my eyesight is blurry. I've been crying. For how long? I rub at the tears and see who's standing over me.

"What happened? I just saw some girl run out of here like the place was on fire..."

I know this man... don't I? I peer at him, trying to match a name to the face.

"Crystal? Are you okay?"

"My head hurts."

"Aw, Christ... can I get you something?"

"Darvocet. In the kitchen."

He disappears and comes back a moment later with a glass of water and a pill. I take the pill, then sit back, waiting for it to kick in.

"Crystal? We need to talk."

"Oh. We do?"

He nods. "About what happened. I... Jesus, I don't even know what to say."

I remember—his name is Jack. The name brings with it a flood of strange feelings, and a tingling warmth in my body.

"Jack..."

"Yes?"

"I was hit. On the head. Did you know that?"

He looks stricken and can't talk for a moment. Then: "Yes, I did. And I'm so sorry, Crystal. It... it should never have happened like this..."

"What should never have happened? Like what?"

He gets up and comes over to sit next to me on the couch. He takes one of my hands, and it sends a shock through me—but not an unpleasant one.

"You know... Greg and Heather..."

I forget the electric hum in my body and look up at him. "What do you know about this, Jack?"

His mouth flops open for a moment, like a fish, a big gutted fish flopping around on a dock as it dies. "I... Crystal... I..." He releases my hand and turns away. "It was a mistake."

There's fire rising in me again, past the numbing painkiller. "A mistake, Jack?"

"Us, Crystal. We were a mistake."

"What does that have to do with my children?!"

Jack looks at me, and his mouth does that silly thing again. Then he stands up. "I'm sorry. This was a very bad idea—my coming here today."

I stand up, too. "What do you know, Jack?!"

He waves his hand and turns away. "I'm outta here."

He tries to walk out, but I grab his arm and hold on. "You're not leaving—!"

Jack yanks his arm free and glares down at me. "Crystal, stop—"

"No! Not until you answer me!"

I grab at his arm again, and this time he bats it away hard enough to hurt me, my arm feels almost like it's broken, and he shouts, "Leave it alone,

Crystal!"

Then he does walk out, slamming the front door closed behind him.

I cradle my arm and just stare after him.

I've never hated anyone so much in my life.

CHAPTER 10: RICHARD

(two days earlier)

I STILL CAN'T FUCKING believe it. Greg and Heather? Dead? How could that be?

They had their third birthday last month. That damned Crystal was so fucking happy. She had this stupid birthday party for them. I put up streamers and we had a clown come in and they had all the neighborhood kids here.

The kids were happy.

But it was all a scam.

All of it. From the beginning. I'm still so angry at her. It's hard to mourn the damned kids, even though none of this was their fault.

Heather had that cute smile. Greg had it sometimes, too, but with Heather, it was almost all the time. Sometimes her laugh would echo through the house. Three-year-old kid noises.

The house is quiet now. Erica is gone for the night. Crystal is all doped up and is sleeping in our room.

Our room. Like I'll ever sleep with her again. Not a

chance. I could barely get it up with her the last time, and I have no intention of trying again.

The living room is so quiet. The TV is off, and I'm sitting on the nice new leather couch she bought last year. Said it would be good for the girls. Whatever. I liked the ratty old couch we used to have. She can take this thing to the loony bin with her for all I care.

I hope she stays doped up and fucked up enough to be put away the rest of her life.

It's Tuesday night. On a normal Tuesday night, she'd cook pork chops and rice. Every Tuesday night. I never needed a calendar; I could tell the day of the week by the smell coming from the kitchen. After, she'd play with the kids and tuck them in to bed at 8:30 sharp and then she'd turn on some damned CSI show. I used to watch them with her, grab a couple cold ones and sit at the opposite end of the couch, but I haven't been able to do that since Jack gave me the news.

Fucking slut.

I watched enough, though. I know they probably have tapped the phone. Maybe *my* cell phone. I know they're watching her. Probably me, too.

I don't miss the kids. Shit, that sounds awful, but it's true. I always loved them. Or was that really love? Maybe I was just used to them being here. They made her happy, and that meant they kept me happy, too.

I like the quiet. I like having control, and she won't be able to take that away from me any more. Just stay on the meds, dear.

Damn, I can feel the cops watching the house. I can't see them out the window, but I know they're there. I need to get out.

My car is an old Toyota Camry. Blue. I wish I'd had life insurance on the kids. I could have bought a new car with the proceeds.

I drive to a bar at the east end of town. Far away from my house. Away from the cops. Away from her. It's quiet. Only a few people there. Some fat girl sits at the bar. She looks at me and smiles as I sit three stools from her. Jeez, I'm not that hard up, am I?

The beer isn't very cold.

"If you were to go anywhere in the world right now, where would you go?" Her voice is a squeaky and it grates on me.

Where would I go?

I stare at her while I think. I suppose she's not that ugly. Way fat. Two hundred pounds, easy.

Hawaii? Somewhere in the Caribbean? France? Shit, it doesn't matter, does it?

"New Orleans," I finally say. "Where would you go?"

She moves to the stool next to me. "New Orleans, with you. We'll go see Coltrain and then visit a witch to buy some dolls to stick pins in, to torture our exes."

"How do you know I have an ex?"

"If you don't, we'll torture whoever you're with. That's okay too."

I laugh. "What if I told you I killed my two kids?"

"With a voodoo doll? Nice work! I wish I could do that to mine."

It's been years since I cheated on Crystal.

"What are you into?" I ask. When I look into her eyes, she knows I'm not talking about New Orleans or voodoo.

She keeps her eyes locked on mine. "I'm flexible. How about you?"

"I need a good blow job."

I thought that would rattle her, but nope. She just nods and added, "You get me off first?"

"After. Tongue."

"Okay."

I want that blow job. Crystal won't do that anymore, even though she knows I like it. She's never cared about what I liked.

The fatty beside me doesn't much care, either. I know it's only a bargaining chip. She takes care of me, I take care of her. It's how the world works.

Except she doesn't know me very well. She should have made sure she got off first, 'cause I have no intention of going down on that tub of lard.

Chapter 11: Crystal

(one week earlier)

It's Sunday, so Richard wants chicken for dinner. Fried chicken, with mashed potatoes, gravy, corn, and cherry pie for dessert. He wants the same thing every Sunday, and I wouldn't even dare consider trying something else. I'd like to cook other things—something French, like Julia Child—but Richard's a real meat-and-potatoes eater.

It's just after five p.m., and I'm about to start on the chicken when I realize we're out of milk. Richard will notice if I make the potatoes without milk. That means I've got to run to the store.

"Richard?"

He's on the couch, asleep—then I see the empty beer bottles on the floor, lined up like the little dead soldiers Richard sometimes calls them. He's snoring. He'll get mad if I wake him.

I briefly consider just taking Greg and Heather with me, so we don't have to wake Daddy... but that's worse, because turning those two loose in the supermarket means we're there for at least thirty minutes, we'll come home with three boxes of cereal, and Richard will be a lot angrier that dinner's late.

He's been angry a lot lately. I think he suspects.

But how could he? We've been so careful, Jack knows what he's doing, this is his profession, after all —

No. I can't let myself think about that right now. Not on Sunday.

"Richard? Honey?"

He grumbles, then finally opens one bleary, red eye. "What the fuck, Crystal...?"

He knows I hate it when he says the "f" word.

"We're out of milk. I have to run to the store."

He rearranges the cushion under his head and closes his eyes again. "Fine. So run."

"Could you just watch the kids? They're upstairs in Greg's room, playing with that fishing game..."

"Playing with themselves, is more like it."

I almost don't go then. I want to tell him to cook his own dinner, I'll take the kids and we'll find a hotel, but... where would I go the next night, or the night after that? I can't depend on Jack, he's got his own family. And my parents... well, I don't think I could stand mom's lecturing about how it's obviously my fault and I just need to go back home and work harder on my marriage.

"I'll only be gone fifteen minutes or so..."

"Fuckin' Fine!" Richard cries out and sits up, running his hands through his hair and making more noises. Finally he looks up at me, and his eyes suddenly go wide. "Go! Jesus Christ, you got me up and now you're just going to stand there?! For fuck's sake, Crystal!"

He's yelling. I look up and see Greg poking his head out of his room, that scared look on his face again. It's been there a lot around Daddy lately.

I call up to him, "It's okay, baby, Daddy's just a little grouchy..."

Heather joins her brother, peeking around his shoulder. "Mommy...?"

"Mommy's going to run to the store, okay? Daddy'll be here. And I'll be right back."

Greg reaches back and takes Heather's hand in his own. What a little Sir Galahad he is. A perfect tiny gentleman.

Hard to believe he could be related to Richard.

I turn and go before Richard can start in again.

The store's crowded, and it takes me longer than it should just to get milk and some fruit for the kids' lunch tomorrow.

In the dairy aisle I see a man who looks like Jack. I almost think it's him, and I start towards him, but then he turns and I see it's someone I don't know.

Jack...

I keep thinking about him. I know I shouldn't, but... I can't help it. The way he makes me feel, when he looks at me, or kisses me, or touches me down there—

I giggle in line, and another woman looks at me, and I feel myself flush.

I should stop this, but... the truth is, I can't wait to see him again.

It's dark when I get home, with my one little bag of groceries, and as I pull into the driveway I notice that none of the lights are on inside the house.

Great. I suppose Richard got tired of waiting and just grabbed the kids and went out for dinner. Without me.

He must know.

He can't know.

I start to put my key into the front door, then realize it's unlocked. Oh, for heaven's sake, Richard—if you're going to take off without notice, couldn't you at least think to lock the front door behind you?! I mean, our neighborhood is a safe one, but you can never be too cautious these days.

"Richard?"

I step into the foyer and reach for the lights. There's no one in the living room, although the television is on, tuned to a sports channel. A crowd is cheering as a player scores.

Now I'm really angry at him. He just heads out, leaves the front door unlocked and the television blaring? I don't care how drunk he is...

I mute the sound. Then I hear a cry. A tiny, strangled whimper.

The groceries fall from my hands and I'm up the stairs two at a time, and it's dark up here, too, and I stumble at the top of the stairs then I run to Greg's room—

"Greg? Heather?!"

—and I slap at the light switch.

I see Heather first. She's sprawled across Greg's bed on her back, her little fingers clawing at the cowboy bedspread, not moving.

"Heather! Baby?!"

I race to her, but I know, I already know, because her eyes are wide, too wide, popped, and her skin is blue, and there's a red mark around her throat, and she's not moving oh god she's not moving and I pick her up and feel her nothing no warmth no sweet breath against my neck no tiny heart beating—

The small whimper comes again.

"Greg?!"

Not thinking, I cradle Heather in my arms and run from the room and I turn on the upstairs hallway light and I see Greg on the carpet outside the room and he's on his back moving feebly his breath coming in short rasps and I rush to him and lay Heather beside him and there's a blue pajama top twisted around his neck and I tear it away and hear that awful rattling noise coming from him and I don't know what to do or how to save him oh god or—

"Greg, breathe, honey, keep breathing for mommy, *breathe*—"

He tries to look at me, and there's such desperation and pain and something like disappointment, as if he's trying to say, *Why did you leave, Mommy? You left, and this happened, you shouldn't have left, and why can't you help me now—*

His breathing stops.

I put my hands on him, thinking about CPR, mouth-to-mouth resuscitation, anything to save him. "Greg, no, don't do this—"

I start trying to push on his chest, rhythmic short jabs like I've seen them do on television, trying to push breath back into him and I know I'm crying and this isn't working and I need to call 911 and I leap up, trying to remember where the nearest phone is and I start to turn and just see a brief glimpse of a man in the shadow of the bedroom and the man has something in his hand and I don't know what it is but he raises it up and then—

I remember a little of the ambulances, the sirens. The trip to the hospital. Nothing that makes sense, really.

Then a woman in a cheap knit top is asking me if I know my name. "I'm... where?"

She tells me I'm in the hospital. That I received some kind of blow to the head.

"My name is... Crystal..."

"Good," she says. "What's your last name?"

"Ellers," I tell her.

She frowns.

I think some more, but it's hard. My head feels... strange. "Oh, I... no, that was my maiden name..."

I can't remember my married name. My own last name.

"What happened?" I ask her.

She looks stricken. And that's when I know whatever it was, it was bad.

Very bad.

Chapter 12: Richard

(concurrent)

Jesus, she drives me so fucking nuts. It's dinner time and she couldn't have done any planning ahead of time to know she needs some damned milk? Christ on a stick, what did I ever see in her?

She finally leaves and I look around to see if there's any beer left in any of the bottles. There's not, but maybe that's for the best anyhow.

No time like the present.

A fleeting lyric passes through my mind: Randy Bachman singing "Taking Care of Business..."

It's time to do exactly that. Time to take care of my own business and get my life back.

The kids are chatting to each other in Greg's room. I can hear them working themselves up into an argument. Well, we'll settle this once and for all.

I take a quick detour to the back yard where Crystal has all of her roses. I almost never go out there, but years ago when I was still interested, I did. I know where she keeps everything.

There's a wooden storage box on wheels in a small shed. There are three drawers and her thin, white nylon gloves are in the middle one. They're one-size-fits-all, but even so, they're awfully tight on me. That's okay. I can live with that.

I pull them on and flex my fingers.

The path from the greenhouse to the house is lined with rocks. Very convenient.

I pick one up and heft it. The sun is starting to set but nobody can see into our yard anyhow. It's very private. Crystal wanted that so nobody could see her fat ass when she worked in the garden.

The rock is jagged and weighs a couple of pounds, so it's perfect. Perfect little killing machine.

The kids are louder when I go back inside. The fight is going to break out any minute. She wants a turn on the game, he doesn't want to relinquish it yet, same old same old.

Sometimes I wonder how I've put up with this shit as long as I have.

I put the rock in our bedroom where I can get to it easily.

Now for the little bastards.

I can feel my blood pressure rising as I think of all the years I had these freaks in my home. Them and their fucking cheating mother.

Greg doesn't react when I come into the room. Heather stops her nattering and smiles at me. "Hi, Daddy."

The boy is big enough to run away, so I have to take care of him first.

Just as I reach for him, though, he glances up and

sees me. He can see the gloves and his face scrunches up into an expression of "What the fuck?" He leans away and I end up grabbing just his shoulder instead of his neck.

"Daddy!" Heather cries out.

"Come here," I order Greg. His eyes widen and he skitters off the bed and starts to run. Shit.

I grab the first thing I see, some clothes on his bed, and jump at him. I manage to get one of his ankles but he claws his way into the hallway since I don't have my balance right. I crawl behind him, Heather's screams eating at my brain from behind me.

"Come here you little shit!"

I finally get a tighter hold and stop him from moving farther.

"Dad, stop! Why are you doing this? Let me go!"

I ignore his stupid whining and pounce onto him, my knee cracking his back. He starts to cry.

The noise is all around me. Heather's screams are even louder, but I take a quick glance back and she hasn't moved.

The clothes I grabbed was a pair of pajamas. I don't hesitate, wrapping it around Greg's neck. I twist it and pull it as tight as I can. He flops around, but at least he's stopped noise.

He keeps trying to get away, but I'm too big, so he can only manage small bumps instead of throwing me off. After a few minutes I figure he's done, and I just slam his face into the floor. He doesn't react.

It's time for the other one. She's still crying but not as loudly. She still hasn't had the common sense to run away. Stupid as her damned mother.

I take a few seconds to catch my breath and stare at her. She's such a pretty girl but that's of no concern to me. She deserves what's coming.

When I stand up and walk towards her, I can see a pleading look in her eyes. I doubt she has any clue what it means to die. Do three-year-olds think of things like that? But she can see that Greg is hurt and surely she knows she's next. She just stares at me, wanting me to take care of her.

I smile and reach my arms out as if to hug her.

Heather reaches back tentatively.

My hands reach to the sides of her head and take a firm grasp.

"Daddy?"

And I twist her head as hard as I can. I hear her neck snap and she collapses. That was a lot easier.

The house is quiet again but not for long. The door is opening. The bitch is back.

I turn all the lights off and move into our bedroom.

Sweet old Crystal finds the bodies after a few minutes. There's a tiny pang of regret in my heart, but it soon passes. The house is full of screams again.

She doesn't care where I am, and so I'm able to come out as she's leaning over Greg's body. I grab her by the hair and slam her as hard as I can into the wall. She collapses without ever seeing me, but she's still breathing. Good.

Now the hard part.

I pick up the rock and try to judge how hard a blow I need. I put my own head against the wall and slam the rock into my temple. Not hard enough.

Again. Still not hard enough. I take a deep breath

and really smash my head.

My face is covered in blood. I'm woozy but still conscious.

I'm able to peel the gloves off and put them on Crystal's hands and put one hand on the rock. Blood is streaming down my face and I have to blink some away.

I do feel very weak and my head is hurting more than I imagined it would. I call 911, then lie down beside Greg and pass out.

CHAPTER 13: CRYSTAL

(a week earlier)

IT WAS ALMOST PERFECT. I did it. I really did it.

The look on Richard's face when he opened the envelope and read the letter was priceless. He was like one of those cartoon characters whose face turns red from the bottom up, filling up with heat.

I'll admit the argument scared me a little at first, but then I remembered my plan, and I laughed at him. And it felt good to do it.

After I said those things to him, he stormed out. I was still shaking with adrenaline, and it took me a few minutes to remember the kids. They were playing in the backyard—Greg was going down the little plastic slide over and over, and Heather was holding a beauty pageant with her dolls. If they'd heard any of the screaming, they didn't give me any clues. In fact, they barely even noticed me when I came out to the yard.

That was good, because I wanted a night away from them. I wanted to celebrate. And I knew just who I wanted to celebrate *with*.

I called Katy, the sixteen-year-old down the street, and asked if she could babysit for two hours. She said she'd be over in fifteen minutes. While I waited for her, I called Jack and told him we had to meet, that something had happened. At first he didn't sound too interested, but then he agreed. He told me to meet him at his office, he gave me the address, and then he hung up.

That was fifteen minutes ago. I'm so excited I can barely stand it. Between what happened with Richard today and what happened with Jack last week, I feel like my life is finally changing.

And then of course, there's that *other* reason I'm excited to see Jack. The one that makes me tingle all over, the one that makes me want to wear bright red lipstick. But I can't do that yet, not with Katy about to show up.

The doorbell rings, and it's her. I tell her I should be back by eight, and then I rush out.

Jack's office isn't far, but I'm so preoccupied that I actually run a light getting there; an angry driver honks at me, but I just keep going. Today's too important to let something like that get in the way.

In fact, today could be the most important day of my life.

Jack's office is tiny, on the second floor of a boring strip mall; half the other storefronts are vacant, and at this time in the evening there are only three other cars in the parking lot.

I run up the stairs and find the sign that reads "214 —Jakobi Investigations." I try the door next to the sign. It's unlocked. I go in.

Jack's office is two rooms: A front waiting area with a few chairs, a battered coffee table, six-month-old magazines and, shoved in a far corner, some old metal filing cabinets; and, through another doorway, the office proper.

Jack's at his desk, playing with something on his computer when I walk in. His desk is cluttered and messy, there are more filing cabinets, two chairs, and a torn old leather couch.

I knock on the open door to let him know I'm there, and his eyes are tired when he looks up. "Oh, Crystal, have a seat." He points at a chair; he doesn't get up.

Because everything else has gone so well today, I'm feeling bold. "Could we both sit on the couch?"

Jack shrugs. "Sure. Whatever."

I feel a small shred of uncertainty. After last week, I thought he'd be thrilled to see me again. I know he hasn't called or e-mailed, but I assumed he was just being cautious.

As he sits beside me on the couch, I say, "I've been thinking about... you know, last week."

He lets out a long sigh, and then says, "So have I, and... it was a mistake, Crystal."

I feel like I've just been stabbed with an icicle. "A mistake? Oh, no, it was... it was wonderful."

"It was good, Crystal, don't get me wrong, but... well, we're both married, and these kinds of things never end up well. God knows I've seen it enough to know—"

I cut him off, smiling. "This one will end up just fine. After today, I know."

Jack eyes me curiously. "Why? What happened

today?”

“Richard told me he wants a divorce.”

Jack’s eyebrows shoot straight up. “Did he now? Well, I have to say, that’s a surprise. How exactly did he tell you this?”

I don’t want to be sitting here on this couch answering endless questions; I want to feel Jack’s hands on me again. So I lean forward and kiss him.

He pulls back, startled. “Whoa, whoa—didn’t you hear what I just said?”

“I heard... and then I told you it doesn’t matter anymore.” Before I can stop to think, I take Jack’s hand and put it under my dress, between my legs, and I hold it there.

He doesn’t take it away. He looks into my eyes, and I’m already so excited that I’m sure he can feel me getting wet, even through my panties. And then he moves his hand just enough to slide them under the fabric, and my legs just fall open. I can’t stop my body from reacting, and I don’t even try. Jack gives in, too, and he tears my panties down and slides two fingers into me, and we both start panting and rocking. I reach for his crotch, and I can feel how hard he is under his pants, and that makes me even crazier. “I want you,” I breathe out.

We make love right there on his couch, in his office, lit only by the glow of his computer screen and a little desk lamp. We never even get undressed all the way, and it’s different from the last time, when we were in bed, but it’s just as good.

When it’s done—when we’re both sitting back with our clothes in disarray and our bodies moist and small smiles on our lips—Jack asks, "So how come he wants a divorce now? I thought he refused the last time you asked him."

"He did. But I figured a way to make *him* ask *me*." I giggle a little, thinking again about the look on Richard's face when he opened the envelope.

"How'd you do it?"

"I got him to think the children aren't his."

"Are they?"

I give Jack a little slap on his arm. "Of course. Richard was the only man I'd ever been with... until you."

Jack stares for a minute, then says, "You're kidding."

"I'm not. Why is that so strange?"

He stands up, zipping his fly and buckling his belt. "Crystal... I'm not so sure that was such a good idea... I mean, Christ, using your kids like that..."

I stand, too, and lean into him. "I don't care about them right now. I only care about us."

Jack pulls away, finishes tucking his shirt in, and says, "I gotta go."

"Jack—"

"We'll talk later."

He ushers me out, without so much as a goodbye kiss. I climb back into my car, warmed by our love but worried, too.

When I get home, Katy looks like she's ready for a drink she's not old enough to have—Greg's throwing a tantrum, hysterically screaming something about Heather ruining his game. Heather's shouting back at him to shut up. Katy's cleaning up a broken glass in the kitchen; she tells me Greg threw it at his sister.

I pay Katy and send her home, and then stare at the two shrieking monsters, and I wish for a moment that I was far, far away from here.

CHAPTER 14: RICHARD

(that same day)

MY COMPUTER HAS THE time always ticking away in the bottom right corner of the monitor. It's like it's mocking me. *Three o'fucking clock! You have two more miserable hours of work, you idiot!*

Two more hours of this shit. I look out to the factory floor and cringe.

One of these days I've just got to win the goddamned lottery or something. I don't know how much many more days I can walk in here and pretend to give a shit.

Every fucking day, five days a week for ten years now. Somehow it wasn't as bad when it was Billy Nazzard running the shop, but this cunt Markie is just too much. He's just this pompous jerk who's so full of himself he thinks his own shit don't stink.

Goddamn it.

"Hey, you're not watching," he yells.

I blink and stare out to the floor. Everything's good. I look back at Markie, who's standing by my workstation and staring down his nose at me. I stand. He always takes it as a sign of respect when I do that, but really it's just so he can't look down at me. I fucking hate him.

Just need to win the lottery.

The only problem is that I don't have a ticket.

I should have a ticket. I should have a thousand tickets from that stupid bitch I'm married to. Crystal has a damned trust fund but not a penny of it do I see. Not a fucking penny. She's never even told me exactly how much she's worth, just waves her hands around like the money means nothing, then goes and spends five hundred bucks on a new wall-hanging for her greenhouse.

One day, I've got to win the lottery. I've got to get my hands on that money.

"The corners aren't coming out smooth."

Markie is holding one of our Walldecs. It's a stylized metal saxophone with a bunch of musical notes in the background. Search me why anybody would want anything like that but maybe somebody in New Orleans has a hankering for art that's guaranteed not to rust over winter. I designed it this morning, based on the e-mail description the customer sent. Stupid thing.

The edges are a little rough, so all I can do was shrug. No point arguing when I'd fucked up.

"I'll re-cut it."

"I want to see it by the end of your shift."

"I *said* I'd take care of it."

He stares at me and I stare at him, and it takes just about every ounce of patience I have not to pull back and hammer his beak. I want to, let me tell you.

Five o'clock couldn't come a minute too soon. The stupid saxophone thing was re-done and sitting on Markie's desk. He'd left already, of course, as I knew he would.

I stop at the Clog on the way home and polish off three quick beers.

"Out of one hell and on my way to the next," I mutter.

There's a woman sitting on the stool next to me. She laughs.

"Sounds like my life," she says.

She's a platinum blonde with big poofy hair that cascades down her shoulders like a snow storm. She turned to me and smiles.

"That right?" I ask.

"I got two teenaged boys, so what do you think *my* life is like?"

"I have no fucking clue. Why don't you just tell me how terrible your life is so I can feel sorry for you and we can be miserable together and go fuck in the closest hotel room?"

Her smile disappeared and she lowers her head. I thought at first she was going to bang her forehead on the bar, but she just leans over and sighs.

I finish my drink and leave a ten spot for the bartender. It's a little after six o'clock and time to go home and face the rest of my own personal hell.

When I get home, the kids are yelling at each other, something about the TV, and I just want to strangle them. Sometimes I can imagine myself doing exactly that. If I was tried for murder, I'd just demand a jury of my peers. Every parent understands wanting to kill the miserable kids once in a while.

"You're home."

I hate her voice. I hate the sight of her.

I don't bother to reply. Of course I'm home. I go to the fridge and grab a beer.

"We need to talk after the kids are asleep," she says.

Oh, joy.

I have three more beers before the talk. I spend the time sitting out on the deck, wishing for a miracle, for some goddamned way to get me out of this miserable life. I just need the fucking money. Then I could be away from Crystal and never have to hear the whining little shitheads again.

I was full of anger even before she comes out and tells me that Greg and Heather are in bed.

"The test result came today."

Test result?

I'd forgotten.

Crystal hands me the letter. It's still sealed. I look at her and can see that she's nervous. Her lips are pursed and there's a sore on the lower one where she's bitten herself. That's her tell. She knows what the results are.

The letter is from Collegiate Labs. It's a mail-in company that does genetic testing. I mailed the samples in myself three weeks ago.

I opened it up and skimmed the introductory crap, not caring about the one chance in a bazillion or whatever it was that they claimed.

The only thing I cared about came near the bottom of the form.

Mother: Match to submitted sample.

Father: Not a match to submitted sample.

I stared and re-read the words. The beer had my mind in a bit of a swirl, but not enough to make me miss out on the meaning.

I'd sent in DNA samples for both us and the kids.

Crystal was their mother, but I was not their father.

Even though it was like a life raft to a drowning man, I still felt a pang of longing. My children had been ripped away from me.

I read the lines a third time, and then a fourth. I wasn't misunderstanding.

Finally I lifted my head and looked at Crystal. She was smiling. And then she started to chuckle.

CHAPTER 15: CRYSTAL

(three weeks earlier)

A DNA TEST.

Bastard.

So he knows. He knows what I did, but not who I did it with. But... so what? He surely can't believe I've been doing... *that*... all the time we were married. He knows I was a virgin on our wedding night. He should know, considering how he made me bleed. And hurt.

Now I've finally been with one other man. *One* man, compared to god only knows how many women Richard's been with. He thinks I don't know—god, he must think I'm just the dumbest, big stupid cow in the world—but even a half-blind heifer couldn't miss the way he flirts with other women, the way he eyes them even while he's standing right next to me. Sometimes he's so open about it that it's humiliating, and I'm sure he likes that, too. To humiliate me, belittle me, drag me down.

Like the Christmas party last year, the one at Jim and Bonnie's house. That was a little more than flirting, especially when I walked into the kitchen to get another napkin and found him and Bonnie in a clinch under the mistletoe. He had his tongue in her ear, and she was moaning as he pushed up against her, and they were so into it that neither of them noticed me standing there, eight feet away, watching. What if I'd been Jim instead, walking in and finding his wife in the arms of another man? Jim's a big guy, likes to go duck hunting, has a rack of shotguns right in the living room. I wondered how long they'd been seeing each other, how long they'd been—the word was hard for me to even think it, unimaginable to speak it out loud—*fucking* each other.

When he slid his hand up under her dress, I stepped back out of the room. I was confused, so shocked I didn't know what to do. Go find Jim and tell him? Barge into the kitchen and demand to know what they're doing?

In the end I staggered off into a guest bedroom, plopped down on the bed, and cried. It was Christmas Eve, and in the living room I could hear "O Come All Ye Faithful" on a stereo, and party guests talking and clinking glasses. I'd always loved Christmas and I should've been happy, mixing with everyone else, making jokes about Santa and Rudolph; instead, because of Richard, I was hiding in a bedroom alone, crying my eyes out.

By the time I finished and went back out to the party, they were done and mingling. How far had it gone, I wondered, there in the kitchen? Had they made each other come, him reaching under her dress, her unzipping his fly and stroking him until he finished?

Maybe it was just my imagination, but I thought I saw them shoot sly, sexy looks at each other.

A week later I forgot about Christmas when I saw Richard sliding a finger along another woman's arm at a company New Years' party. I had no idea who she was... but, when she excused herself and left the room, and Richard followed a minute later, it didn't matter what her name was or who she'd come to the party with.

That was when I put it all together: Richard had been cheating with other women—*a lot* of other women—for years. Maybe even right from the beginning of our so-called marriage.

Now he's gotten a taste—a *tiny* taste, by comparison—of his own medicine, and he's not happy. He made me run a swab around my mouth, then took it from me, sealed it in a little bag, and dropped the whole thing into an envelope addressed to some lab. I think he knows our children must be his, but he's doing this for the same reason he does a lot of things: to intimidate and humiliate me.

Well, darling Richard, two can play that game. And if I play it well enough, perhaps you'll finally decide that my trust fund money isn't worth it any longer, you'll leave and I'll be free of you at last. Especially if I can convince you about the children...

So I wait until the clock says it's after two a.m. I made sure Richard had plenty of alcohol with his dinner tonight, and now he's snoring away. I've been still and quiet in the darkness for three hours, planning this, making sure it's done carefully, and now at last it's time.

I dress quickly and steal from the room. I tiptoe down the stairs to his study, and there on the desk I see the test, all sealed and ready to be mailed in the morning. I use a knife blade to pry the envelope open; it takes minutes, because I'm so cautious, but at last it's free and I haven't even torn the flap. I take out the sealed bag with Richard's name printed on it; inside is his swab. I open the bag, pull out the swab, and put it in a pocket of the bulky jacket I'm wearing. I grab my purse and keys, then slip out the front door.

I'm sure Richard's drunk enough that he won't hear the car engine, but my heart's still hammering as I start it up; it sounds like an earthquake, or a war. I back it out of the driveway; it isn't until I'm a block away that I breathe a little easier.

My first stop is a twenty-four-hour drug store. There's one closer to us that we both go to often, but I've already decided someone there might recognize me, even at this time of night. It's too risky.

Instead I drive to one a few miles farther away. I park and go in, looking for swabs. The only other customers are a pair of giggling, skinny twenty-somethings who are probably high. One of them mutters something as I go by, and the other laughs. I try to ignore them. I find the swabs and check out; when I leave, they're standing before a display of condoms, trying to make a choice.

Idiots.

Now comes the part I don't like, but it has to be done. I tuck a twenty-dollar bill in a pocket, hide my purse, and start driving. There's a convenience store nearby that I try to avoid because there are always filthy transients hanging around it, begging change from passersby.

As I approach the convenience store, I see tonight is no different. There are two men standing outside, bathed in the harsh fluorescent lights: One is well-built, young, smoking a cigarette, eyes darting around. The other is rail-thin, dressed in threadbare clothing, beard growth hiding a leathery face.

I decide on him.

I park. I gulp down panic. He's already eyeing me before I even open the car door. I grab the box of swabs in one hand, my keys in the other. I climb from the car.

His hand reflexively goes out as I approach. "Can ya spare any change?"

I stop and glance around. There's nobody inside the store but a clerk, bored and playing with a smart phone. The muscular man on the other end of the store's parking lot looks us over, then decides I'm not who or what he needs.

I pull the twenty from my pocket and hold it up before the homeless man; the reek from his body nearly makes me turn and leave, but I force myself to stay. "This is for you..."

He starts to reach for it, grubby fingertips poking from fingerless gloves. I yank my hand out of reach. "...but I need you to do something for me first."

His brow furrows. "What? I'm not goin' anywhere with you, so unless it involves me staying right here—"

"It does." I hold up the sealed box of swabs. "It's simple: I just need you to open this box, remove a swab, run it around the inside of your mouth, and hand it back to me."

"Uh-uh," he says, his voice rising. "No fuckin' way! I know about you crazy fuckers out there in the suburbs, crazy rich fuckers think you can just poison a guy who's down on his luck—what is that, fun for you?! A fuckin' party game, bitch, is that it?"

By the time he finishes, he's shouting. The muscular man looks at us again, then shakes his head, smiling. "Shut the fuck up, Charlie, you crazy old bastard," he mutters.

I should leave. Find someone else, someone who won't scream curses at me, who'll be happy to take my money for something so simple. But I want this to be done, so I wave the box of swabs before his eyes. "Look—the plastic hasn't been opened. Nobody's poisoned anything."

"So why the fuck you want me to do it? You gonna use it to control me, or frame me, or...?"

I think fast, and almost just tell him the truth. "It's a practical joke. I have a friend who needs a DNA sample from me for... a science class. I just want to fool him, that's all."

Charlie coughs, great wracking, phlegm-filled expulsions that release even worse-smelling air and make me gag. When he quiets again, he snatches the box of swabs from my hand. "Lemme see that..."

He examines it carefully, then rips the plastic away and opens the box. He pulls out a single swab and holds it up to the light, turning it slowly. "Twenty bucks just to rub this around my mouth, huh?"

I give the bill a little wave.

And he does it. Quickly, but he does it. He tosses

me the swab, snatches the twenty, and heads into the convenience store.

I nearly fumble his toss and drop the swab, but finally grab it and slide it into the little plastic bag, which I seal. I get back into the car and start it up. Inside the convenience store, Charlie is heading to the front counter with two bottles of cheap wine.

Looks like we're both going to have a good night.

I make one last stop on the way home, although it's not really a stop; at an intersection, I roll down my window and toss out Richard's swab.

By four a.m., I'm home again, Charlie's swab is in the bag with Richard's name on it, and the bag is inside the envelope, next to the bag with my name and my swab. I use some glue to re-seal the envelope, eye it critically, it passes inspection, and I head back up the stairs.

Before I reach the second floor, I can hear Richard still snoring away.

I undress in the hallway, just to be safe. In the bedroom, I toss my clothes into the closet, pull on my nightgown, and climb into the bed.

Because I've completed my little charade, I'm happy, and being happy naturally makes me think of my afternoon last week with Jack, and that makes my body grow hot and tingly until I can't stand it any longer and I touch myself, imagining my fingers are Jack's, remembering his tongue and... the rest.

When it's over, when I'm still throbbing, I think about how good it's going to feel to watch Richard's face when he gets the results.

It's the only time that I've ever felt a deep

satisfaction in bed next to Richard.

CHAPTER 16: RICHARD

(the day before)

I KNOW THE MINUTE I walk into Jack's office that he has something. Bastard. The smug look on his face tells me everything I need to know. He'd found something.

"You want a drink?" he asks.

I nod. I don't really need the drink but want to be sure to get my money's worth. All of a sudden I realize I was paying this guy way too much. He'd found it too fast and hadn't earned the thousand bucks at all. How could he have? It'd only been a couple days.

He pours me a glass of something and I shoot it back and hold out the empty glass, demanding more. He obliges and then tells me to sit.

"Are you sure you want to see this?"

"Jesus, Jack, stop fucking around."

He laughs then. Actually laughs. If he intends to humiliate me, well, he doesn't really know who he's dealing with.

"Can we please get this over with?" I ask. I shoot back the second whisky and spread my hands apart as if to say, "Well?"

"Okay, then. This was yesterday. I set up the camera outside behind my car. I didn't attract any unwanted attention, in case you were wondering."

He waits to see if I'd complain, but I don't really know what he was talking about. I just stare at him.

He has a monitor on his deck that he swivels around so we can both see it. He's already set things up so he could just click the video to play.

The feed starts and at first it was just focused on a window. I didn't clue in immediately that it was the window of the master bedroom in my own house. The camera could see the bed and the bureau beside it.

Jack must have been filming from a rooftop or something. He'd lied about the camera being behind his car.

Whatever.

It didn't take long before Crystal came into view. She was smiling. *Bitch.*

Even though I'd asked Jakobi to investigate Crystal, I actually didn't believe he'd find anything. Pure, sensitive little Crystal? I'd expected he'd spend a week farting around, following her while she bought tulip bulbs and fertilizer and then come back to me and say, "Sorry, she's clean."

On the monitor, though, that wasn't the story at all. A man came onto the image, but not very clearly because his back is to the camera. But I can see enough, oh, yes. I see him undress her, I see him kissing her and fondling her, and then he goes down on her, and the camera is perfectly positioned so I have no doubt what was going on.

I fucking want to kill that bitch.

"Who is he?" I ask after the clip ends.

"That wasn't part of my job. I didn't follow him to see who he was. I just got what you paid for and left."

"You enjoy filming this?"

He just shrugged. "I'll enjoy cashing the check."

"Play it again."

He clicks a couple of keys on his computer and I watch again, looking for some hint of who the guy was. No clue.

"I wonder how many guys she's been with…"

"Well, you know what they say," says Jacobi. "A leopard never changes her spots."

"Years?"

And then for some reason, the video makes me really wonder about that. How long has the bitch been sneaking around? Could it really be years, without me realizing it?

What about the kids? Were they even mine?

Cunt.

"Are you satisfied I've completed my work as you asked?"

This time it was me who poured the drink. I glanced at the label and decided I'd never drink this shit again.

"You did what I asked."

"Here's my invoice." He hands me an envelope.

"I'll pay you next week," I say.

"You agreed to pay when the job was done."

"So, sue me. I'll fucking well pay you next week."

I hadn't intended to move so close to him, but we were almost chest-bumping, and he likely sees the anger written all over my face.

He nods and moves back a step.
"Next week is fine."

CHAPTER 17: CRYSTAL

(a day earlier)

IT'S MID-AFTERNOON, and quiet in the house. Greg and Heather are down the street having a play-date at the Jordans', and I'm taking advantage of their absence to wash their clothes and clean their rooms.

There's a knock at the door.

I'm not expecting anyone, so I figure it's probably a salesman, or maybe a Jehovah's Witness. I almost don't answer it, but then the knock comes again. I sigh, drop an armful of Heather's little dresses, and trot down the stairs.

I peek through the peephole, and am surprised to see Richard's friend Jack. We met him at the infamous Christmas party, the one where Richard apparently made sure the hostess personally licked his candy cane. Jack said he was an independent contractor who'd done a job for the company Richard works for, but he didn't say exactly what it was. I thought he was very nice, and very good-looking, especially for a man in his forties.

I open the door and smile. "Hi—it's Jack, right?"

He returns my smile. He looks good in a simple windbreaker and jeans. He's carrying a large black case. "Yes—hi, Crystal. I'm glad you remember me. It'll make this easier."

"This...?"

He holds the case up. "Your husband, Richard, hired me to install some security cameras in your home."

"Oh. I didn't know that's what you do."

"Yeah. Security. Private investigations. Stuff like that."

I open the door wider and step back to let him in. "Oh, okay, then. Come on in."

He walks in and looks around. "You have a lovely home."

"Thank you. Can I get you something, some coffee, or...?"

"No thanks, I'm already over-caffeinated today, I think." He sets the case down and starts digging through it.

"So... Richard hired you to install security cameras?"

Jack grins nervously, and it seems like a strange reaction. "Yeah."

"Did he say why? I mean... it's a safe neighborhood, I haven't heard of anything like break-ins, or..."

"I... uh..." Jack turns to look at me, and I don't remember his eyes being such a lovely shade of hazel, with hints of green. "To tell you the truth, Crystal... I don't think it's robbers he's worried about. It's *you*."

"Me? Why?"

"Can we sit down to talk?"

I nod and lead him to the living room couch. We sit just a few feet apart. He leans forward, and when he gestures with his hands I'm struck by how attractive his fingers are—long and graceful, not blunt and thick like Richard's.

"Look, Crystal, I'm going to level with you: Richard thinks you might be... seeing someone else."

That actually makes me laugh. "Well, that has to be the biggest case of the pot calling the kettle black that I've ever heard of."

"So... you're not?"

I stare at Jack; I'm getting more than a little angry now. "No, I'm not. And why would anyone think I am? I've never..." I break off—what I was about to say is more confession than I'm willing to share with this man I barely know. I was about to say, *"...I've never even been with anyone but Richard."*

Jack waves those elegant hands in a placating gesture. "Hey, listen, I believe you. Even though..."

"What? 'Even though' what?"

He smiles, right at me, and his teeth are white and perfect. "Well, even though you are a very attractive woman."

I feel heat rush to my face, and I turn away so he won't see. "Don't be silly. I'm a thirty-eight-year-old housewife, not some glamour queen."

Jack leans forward, trying to catch my eye. "You don't have to be a glamour queen to be attractive. Come on, don't you know how pretty you are? Doesn't Richard ever tell you that?"

"No." I almost add, *Of course he doesn't.*

"Well, then—at the risk of insulting your husband, he's an idiot. Because you're very pretty. And you have a great body."

The fire in my cheeks feels like it could burst right through my skin now. "Jack..."

He takes my chin in his fingers and turns my face towards him. "Don't you know any of this?"

I can't speak. I can't move. I've never been touched by a man like this who I wasn't related to. It's both electrifying and terrifying.

Jack leans in closer and speaks softly. "When I first saw you at that party, I couldn't take my eyes off you. I've thought about you so many times since that night. If you were my wife, I'd tell you every day how gorgeous you are, and how much every man who sees you must want you."

The heat I feel on my cheeks now isn't blood, but tears. Jack sees it and pulls his hand away, and it's as if the sun has disappeared behind the moon. "I'm sorry," he mutters, "I didn't mean to upset you..."

"No, I'm not upset." I surprise myself and reach out to take his hand in mine. "I'm happy."

He looks from our interlocked hands to my face, and then he leans in, slowly, giving me time to pull away, if I want to... but I don't want to.

We kiss. It's tender and sweet, and like some hole has opened up in the universe and I've fallen in. Time stops. I stop. There's nothing but the kiss.

He pulls away, but only a little. "Crystal..."

I know it's partly a question, and so I answer, "Please don't stop."

He kisses me again, but it's different this time—his

mouth is open slightly, the pressure is more demanding, insistent, and I respond. Tongues meet. My pulse beats hard.

"Are you sure?" he asks, his hand on my breast.

"Yes," I can barely answer.

Soon we're upstairs, in the bedroom, already half-undressed. He stops for a moment and goes to the window, arranging the drapes. He doesn't close them completely, but lets some light stream in. "I want to see you," he says.

I'm shy. I cover myself when he undoes my dress and my bra. But he gently pulls my arms down. "You're beautiful," he says, before burying his head in my breasts and lowering me to the bed.

He's naked, too, and the feel of him hard against me excited me even more. But he won't put himself in me. "Not yet," he says. "You first."

He moves his mouth down between my legs then. Richard's never done that. I've never felt anything like it. I'm dimly aware of my hips moving, my breath coming faster and faster, and then everything explodes. I'm gasping and then he's holding me while I cry. I cry because I realize now what a complete and utter lie my life has been, how I've been married to a man who has never shown me the slightest bit of real warmth or desire, who has never cared about anyone's pleasure but his own. Seventeen years of my life, gone, impossible to reclaim.

"I hate him," I say at that point as I sob into Jack's chest.

He pulls me tighter against him. "I know."

And right then I realize that I can't stay with

Richard. Even for the children.

Chapter 18: Richard

Another crappy day at the factory. Sometimes it just feels like shit is raining down on me, and when my shift is over all I have to look forward to is going home to the screaming brats and their moron mother.

I choose instead to go to a bar. It's not one I've got to very often, because there's no strippers and not many girls go there. Stupid name too. *Havannah.* I think it's supposed to be a cute combination of the Cuban capital and a southern Gothic kind of thing. Whatever, there's no cuties that show up to drink, just a bunch of fat old white men who have nowhere else to go.

I order a couple pints and just stare vacantly at the television hanging on the wall behind the bar. Maybe if I stay long enough, at least one of the kids will be in bed before I get home.

"Hey!"

The hailing is aimed at me, but it takes me a minute to realize it. When I turn around, I see a man who looks somewhat familiar, but I can't immediately place him.

"Richard, right?"

"Yeah. And you're—?"

"Jack. Actually, Peter Jakobi, but nobody calls me by my first name. Just Jack."

"Hi, Just Jack."

"We met a few months ago, that Christmas thing at the Beltons. Remember?"

It did seem to ring a bell. I stared at the guy and then I remembered, "You're a private investigator. You were talking about some of your cases. I remember my wife staring at you."

He chuckles. "The girls do like the stories."

I shrug. How would I know? And why the hell would I give a crap?

But then...

I think about it and slug back some more beer. Somehow both glasses are empty and I wave to the bartender to get a couple more.

"And one for my friend," I call out.

"Why, thank you, Richard. I never turn down a free drink."

We toast and I ask what he's working on. Turns out things are a little slow right now. I guess there's only so many people who need slimy investigators at any one time.

But one of them is me.

"I might have something for you," I say.

Jakobi nods and sips his beer before answering. "What's up?"

"I think my wife is screwing around. I just think she's too fucking happy. Our life together is a goddamned mess, but she's fucking happy. How the hell does that work?"

He just stares at me.

"What would you charge to find out if she's sleeping around?"

"Well, my standard rate is a thousand bucks. That'll buy surveillance for up to five days. If she's screwing around, I'll find it by then."

"That's pretty damned expensive. What if you find something the first day?"

"Then you stop fretting earlier and know the truth."

"Shit, I don't know."

"Peace of mind, brother. Maybe she's just a happy little clam."

"Yeah, right."

"I think I remember her. Pretty, blonde girl, right? About 35? Medium build?"

Pretty? Well, maybe I used to think so.

"I'll pay you when you deliver."

"That's not really how it works. Half now, half when the job is done."

I hesitate and try to knock his price down, but we both know the deal is done.

CHAPTER 19: CRYSTAL

(a month earlier)

HAPPY NEW YEAR.

That phrase has never been more ironic than it is today. It's anything but happy.

Richard wakes up late, hungover. I've been up for a couple of hours already; the kids have already had their breakfast and are watching the parades on the television in the living room. Richard comes downstairs in a stained T-shirt and his shorts, sits down at the kitchen table, and groans. "Christ, I feel like hammered shit. Get me some coffee."

Without a word I pour him a cup and do my best to slam it down in front of him before I turn away. I hear him slurp it before he says, "What's that about?"

"Who was she last night, Richard?"

I turn to look at him. The bastard smiles. He *smiles*. "Who was who?"

"The woman you..."

"What?"

"The woman you had sex with last night."

He feigns outrage, but he's still smirking. "We were at a party... *together*. Or did you have even more to drink than I did?"

"Who was the woman in the red dress with the black blazer?"

"I don't remember."

Liar.

I pretend to busy myself with scrubbing the counters. "Really? You don't remember stroking her arm and then following her out of the room? You don't remember taking her into the guest bedroom, closing the door, and having sex with her right there?"

Richard turns to stare at me and there's a new fury in his eyes. "Did you follow me?"

I don't answer. He gets out of his chair and comes over to put his face in close to mine. "*Did you follow me?*"

"Yes, I followed you, because I'm so stupid that up until that moment I didn't really believe you were cheating on me."

He slaps me. Hard.

It staggers me. My back slams up against the stove, tears spring to my eyes from the sharp pain, and my hands fly to my face. He glares at me for a second, then ambles back to the kitchen table, where he sits and sips his coffee as if nothing has happened.

After a few seconds, I say, "I want a divorce." I hate the way my voice shakes.

Richard swallows, then answers, "And I want your daddy's money. Too bad for you, I guess."

"But you don't even love me..."

He looks up at me, placid. "Why should I? You're a

simpering little bitch and a lousy lay."

"I'll file anyway."

He sets the coffee down, gets to his feet slowly, and walks back to me. I start to shake. I think he might kill me this time. Instead, he says, very softly, "If you do that, I will make sure you never see your children again."

I hear them in the other room, squealing in delight over some float or marching band, and my instinct is to run in and grab them, flee this house, go somewhere, anywhere away from *him*.

"Do you understand me?"

I glance down and see he's holding a knife. It's a butter knife, a small, dull thing... but it's enough. I nod.

"Good. There's not going to be a divorce."

He turns and walks back to his coffee. "Now get me some breakfast," he says, sitting down again.

My tears sizzle in the skillet next to his bacon and eggs.

I believe him when he says I'd never see the children again. He's never loved them. I've always known that. He can barely tolerate them. I don't think it would be that hard for him to hurt them.

Or me.

So I'll stay married to him. I'll stand by in silent embarrassment as he fucks other women right in front of me. I'll endure night after night of sharing a loveless bed with a man I despise and fear. There will be no one for me—my mother long gone, my father dead last year, his money tied up in trust funds and probate. The money that's making my life into a hell.

And Richard is my Devil.

CHAPTER 20: RICHARD

(twelve year earlier)

THE HOUSE IS—WELL, I'm not even sure I have words for it—huge, rustic, beautiful, roomy. And it's... free?

Really?

Who can afford to just give a house away?

Apparently Crystal's parents can.

Jamie and Elisha Ellis can. I had no idea they were that well off. Of course I knew they weren't hurting, but to give a fucking house as a gift?

The baby is colicky. Her name is Heather, and she drives me fucking bat-shit crazy with her crying. The grand-parents, who have spent a total of about four hours in her company decide that an appropriate baby shower give is to give us a new home.

I hope they don't expect me to feel some kind of debt toward them, because that just isn't in the cards. Crystal can be a bit of a challenge to live with and although we're more or less happy, the baby has thrown a monkey wrench into things.

The new house reminds me. Crystal has some kind

of trust fund or something. I remember her mentioning it and her father demanded a pre-nup that specifically excludes that from any settlement if there's a divorce. I didn't care, because I loved her, but now I'm just curious. How much money are we talking about here? Crystal never wants to talk about it, but I go out and work eight or ten hours every day to put groceries on the table, and I can't help but think there's an easier way if she'd just pop open that sucker. It's got to be a lot of money.

I stare at the master bedroom. It's huge. I mean, you could play tennis in here. We each end up with an office, Heather gets her own room and there's a spare room. I know Crystal wants to fill that one up with another kid. I suppose one day that'll happen.

One day...

CHAPTER 21: CRYSTAL

(five years earlier)

I GOT MARRIED TODAY. It's supposed to be the happiest day of a woman's life.

Isn't it?

I don't feel so happy right now.

The ceremony itself was nice enough. Mom and Dad made sure I had the prettiest gown and the nicest church and the best food at the reception. Richard and I said our vows and kissed and then danced at the reception and ate cake and drank champagne together.

But even during all that, something felt wrong. I felt like we were the little plastic bride and groom on top of the cake—we looked right, we did the right things, but we were lifeless somehow.

Now we're in our hotel room. I'm in the bathroom changing while Richard waits in the bed, and I'm so nervous my stomach's in knots.

We haven't had sex yet.

I know that's strange. I'm twenty-one. Richard's

three years older than me. I'm the only one of my friends who's still a virgin. Richard and I haven't even fooled around much; we've kissed a little. One time he made me stroke his... you know, his *thing*. But he seemed to get bored after a while, and he put it away.

At first I thought maybe he was old-fashioned and wanted to wait until we were married... but then I caught him with my friend Allison. I saw them kissing in his car one night when I came over to his place. They kissed for a long time, and his hand was under her blouse, and her mouth was kind of open. It looked like she was moaning.

Maybe he'll leave me alone tonight. Maybe he'll never want to touch me again.

Before I leave the bathroom, I look at the ring he put on my finger today in front of all those people in that church. He told me in the limo that it was three real diamonds. Now I look at it in the bathroom light, and I'm not so sure. I'm tempted to smash my hand against the wall to find out.

Instead I take a deep breath and open the door, hoping he's already asleep.

But he's not. He's in bed waiting for me. "Get over here," he says, pulling the covers back.

I'm wearing a nightgown my friend Terry got me. It's sheer and tight, and I'm hugging my arms over my chest as I walk forward. I'm about to climb into bed when he says, "No, no—take that thing off first."

I stop, stunned. I have no idea what I'm doing here.

He chuckles and says, "Look—do you see any clothes on me?" He holds up the covers. He's naked. I've never seen a naked man in person before. My face gets hot.

He lowers the covers and reaches for the light on the side table. "I'll turn out the light, okay? That way you can undress in the dark."

Richard turns off the light. I'm shivering as I pull the nightgown over my head, drop it, and crawl under the covers.

What happens next is terrible. The worst night of my life. Richard doesn't kiss me or say sweet things. There's no affection, no love. It hurts. A lot.

At least it's over quickly. Richard rolls away onto his back. After a few seconds he says, "What are you crying for? I'm the one who did all the work." He goes to sleep after that.

I don't. I lie there in the dark hotel room, still hurting, and I know some of that hurt will never go away. I'm twenty-one and my life is already over. I went right from nannies—my parents were barely there, and seemed to only find me interesting when they dressed me up like a little prize dog and trotted me out to show off to their rich friends—to Richard, who treats me as something worse than a dog.

I tell myself I won't take this forever. Things will come to a head. It will end.

But I know this is only the beginning.

Chapter 22: Crystal

(present day)

Dr. Reeves is happy with the journal and says I did a good job of capturing Richard. But she says I need to do it over again, because I "need to be honest about what I did to the children and Richard in the greenhouse."

I don't feel very good right now. ⋊

About The Author

John R Little is a Canadian writer of dark fantasy and horror. He's been publishing his unique brand of fiction since 1982. John won the Bram Stoker Award for his novella, "Miranda," and has been nominated three other times.

John loves to hear from his readers, so feel free to drop him an email to John.Little@telus.net and let him know what you thought of this book. He is married and lives in the village of Ayr in southern Ontario.

The Collected Works of John R Little:

Vol I: Little by Little

Vol II: Little Things

Vol III: A Little Bit More

Vol IV: Lost Little Tales

Fully Illustrated Paperback and Full- Color
Hardcover Editions

Ebook and Audiobook Editions Coming Soon!

Available at LycanValley.com